ZIGGY

KINKY BOYS BOOK 2

NORA PHOENIX
K.M. NEUHOLD

Ziggy (Kinky Boys book two) by K.M. Neuhold and Nora Phoenix

Copyright ©2020 K.M. Neuhold and Nora Phoenix

Cover design: Vicki Brostenianc www.vickibrostenianc.com

Editing: Tanja Ongkiehong

All rights reserved. No part of this story may be used, reproduced, or transmitted in any form by any means without the written permission of the copyright holder, except in case of brief quotations and embodied within critical reviews and articles.

This is a work of fiction. Names, characters, places, and incidents either are the products of the author's imagination or are used fictitiously. Any resemblance to actual persons, living or dead, businesses, companies, events, or locales is entirely coincidental. The use of any real company and/or product names is for literary effect only. All other trademarks and copyrights are the property of their respective owners.

This book contains sexually explicit material which is suitable only for mature readers.

1

MARSHALL

I lift my sweat-drenched T-shirt, exposing my chest and stomach to the slight breeze created by my movement, and wipe some of the sweat off my forehead before it can reach my eyes. That shit burns like a motherfucker.

I don't miss a beat, my feet hitting the pavement rhythmically as I let my shirt fall back into place. The morning sun scorches the back of my neck and the top of my head. I thought seven in the morning would be early enough for a run, but I still have a hell of a lot to learn about living in the damn desert. Tomorrow I'll have to try for five a.m. and hope that's a better time to get my run in for the day.

I come to a crosswalk and stop at the command of the big, red hand that says it's not safe to cross yet. I take the opportunity to chug half my water bottle and wipe my face again, although my shirt is so wet at this point, it's not doing much good.

I glance over and catch the interested gaze of a beautiful woman. She's dressed to kick ass and take names: a crisp power suit, paired with bright red pumps and a confident smile on her lips. My cock takes interest, which isn't ideal when wearing a pair of thin running shorts.

The light changes, and I consider asking for her number, then think better of it. I moved to Vegas for a fresh start, not to fall right back into my old patterns of failed relationship after failed relationship. Even if she is *exactly* my type. Some Doms like sweet and a little bit helpless. Others like bratty, but nothing turns my crank harder than confidence. A sub with their shit together, giving me the gift of their submission...pure fucking bliss.

I settle for shooting her a flirty wink, then take off again, going hard for the final few blocks until I reach my apartment. As soon as I step into the building, I curse myself for renting in a building without an elevator. I normally don't mind the few flights of stairs, but that run took it out of me.

I take a breath, my chest heaving with the effort of my run, and then push myself to sprint up the stairs, using the last of my energy reserves but being rewarded with a burst of endorphins.

As soon as I'm through the door of my apartment, I strip my shirt over my head, beelining for the bathroom. A glance at the time tells me I'll be cutting it close to making it to the team building Hunter—no way in hell am I calling him *Daddy*—has planned for today.

I start the shower, turning the knob a few degrees cooler than lukewarm, and hop right in. The cold water feels like heaven against my overheated skin, sending goose bumps skittering over my body as the sweat and dust from the run are washed away.

I grab the bar of soap off the little ledge, lather it up between my hands, and rub the suds on the top of my smooth head and then over the rest of my body. I wasn't always so fit. In fact, ten years ago, I would've laughed if someone would have told me I'd ever have six-pack abs.

I was a chubby kid who loved food, and I never had a problem with that. My weight never hindered me in any way and certainly never made it difficult to get a date, but then my dad died of a heart attack unexpectedly at the age of forty-seven. Technically he was my stepdad, but he was more of a father than my biological one. It was a wake-up call when he passed. I started eating healthier and discovered running isn't actually as bad as I always thought it was. Don't get me wrong. I can still throw down a couple of cheeseburgers with the best of them, but I add in salads and shit now too.

I finish rinsing off the soap, turn off the water, and jump out.

I don't live far from Kinky Boys studios, so once I'm dressed, it doesn't take long for me to haul ass over there.

"Nice of you to join us," Hunter calls out as I stride into the studio, finding everyone else already gathered there, clearly waiting on me. Oops, guess I'm a little late after all.

"How was I going to capture the attention of everyone in the room if I got here on time?" I joke, smirking at the man I simply can't see as my boss, even if he *is* signing my paychecks these days.

When Hunter called me a few months ago and told me he was starting a gay porn studio focusing on kink here in Vegas, I thought he was crazy. But I figured taking the consulting job he was offering was as good of an excuse as any to get out of New York and have a fresh start in a whole new state. I just wish I'd realized how god-awfully hot it is out here.

"We were just discussing what kinks we already have experience with and what we're most excited to try on-screen," Glam explains, leaning forward to shoot me a flirty smile.

"Cool." I'm not entirely sure why Hunter wanted me here this morning. I get why he wants the models to bond. They're going to be doing scenes and having sex with each other, so a level of comfort is important for safety as well as for the quality of the final product. But I'm nothing more than a kink consultant. "I guess talking about everyone's kink is better than trust falls or some shit."

Byron, one of the models, laughs, a loud snort coming through his nose. His cheeks turn pink, and he slaps a hand over his mouth. "Sorry," he mutters.

"Please, that was adorable," Ian assures him.

Hunter calls everyone's attention back, and I take a second to assess the group he's assembled to get this studio off the ground. They all have the look, that's for sure. The subs are cute and sweet, and the Doms are all typical Doms. I'd like to talk to him about finding men to break those stereotypes down the road, but these guys will do to start with. Although who knows if there will be a "down the road." Not that I don't think the studio will do well. It has the backing of the Ballsy Boys after all, so I'm sure it'll do great. But I only committed to being here for six months. Whether I'll decide to stay past that...well, time will tell.

Ziggy

I DIDN'T EXPECT Marshall to have a sense of humor. I mean, come on, he looks like Jason Statham, for fuck's sake. Hot, but in a badass, aloof way that radiates he's miles above everyone else. Not that he wants to be, don't get me wrong.

It's the difference between arrogance—which I detest—and being innate cool. He's the latter.

But god help me, he has a sense of humor too, and that's always been my weakness. I can resist charm or a smoking hot body, lord knows I have, but the looks combined with a sense of humor? It's my kryptonite. Which doesn't bode well, since it's technically my first day on the job, and I'm supposed to make a good impression. Thank fuck he's only a consultant and not someone I have to do scenes with. Otherwise, things could get awkward fast. For someone who is as fabulous as me, I sure major in awkward situations. Sigh.

"Would that work for you, Byron?" Daddy says, and oh boy, I must've tuned out because I have no idea what I would or would not be agreeing to.

"Be the main star in the Experimenting with Kink series," Glam whispers, and I could kiss him for that.

"Sure," I agree.

Daddy studies me with narrowed eyes for a few moments, maybe to make sure I actually know what I'm agreeing to. I can't blame him, since I clearly wasn't paying attention. "Okay," he says finally. "You'll be paired with Harley for the whole series, so I suggest you two get to know each other before the first scene. He's an experienced Dom, so you're in good hands, Byron."

I nod, then steal a glance at Harley, who is leaning back in his chair, observing everyone. When he catches me looking at him, he winks, and my mouth pulls up in a cheeky grin as I wink back.

He and I will get along just fine. I kinda like that he's an experienced Dom. That means no entanglements. A pro. He must've had inexperienced subs plenty of times, though maybe not on camera, and he's used to hit-and-run meetups, or whatever they call that in the scene he's from. That makes it purely physical, and that sounds hella good right now.

No relationships for me, thank you very much. I'm still digging my way out of the hole the last one shoved me in. But I'd better not think of TJ because that will put me in a sour mood for the rest of the day. Motherfucking asshole. Backstabber. Lying, cheating son of a bitch.

See? Not good for my mood.

"Byron, is that your real name or your porn name?" Ian asks. His question pulls me back into the present.

I snicker. "My real name. I wouldn't have picked something quite so posh as a porn name."

"Ian brings up a good point. We have a lot of newbies here, so you may not be familiar with this, but make sure to choose your porn name in the next few days. Once you've picked it, that's how we will all call you, just to avoid slipups during filming," Daddy says. "So for those of you who don't have an alias yet, have you given any thought to what name you want to use?"

"I'm gonna go with Baby," Ian says. "Because nobody puts Baby in the corner."

I laugh along with everyone else. "Sweetheart, no one would ever put you in a corner," Harley says, and Ian bats his eyes at him.

"Why, thank you, Sir."

"How about you, Max?" Daddy asks.

Max—a gorgeous redhead I wouldn't mind being paired with at some point—shrugs. "Benton, my best friend, suggested Thunder."

"Thunder?" I ask.

"Yeah. 'Cause he says that when I fuck people, they'll see lightning and hear thunder."

Laughter explodes around the table, and it takes a while before everyone has calmed down again. "You're feeling that confident about your abilities, boy?" Marshall says good-naturedly.

Max shrugs again.

"We picked Max for his...physique," Daddy says. I'm sure I'm not the only one who immediately focuses on Max's crotch. He wears his shirt pulled out of his shorts, though, so I can't tell, but surely, Hunter had to be talking about his dick, right? The guy has a nice body, and I love me some gingers, but he's not extraordinarily ripped or anything. That leaves his dick, which, I have to admit, would be a prime asset in porn. Also, yummy.

"I volunteer as tribute," I quip, and that brings on a new round of laughter.

Max grins, looking a little embarrassed.

"Eager to start, huh?" Harley says, and he gives me another wink. "You replacing me before we even had our first scene, boy?"

"What can I say? I could use a good dicking."

"Oh, don't you worry, boy. I got you, and I promise you won't complain about my performance," Harley says. I'm liking him more by the minute.

The contrast with the last work meeting I attended couldn't be bigger. That was before I got fired, of course, and I was in a room full of elementary school teachers, all of whom would've had a conniption if they heard me use words like *dicking*.

Hell, Bruno, the principal, would've dropped dead on the spot of a heart attack, I'm sure. We're talking about the judgmental asshole who got me fired after he heard about my video. Yeah, I prefer this banter and flirting. The pay is better too.

"So what about you, Byron? Picked a name yet?" Ian—and I'd better start calling him Baby from now on—asks.

I nod. "Ziggy."

"Ziggy?" Daddy asks.

"After Ziggy Stardust. I'm a huge David Bowie fan."

"I love seventies music," Harley says. "Music was so creative and diverse back then, everything from glam rock to funk, soul, reggae, and of course, some of the most iconic rock songs ever recorded. Some of my all-time favorite songs are from that era."

"It appears you two have a lot in common," Daddy says, sounding happy.

"You mean you actually want us to talk while shooting?" I joke and earn me another round of laughs. I'm on a roll today.

"I'm gonna have my hands full with you, aren't I?" Harley says, but he's smiling, so I don't think he means it in a bad way. "A high-maintenance sub. I'm always in for a challenge."

A *sub*. Right. That's the part I've conveniently pushed down. I'm supposed to be a submissive. For someone who's never taken orders very well, that's gonna be the challenge of the century. I'd better hope that either Harley can make me want to submit or that my acting skills have improved since I got a C in drama class in high school because otherwise, I'm in trouble.

2

MARSHALL

After the bonding session at the studio, Hunter had pulled me aside and asked if I would mind leading a brief kink talk—mostly as a way to cover his ass—and then sit down with each of the Kinky Boys to go over their contracts and limits ahead of any of their scenes being filmed. He thought it would be a good way to sidestep the issue of some of the more inexperienced subs feeling pressured into agreeing to things they might not be fully comfortable with.

It's an interesting position to be in, and one I certainly never expected before I took this job. I've lost count of the number of times I've sat down with a sub to discuss a contract, safewords, and limits, but preparing for a limits negotiation with a handful of subs I'll never touch? It's strange to be sure. Of course, I'll be having the same conversation with the Doms, which will be even more outside my comfort zone. But that's why I took this job, isn't it? Comfort zones are for cowards.

I pull into the parking lot of Kinky Boys studios to find a

couple of cars already here. I check the time and realize I'm a few minutes late, and I sigh. I could've sworn I left with plenty of time. Someone must've changed the clocks on me because there is no way this is my fault yet again. All right, fine, my stepfather is probably rolling over in his grave at the continuance of my chronic lateness, but we all do the best with what we're born with. Some people are blond or brunette, some have blue eyes or brown, and some people are punctual, while others can't manage to be on time if their life depends on it. Variety is the spice of life and all that shit.

As soon as I step inside, I can hear the sound of excited chatter echoing off the walls of the repurposed warehouse. The acoustics in this place will be amazing for filming scenes.

My footsteps seem to thunder as I stride toward the correct sound stage, the laughter and talking tapering off as I near. The hush that falls over the group is exactly the kind of easy power and control over a situation that first got me interested in the kink scene back in my early twenties. Nothing is more arousing than walking into a room full of subs and instantly having their full attention.

"Sorry I'm late," I apologize.

Several sound stages are set up for various scenes, and luckily one of them looks exactly like a living room, complete with a couch, a loveseat, and a couple of chairs. In another sound stage stand a spanking bench and a suspension tripod in case anyone forgot we're here to bring a greater understanding of kink to the world.

Harley sits on the couch in the center of the set, his legs spread and his arms thrown wide over the back of the couch. Everything about his body language says *confident* and *in control*. Baby is on the same couch, a self-satisfied smirk on his pretty pink lips, leaning against the armrest, his legs stretched out in front of him just enough to encroach on Harley's territory.

I mentally jot the word *brat* next to Baby's name and continue my perusal of the room. Max, or Thunder as he's going by now, is relaxed in one of the chairs, a laid-back smile tilting the corners of his mouth. Glam is on the floor, his arms over his head and his back arched in what I'm *hoping* is a yoga pose. Otherwise, he's getting way ahead of the rest of us.

I arch an eyebrow at him, and he shoots me a flirty wink. It seems like Hunter decided to forgo sweet, pliant subs altogether and stick with a bunch of brats. Except...I keep looking and finally spot Byron sitting with his legs pretzeled on the spanking bench. As soon as my eyes meet his, a light blush creeps into his cheeks.

"Great, everyone's here." I bring my hands together and rub them. "So let's get started."

"Started on what exactly?" Harley asks. "Hunter wasn't clear about what we'd be doing today."

"Of course he wasn't. Where would be the fun in that?" I joke. "He asked me to lead a brief talk, and then he gave me access to his office so I can sit down with each of you to go over contracts."

"Contracts?" Byron pipes up. "But didn't we already sign our employment contracts? In fact, I'm sure we did. I spent a whole night reading mine over carefully."

"Not that kind of contract, boo," Glam says before I have a chance to.

"No, not employment contracts," I say. "Any of you who have had a contracted relationship before, this will be similar to what you're used to, except the discussion will be with me rather than with your scene partner."

Byron looks a little uncertain but nods. I glance around to make sure no one else has any questions. Then I press forward.

"First things first. Hunter and I decided it'll make the most sense if for the scenes you do here, we all use the stoplight method for safewording. It'll be much easier than everyone trying to memorize half a dozen different safewords, and it will minimize the risk of any of you who are newer to practicing kink forgetting your safeword."

"The stoplight method, is that just like red to stop?" Baby asks.

"Red means stop, yellow means slow down or that you're approaching your limit, and green is good to go," I say. "Doms, we want you checking in on your partner as frequently as you would in any other scene. Hunter's goal is to portray kink as realistically as possible, which means don't be afraid to check consent throughout the scene."

Harley nods, his expression serious. I look over to Thunder and find him with a blank expression.

"Are you good with that, Thunder?"

"Me?" He sits up a little. "Oh, yeah, I'd be a Dom, right?"

I frown. "I'm sorry. I shouldn't have assumed. Are you a sub?"

"Daddy implied that I'd be a Dom when he hired me, but I'm fine either way." He shrugs. "I'm here because I have a massive dick, not for my personality," he jokes, but there's the slightest hint of self-deprecation behind his words. I make a mental note to discuss this with Hunter later.

"It never hurts to have a switch." I move on to discuss the philosophy of safe, sane, and consensual kink.

Once I've covered all the topics Hunter wanted me to go over, we get to the contracts.

"Whoever wants to be my first victim, let's head to Hunter's office, and we can get the first contract hammered out," I say with a wolfish grin.

"Well, if that doesn't sound suggestive," Glam teases.

"Hammered out *professionally*," I say. This may be a porn studio, but the last thing I want is anyone to think I'm inappropriate with them.

"Disappointing." He sighs, fluttering his eyelashes at me flirtatiously. I've spent almost no time with any of these men so far, but something tells me that *flirty* is Glam's default, so I don't bother to acknowledge it.

"Byron, why don't you come with me first." I decide when no one makes a move to volunteer.

His eyes go wide for a fraction of a second. Then he hops up off the spanking bench and trips over his own feet. He catches himself on the back of the couch just in time. Harley leans forward and offers a hand to make sure he's okay.

"I hope the judges won't deduct any points for that dismount," Byron jokes quietly, and Baby and Harley both chuckle. Byron sweeps his hair off his forehead, squares his shoulders, and follows me.

We step into the office, and I round the desk and take a seat in Hunter's soft, leather office chair. Byron hesitates near the door, shuffling his feet, looking a little uncertain.

"Feel free to leave it open. I wanted to discuss contracts away from the others so no one would worry about what the others might think, and feel pressured to agree to anything they're not comfortable with."

He closes the door with a soft click and then sits down in the chair opposite Hunter's desk. He wiggles a bit as if finding a comfortable position, and I take that time to study him. He's an interesting mystery. Every time I've seen him interacting with the other models, he seems relaxed and carefree but turns into a nervous chihuahua around me.

He's beautiful—soft blue eyes, a sweet angel face, and dark hair, somehow both styled and messy at the same time. I'm sure it takes an endless amount of time to achieve. He's petite, the kind of sub who's perfect for manhandling. My cock stirs at the thought of having his lithe little body pliant under my hands.

He looks at me expectantly, waiting for me to pull my head out of my ass and start discussing the contract with him. Clearing my throat, I grab the top contract and pass it across the desk to him while mentally scolding my dick for getting such an unprofessional idea at a time like this. It's been months since I've played with anyone or gotten laid, but that's no excuse.

"I know you're not familiar with a contract like this, but we want you to blatantly spell out what you would be comfortable doing and what your hard limits are. In most contracts, several clauses will go over how many scenes a Dom and sub might do together or how long the contract term will be, things like that, but since this is for the studio, we've left all that out," I explain.

Byron scans the papers I prepared and printed a few days ago. To make it easy, I made a checklist so each of them could check off what they're willing to do for a scene, and then a separate section allows them to circle their hard limits.

"I don't know what a lot of this is," he admits after a few minutes, that delicious blush returning to his cheeks.

"Why don't you start by checking the things you are

familiar and comfortable with, and then we can go over the rest," I suggest.

He picks up a pen off the desk and hovers it over the papers for a few seconds, then glances up at me again. "If I've never done most of this, how will I know if I'll like it? Can't there be a third section of things I'm okay trying but I might change to a no later?"

"That's what the safewords are for. If at any time you're in a scene and you decide you don't like what's happening, you can safeword and everything stops. I know it's a little strange because you *are* being paid for it, but I can assure you, Hunter doesn't want any of his boys to be uncomfortable. You can fill this out with things you're willing to explore right now, and if you want to sit down after each scene and reevaluate, I'm happy to do that with you."

"Really? Wouldn't that be kind of a pain for you? I'm sure no one else will need that much...coddling." He wrinkles his nose and says the last word with distaste.

"Making sure all the kink practiced here is safe, sane, and consensual, as well as accurate, is my entire job. I'm being paid to *coddle* all of you." I emphasize the word so he can hear how silly he sounds. "Besides, I'm not sure how much you know about Doms, but we get off on taking care of subs." As the words leave my lips, I realize how inappropriate that seems. "Shit, I meant that figuratively."

Byron giggles, and it settles pleasantly in my chest. "I get what you meant."

"So fill that out the best you can, and we'll check in after each scene."

"Okay."

Ziggy

. . .

I'VE MADE some impulsive decisions in my life, and luckily, most turned out well. The crazy idea to do highlights worked out surprisingly well, for example, even though everyone called me crazy for even trying it, considering how dark my hair is. And losing my virginity on a whim to a guy I'd met hours before in a gay club wasn't a bad call either. He took his time prepping me and made it into a wonderful first experience. The fact that I can't remember his name is a small detail.

A few impulsive decisions had less stellar results, like me enthusiastically embracing the idea of shooting a little home porn with TJ. For our own *personal enjoyment*, he'd stressed, giving me a cheeky wink. And me, the idiot that I am, fell for it hook, line, and sinker.

But as I'm reading through this list of kinks, my heart rate speeds up, my palms get sweaty, and the fear that I made the biggest mistake of my life by signing up for this coils in my stomach. What the hell did I do? And more important, why the fuck didn't I do more research?

I've focused so much on the *sex* part of going into porn that I forgot to consider the kinky part. Maybe I should have applied with the Ballsy Boys after all, but I wanted out of California. A fresh start, that was the goal. Las Vegas sure qualifies, but as I'm contemplating what the fuck *cock and ball torture* implies because the word *torture* does not inspire much confidence, I'm questioning my decision to do this.

"Scared?" Marshall asks softly, his voice kinder than it's been so far. Not that he was unkind before. More like strict. Dominant.

The denial almost falls off my lips automatically, but I swallow it back. "You know that feeling when you thought you were prepared for a test but then see the questions and none of it seems familiar?"

Marshall grins. "Aka high school math trauma." He shudders.

"That's how I feel reading this."

Marshall lifts an eyebrow. "You didn't do research before you signed up?" His voice has that tone again, that low timbre that does something to me.

"Of course I did," I snap, my defenses going up at what I assume is criticism on his part. "But reading about something and agreeing for someone to do it to you are two completely different things."

"Harley is an experienced Dom," Marshall says. "I've known him for years. You're in good hands, so you don't have to worry about that."

I bite my lip. "What if I don't like it?"

"Don't like what?"

I gesture vaguely at the papers in front of me. "Any of it. All of it."

"If you don't like certain elements, you can use yellow to slow down. That means Harley will talk to you and ask you why you need to go slower. It may be because it's too much, too intense, but you can also use it when you're not sure if it's working for you. And Harley will either stop the scene or take it in a different direction."

A wave of relief washes over me. I must have missed the part about using safewords. I thought I could only use them if things got too painful. Not that I'm telling Marshall this. He must already think me a complete idiot.

"And if something happens that truly crosses your boundaries, your limits, call out red. Harley will stop everything right away."

"Okay." I'm feeling more confident now. "And Daddy said it's a series that focuses on beginner's kink, right?"

Marshall smiles, his eyes sparkling with something wicked. "No worries. He's not gonna flog you on your first try."

I refocus on the list in front of me. Flogging. Right. That's one of the options I actually recognize. A soft limit, I decide. Paddling, what do I think of that? Getting smacked on the ass with a wooden paddle? I can take that.

Oh, spanking. That's a "hell, yes." So is getting tied up. It's not like he could do anything too weird in front of a camera. I guess that's at least one advantage to this setup. I pick a few more I'm certain I can do, like being blindfolded, sensory play, and of course, all sexual acts.

Marshall seems to be reading with me as I check things. "You're aware anal play involves more than anal sex?"

I look up from my papers. "I assume you mean dildos and stuff?"

His mouth quivers, but he doesn't smile. "Define 'and stuff.' We're all about specifics here."

I shrug. "Dildos, vibrators, butt plugs, the occasional cucumber…"

"We usually try to stay away from vegetables."

"Really? I'm a pescetarian, so I'm all about the vegetables. Although I prefer a thick zucchini over a cucumber, but that's just me."

That gets a smile out of him at least. "No veggies, sorry. But you're right about the butt plugs, and they may contain some enhancements."

"Enhancements?" He makes it sound like some futuristic gadget where they add something to my butt that can make it do amazing things. I mean, I'm all down for that, but I've always liked my ass, so I'm a tad protective of it.

"A tail, for example."

"A tail."

"Are you gonna repeat everything I say?"

"Until you use enough words to actually explain something, probably."

"A tail, as in a cat's tail or a dog's tail or a ponytail. Pet play, that's what I'm talking about. It's in the third or fourth scene of your series, though Harley hasn't narrowed it down yet what kind of pet. I think he wants to get to know you a bit first."

The part about the tails is so surreal that I latch on to his last words first. "I wouldn't mind getting to know him better at all."

Marshall's jaw tightens, and his eyes darken. "While Hunter doesn't have a policy against coworkers dating, I wouldn't recommend picking the guy you'll be working with for the next few months. If things go south, it might be hard for you to do scenes with him."

"Dating? Who the fuck said anything about dating?"

"You said..." He stops talking, shifting a little in his seat, his eyes still dark and cloudy, and my temper flares up.

"I said getting to know him better, not dating. Not jumping into bed with him, though why you'd have an issue with that, I honestly don't know. Hell, he'll be fucking me by next week anyway, so what the hell is the problem?"

Marshall's jaw ticks, but he stays silent, which I count as a victory. After staring at him for a few seconds, keeping my expression as stern as I can, I turn my attention back to the papers and check off boxes. "There, done." I hand them over to him.

He glances at it. "You have a lot of soft limits."

I shrug. "Until I know exactly what everything entails—

pun intended because the tails are actually fine with me—I'm not gonna embrace a damn thing."

He looks at me for a few beats, his expression unreadable. "I'm not comfortable letting you start when you don't know what you agree to. You and I are gonna go on a little field trip."

A field trip with bossy Marshall? That should be fun. Yay. Note the sarcasm.

3

MARSHALL

A *field trip*. If I'd considered my words before they left my mouth, I might not have suggested it. Obviously, I find Byron attractive, and I can't imagine taking him for his first taste of a kink club is going to convince my dick that getting involved with him is a bad idea. And not only because he's a Kinky Boy. That's only one of the many, many reasons I don't need to do what I always do: getting all heart-eyed over a sub who isn't meant for me.

On the other hand, I *am* the kink consultant for the studio, and the way Byron was studying the list of kinks with wide-eyed innocence and a hint of fear, I would be remiss in sending him into the lion's den without at least a hint of what to expect.

As I get out of my car at the studio, I pull out my phone and type out a quick message.

Marshall: Wear something comfortable. Don't worry about looking sexy. We're just going to observe. I'll be at your place in twenty minutes.

. . .

I press Send and cringe as I reread my words. They're entirely too bossy. My fingers hover over the keyboard. Should I send a second *softer* message? Then again, part of me is eagerly waiting to see how Byron might respond to the tone.

Byron: yes, Daddy

Byron: or is it *yes, Sir*? Lol

Byron: yes, Master?

Byron: omg, I can't believe I just said that. Please delete those messages without reading them. I'll be ready when you get here.

The messages come through in a rapid flurry, and the grin plastered on my lips grows wider with each one. I can imagine the blush that must be staining his cheeks right now. I stand next to my car and reread the messages a couple of times, trying to decide why I like them so much. Obviously, they're adorable, but it's more than that. I picture him standing in front of me, the awkward babble spilling from his lips before he giggles at himself.

Then it hits me. The messages aren't shy like he usually is with me. They're funny with that combination of awkward and confident he seems to have around everyone else.

I don't bother typing a reply but shove my phone into my pocket, satisfied I cracked that mystery, and I head inside.

An hour ago, I called Hunter to ask if I could talk to him, and he told me he'd be at the studio for a bit, organizing the lighting and everything for Byron and Harley's first shoot, which is only a couple of days away. I'm sure everything has been set and ready to go for days or more already, but I don't blame him for being a perfectionist when it comes to launching a business like this.

I step inside the dark studio, listening cautiously for any sexy sounds that might suggest that Hunter and his boy, Joey, are testing out the lighting and equipment in the most fun way possible. When I don't hear anything but footsteps, I figure I'm safe.

I find the two of them plus Silas, the other cameraman, who's looking rather put out as he hauls a large, presumably heavy light across the sound stage.

"Hey," I greet them.

Hunter glances up and grunts in acknowledgment, then turns his attention back to the set.

"Do you have a minute?"

"Sure, what's up?" He waves me over, still clearly distracted.

"I was hoping you could tell me what Ziggy's deal is."

He finally gives me his full attention, his eyebrows raised. "Care to clarify?"

Not particularly, no. I sink my teeth into my bottom lip. Maybe it's better to drop the subject. It's nothing more than errant curiosity, really, not worth making Hunter think I'm trying to mess with one of his boys. His dating policy states that he'd be okay with relationships within the studio. Not that I'm looking for a relationship with Byron, but I'm in a bit of a power position, so I need to be careful about how things might be perceived.

"He seems pretty vanilla, is all. I was curious about why he'd want to work for a kink studio."

"He needed money fast, and he's a friend of Rebel's. I didn't ask any questions beyond that because frankly, it's not our business," he answers pointedly.

Money fast. The phrase deflates me. He must be one of

those subs. Not that he's truly a sub outside of the scenes he's going to be paid for. I've known too many just like him, though, in desperate need of someone to put their lives back together for them. I'm not judging. I get that not everyone is well suited to responsibility, just like not everyone is suited for dominance or submission or anything else. But being a white knight kind of Dom has never been my kink.

"Hmm." I make a noise of acknowledgment and angle myself slightly away from Hunter, the conversation having lost all its appeal.

"There a problem?" Hunter is perceptive as ever.

"No, I was curious. Now I understand."

He frowns. "When I was hiring these guys, I promised myself I wouldn't take on any boys who were *only* here for money. I don't know his full story, but he's a good kid, and his intentions aren't bad."

"I wasn't questioning your integrity." He nods, and then Joey approaches. The perfect time to escape the conversation before I dig myself an even deeper hole.

I leave the studio, and within fifteen minutes, I'm pulling up at the address Byron gave me. He lives in a decent part of town, and the building doesn't look particularly sketchy, which is good news if he is, in fact, down on his luck financially. He's already waiting on the sidewalk. I park, hop out, and hustle around the car to open the door for him.

"Thank you," he says primly, slipping into the car and buckling himself in. I'm pleased to see he followed my instructions and didn't try to guess what one might wear to a kink club. He's dressed in a plain blue T-shirt and a pair of jeans.

I get back in the car and study him for a second. "You sure you're up for this?"

He rolls his eyes and makes a *tsh* sound with his tongue.

"I may be new to all this, but I'm a big boy. I can handle myself," he assures me. I bristle a little, resisting the urge to tell him to watch his tone. "Besides, two days from now, I'm going to be bent over Harley's lap, getting spanked with god knows what and then fucked into next week. This is no time for me to be a prude."

I'm not about to argue with that, so I simply nod and put the car back into drive. The nearest kink club, Ball and Chain, is just outside the city limits in a large, nondescript building.

"Huh, this is *not* what I was picturing," Byron says, looking up at the building as we get out of the car.

"What were you picturing?"

He shrugs. "More like a regular club, I guess? I thought there would be lights and music, maybe a line outside?"

I chuckle. "Kink clubs typically try to be more discrete than that. And there's never a line because any reputable BDSM club has a list of prescreened guests. No need to wait in line."

"Oh. I didn't get prescreened, though."

"No, but I did, and tonight you're mine," I tease, shooting him a wolfish grin and enjoying it way too much when his eyes go wide and his cheeks darken.

"I'm not sure I read the fine print on this one," he mutters, and I laugh.

"Don't be afraid, my little lamb chop. I only bite after careful negotiations." I snap my teeth at him playfully.

"Good to know."

I put a hand on his lower back to guide him inside. Not that he can't make it to the door on his own. I'm sure he's perfectly capable, but old habits die hard.

I greet the doorman with a friendly handshake. We've met on several occasions when he visited the club I used to frequent in New York, and we struck up a long-distance friendship.

"Marshall, it's good to finally see you in my neck of the woods. How's Vegas treating you so far?"

"Hotter than hell. But otherwise, not so bad."

"Glad to hear it. Have a good night, and give me a call soon so we can grab dinner and catch up."

"Will do." I pat his shoulder as we pass, leading Byron down the hallway to the main room of the club.

He looks around in awe. The main room of the club seems to be fairly tame, as I expected. Plenty of subs are kneeling for their Doms, some acting as a footrest or simply existing happily at their Masters' feet. Several people meander in various states of nudity, but no obvious sex is taking place.

I'm sure most patrons use the bar mostly for water or soda. I'm impressed by a large sign behind the bar warning of the danger of playing while intoxicated. Many of the patrons come here at nights not to play but just to relax, and then they're more likely to have something stronger to drink.

I nod toward the bar. "Are you thirsty?"

"Maybe just some water?" His look with the slightest hint of helplessness goes straight to my dick. My fingers flex against the small of his back.

"Go sit down there." I point at an empty booth a few feet away. "I'll be there in a minute."

He nods and licks his lips, heading straight for the spot I indicated, and I buy us a couple of bottles of water.

Ziggy

. . .

Ziggy

I SLIDE INTO THE BOOTH. My eyes are glued to Marshall as he walks off to the bar. He knows how to fill a pair of jeans, that's for sure. Holy cow, those tight denims hug his ass in a way that's probably illegal in a few countries. I make a mental note to catch a glimpse of the front as well.

Not that I'm interested in Marshall's package or anything. Let's call it professional curiosity. I am a porn star now after all. Or don't I get to call myself that until the first shoot? Semantics. It's only a matter of days now anyway.

I'm strangely looking forward to it. Harley seems like he knows what he's doing, so all the hallelujahs for that. Trust me, the best equipment or even packaging in the world can't compensate for not knowing how to use your *tool*.

Once Marshall is out of sight, I take in my surroundings a bit more. Across the aisle from me, I have a full view of a booth where a sub is kneeling under the table for his Dom, his face pressed against the Dom's crotch. He seems blissed out, sporting a happy, almost goofy smile, his eyes heavy lidded. The sub, not the Dom, though his smile is satisfied as well.

Next to them, a man is on his hands and knees, his back almost perfectly straight as he balances a bottle of water and a glass on it. His Dom is chatting with another guy, also a Dom, judging by the power he radiates. They basically ignore the sub, and I frown.

"It's humiliation kink." Marshall puts down my water in front of me and takes a seat. "He's using him like a piece of furniture, and the sub is not allowed to move or talk unless it's to use his safeword."

I twist off the cap and guzzle some water down. "Why would someone like that?"

Marshall studies me intently. "Why do some men get off on bottoming and others on topping or no anal sex at all?

Why does one man fly high if you so much as touch his nipples, and others could take it or leave it but go crazy when you suck on their earlobe? We're all wired differently. The challenge is to find what makes you tick."

Hmm, fair point. I shrug. "I'm easy. I like sex. All sex. As long as a guy knows what he's doing, I'm not hard to please."

Marshall lifts an eyebrow. "Not *hard*?"

I wave my hand dismissively. "Unintended double entendre. All I'm saying is that I'm easily aroused, and it doesn't take much to make me feel good."

"I'd pegged you as more of a high-maintenance guy."

"In the bedroom? No. Personal hygiene, a strict condom policy, and knowing how to use your dick. That's all I'm asking for. Outside the bedroom is a whole different matter."

Marshall studies me a bit more, then changes the subject. "Have you had a chance to read through the scripts for the first scenes you'll be doing?"

"Yes, Sir."

I meant it as a joke, but Marshall's reaction to that expression makes me realize I'd better be careful throwing those two words around casually.

"Tell me what the first scene looks like." Marshall's voice rumbles with authority. I've never been a "yes, Sir" person in my life, but I have to admit he's getting to me when he talks like that.

"Bondage," I respond promptly. "Harley will experiment with me with tying me to a bed and then fucking me."

"You're saying that as if you'd be more worried about tomorrow's weather forecast."

"I'm from California. The weather is not something to get stressed about, since it's always hot. It's just a matter of degrees between hot and hella hot. Much like here, actually.

But no, I'm not particularly worried about the scene. I mean, what's there to fret about? It's just some ropes or some shit. He'll tie me to a bed, hopefully, fuck me real good, and then we're done."

Marshall doesn't say anything, but his eyes radiate displeasure. I squirm a little on the bench, forcing myself to stay still. My dad used to employ that tactic when I was smaller: say nothing and stare me down. Until I learned better, he'd get me to spill whatever I had done wrong every single time.

"Stay here for a moment," he finally says, and with the authority of someone who's used to being obeyed, he slides out of the booth and walks away without even waiting for my answer. The fact that I find that somehow hot is concerning. Still, when he returns a minute later, holding something in his hand I can't see, I haven't moved a muscle.

He sits back down into the booth, then crooks his finger to gesture me over. I'm on my feet before I even consciously register it, which sends a wave of annoyance through me. Dammit, I've worked too hard at becoming independent and strong to allow another man to take charge of me like that.

But I've gotten up already, so I may as well continue now, and I stand where he points his fingers.

"Can I do a little experiment with you?" Marshall asks.

Something tells me I may regret this, but I'm also curious. "Sure."

"Yes or no, please."

"Yes."

"And your safewords?"

Safewords? What the hell does he have planned? I swallow. "Red to stop, yellow to slow down."

"Kneel," he says.

"Excuse me?"

"Rule number one. You address your Dom as Sir."

"You're not my Dom."

He raises an eyebrow, and it's amazing how effective he can utilize that one gesture. Even the man's damn eyebrow is dominant, for fuck's sake. "Is that what you're gonna tell Harley, boy?"

Boy. Even though I'm sure he said it to remind me of my place in our particular pecking order, it still hits me hard. That word has meaning. A deeper layer I can't quite put my finger on. All I know is that it sinks inside me, touching someplace inside me that's hungry for more. Am I really that desperate for a bit of attention that it's come to this?

"I don't see how it's any of your concern what I will or will not call Harley."

Marshall rises from the booth, and I scramble back, but a strong hand around my wrist prevents me from stepping back farther.

"Stay here." Much to my surprise, he doesn't sound angry but...intrigued? His eyes burn dark, intense. My brain is struggling to come up with a coherent sentence in response but coming up blank.

His left hand is still circling my wrist, holding it in a way that doesn't hurt but makes crystal clear who's in charge here. His right hand comes up to my face, and he grabs my chin between his thumb and index finger, making me look him in his eyes.

"I will decide what is or is not of my concern, boy. That's not your call to make. Hunter has hired me as a consultant, which means I'm in charge of all shoots. To make things easier from now on, consider me your boss. That means if I tell you something, you obey."

Yeah, no. That's not gonna fly with me. "Pretty sure that's

not how it works, according to not only my employment contract but also the state of Nevada, let alone the constitution. Nowhere does it say that when you tell me to jump, I have to ask how high."

Marshall's mouth pulls up at one corner, and his eyes narrow just a bit. "I didn't tell you to jump, boy. I told you to kneel."

I swallow. "Same difference."

"Boy, if you can't even follow a simple order, how the fuck do you expect to make it through these shoots? What do you think Harley is gonna ask you to do?"

He's got a point, of course. Not that I intend to admit it. I shrug. "I'm willing to concede he's my Dom, at least during those scenes. So that's different."

"Is it now?"

I raise my chin. "Yes." I almost tag on Sir out of habit but hold back at the last moment. Thank fuck. I wouldn't want to give him the satisfaction.

He slowly shakes his head. "Boy, you're in so much trouble with all this. I don't even know where to start. But you know what? I'll let Harley sort that shit out. For now, humor me for a five-minute experiment, if you would be so inclined, please, and thank you?"

Fear sloshes in my stomach, and I regret my bratty attitude, but there's no turning back now. "Sure. What can I do for you?"

"Kneel," he says, then steps behind me.

Yeah, I walked straight into that one. I can't refuse now, and I sink to my knees, almost hitting the table and but correcting myself. Ouch. "Okay, kneeling. Now what?"

"Hold your hands behind your back."

By now, I'm kinda forced to go through with it, so I do as he says.

"I'm gonna tie a rope around your arms and chest and immobilize you."

He crouches down, loops a rope around my hands, pulls it tight, and knots it faster than I can blink. But he's not finished yet, and before I can say a word, he winds the rope around my shoulders and chest, then under my arms, and around my waist. When he's done, my upper body is trussed up like a stuffed turkey.

"What is this for?" I ask, uneasiness settling in my stomach.

He steps in front of me, looking at me with brooding eyes. "How does it feel?"

I instinctively try to move my hands, and I can't. The rope is so tight around me I can't lift a finger. A sliver of panic infuses the uneasiness now. "I don't like this."

"Are you safewording?" Marshall asks, and it eases some of my discomfort, though my heart is still racing. I do have a way out.

"No," I whisper.

He studies me for a moment, then steps closer, bringing his crotch within an inch of my face. "If I were so inclined, I could fuck your mouth until you choked on my cock, and you couldn't do a damn thing to stop me. No one here would interfere because they'd assume we both know what we're doing unless you utter what could be a safeword."

Sweat breaks out all over my body, but it's a cold sweat. "Marshall..." My voice quivers.

He takes one look at me, then reaches over and tugs on the rope. Somehow, the whole construction falls free of my upper body. With another flick of his wrist, my hands are free as well. I'm shaking a little. He pulls me up on the bench and wraps his arm around me. "Drink some water," he says, his voice kind now.

It takes me a minute or two to get rid of the fear in my system and my heartbeat is back to normal. All the time, Marshall holds me close, his body providing a comfort I don't understand.

"Why did you do that?" I finally ask.

He lets go of me but tilts my chin so I meet his eyes. "Because you seem to think this is all a joke. There's no such thing as *just* ropes. Being tied down and helpless is one of the scariest sensations there is, and it requires a great amount of trust in your partner, your Dom. You're at his mercy, and it'll fuck with your head like nothing else. You couldn't last even a minute on your knees for me, so think of that the next time you wave off my concern."

4

MARSHALL

To say I'm uncomfortable is an understatement. After I showed Byron just how helpless bondage makes a sub, just how serious participating in kink is, we didn't stay at the club much longer. In all honesty, it was a risky move on my part, but I wanted to get it clearly across to him that this isn't a game. He seemed anxious after that, and I don't blame him. He *should* be anxious. He's playing with fire, and he doesn't know the first thing about it.

I contemplate the situation as I run, my feet slapping against the pavement, the sun only now starting to crest over the horizon. I was right. My morning run is *far* more enjoyable before sunrise, and it turns out this time of the morning is surprisingly peaceful.

I understand Hunter hired Byron because he has connections to the Ballsy Boys, but I'm not convinced hiring someone completely new to kink was the way to go. And Byron isn't the only one. When I went over contracts with the rest of the boys, it was clear both Max and Ian are complete newbies as well. Although it seems like Ian has some major submissive tendencies. I think that once everything gets rolling, he'll take to this like a duck to water.

My pulse thunders in my ears, and my lungs burn with exertion. When I first started running, I hated this feeling. Now it's the second-best feeling in the world. Obviously, the rush of the perfect little sub giving themselves to me is an unbeatable number one. As I run, I wrestle with whether it's my place to question Hunter's hiring practices.

On the one hand, he owns the studio, and I respect him as both a Dom and a businessman. I want to think he knows what he's doing. On the other hand, he *did* hire me as a consultant, and I'd be shirking my duties not to bring this up to him.

By the time I slow my steps in front of my apartment building, I've decided. I take the stairs to my floor two at a time. As soon as I'm inside my place, I whip my sweaty shirt over my head and head straight for the shower.

I start the shower, strip off my shorts and underwear, and toss them into the hamper as I wait for the water to heat up. I run my fingers through my beard. Is it time for a trim? There's such a fine line between a sexy, neat beard and mountain man beard, and I try to err more on the neat side when I can manage. A trim can wait a few more days. I push back the shower curtain and step inside.

The hot water cascades over my body, relaxing my tight muscles and drawing an appreciative groan from me. I'd kill to have an eager-to-please sub in here with me right now. I can practically feel a pair of confident, obedient hands soaping my body, massaging my neck and shoulders, vibrating with their need for praise. Fuck, do I love a praise slut. My cock thickens against my thigh, hardening and slowly standing at attention as I run my soapy hands all over my body, imagining needy sighs and impatient whimpers echoing off the tiled walls.

"Am I doing a good job, Sir?" a little voice whispers in my ear, and my whole body jolts. No fucking way does Byron belong in this fantasy. Unfortunately, my cock doesn't seem to get that message because it only gets harder.

"Fuck," I mutter, slamming my eyes shut and trying to conjure the image of the last sub I played with before I moved to Vegas. Except, nope, not going there. My brain decides to replace images of Vince with Byron on his knees at the club, his hands bound, his cheeks flushed.

I wrench my eyes open and turn around to face the showerhead, pushing my face under the stream and then using my hands to clear it away. I'm not going to stand here and jerk off to Byron. It's unprofessional, and I won't be that guy. I finish rinsing off, shut off the water, and climb out of the shower. It's been too long since I've played with anyone or done any scenes, that's all. It has nothing to do with Byron.

Once I'm dried off and dressed, I grab my phone and call Hunter.

"Hello?" he answers gruffly.

"Oh, shit, it's early. Sorry."

He chuckles, and I hear fabric rustling and what sounds like the soft, sleepy protest of his boy as I'm guessing he climbs out of bed.

"Is everything okay?" he asks after a few seconds.

"Everything is fine. Sorry, I was up early for a run and didn't realize how early it still was."

"You can't manage to be on time if your life depends on it, but you're up at the ass-crack of dawn?" He sounds more amused than annoyed, which I'm grateful for.

"Yeah. Listen, there is something I wanted to talk with

you about, but I think it would be better to sit down in person rather than over the phone."

"So, there *is* something wrong?"

"Not *wrong* exactly," I hedge, running my hand over my mouth and sighing. "Can we meet for coffee in a few hours? And if it's okay with you, I'd like to invite Harley to join us."

"Sure, we can do that. Why don't we say ten o'clock at Higher Grounds?" Hunter suggests.

"Great. Sorry again. I'll let you get back to your boy, and I'll see you at ten."

Hunter laughs one more time. "Knowing you, it'll be more like ten fifteen, but I'll see you then."

We say our good-byes, and I hang up. I opt for texting Harley so I don't risk waking him like I did Hunter. He responds immediately, agreeing to meet, and I breathe a little easier.

∽

"Ten oh five, I'm impressed," Hunter jokes as I approach the table where they're already seated with drinks in front of them.

"Oh, come on. Five minutes past counts as being on time." "Ten minutes early is on time," Harley counters, taking a sip from his coffee.

"Well, there's no way in hell I'll ever achieve that, so I guess I'll just have to love myself for the constantly late asshole I am."

"It's okay. We love you anyway," Hunter assures me.

I go to the counter and order some coffee, then join them at the table.

"So, what was so important that you dragged me away

from my warm, sleepy boy this morning?" Hunter quirks an eyebrow at me.

"I'm concerned about Byron's first scene." I lay it out there without any pretense. "The kid doesn't have the first clue what he's getting himself into, and I don't think he knows what he's even consenting to."

"Hm." Harley makes an unhappy noise. "That certainly doesn't sit well with me."

"Exactly. "Does this have to do with the contract discussions you had with him yesterday?" Hunter asks.

"Yes. He didn't know what most of the things on the list were, and then I took him to Ball and Chain last night so he could get his feet wet, and he was entirely too flippant about the idea of bondage and submission. I tried to open his eyes to the fact that kink isn't a game, but I think I may have just made him nervous."

"What did you do?" Harley asks, his eyes sharp.

"Relax. You know I wouldn't do anything out of line. I used a quick slipknot on him so he could feel exactly what it's like to have to trust someone with his safety. To be honest, I don't think he's even a submissive at heart, which could make his scenes extremely difficult and possibly even unsafe."

"What's your suggestion? Do you think I need to let him go completely?" Hunter asks.

I'm not sure how to answer. With everything I've said, it seems like releasing him from his Kinky Boys contract would be the right thing to do, but I hesitate to go that far.

"He needs a better idea of what being a submissive entails before he gets in front of that camera. And it wouldn't hurt if you took some time to get to know him better," I finally say.

"I'm way ahead of you on that. I already asked him to

dinner tomorrow night so we could talk and get more comfortable with each other. Ziggy may be new to the scene, but you know I know what I'm doing." Harley levels me with a look that says he doesn't appreciate my lack of faith in him.

"I trust you. I'm sorry. This is a weird situation for me to be in because I know in the scenes you're doing with these boys, you're their Dom. But I'm responsible for their safety and well-being the rest of the time, which triggers my Dom side as well."

"I get it," he assures me.

"I'm glad you're taking the job seriously," Hunter says. "Why don't we do this. We can take another field trip to Ball and Chain as a group. I'll talk to the owner ahead of time and make sure we go on a night when there will be some enlightening scenes for them to observe."

"Good," I agree. "I feel better now that we're on the same page at least."

With that decided, the three of us finish our coffee and chat for a while about a variety of topics before parting ways again with plans to organize a trip to the club.

Ziggy

NOT ALL DOMS are created equal. I study Harley as he sits across the table from me in the steak house he picked for us to have dinner. I probably should've mentioned I'm a pescatarian, meaning I do eat fish occasionally, and I spotted grilled salmon on the menu, so I'll get that. I need the proteins anyway, and getting them in another way is not easy when you're a no-budget pescatarian. Hell, if Harley hadn't told me he'd pay for this, I'm not sure I would've been able to afford it.

Harley is perusing the menu, which allows me to get a good look at him.

He's hot. I doubt a single person in this restaurant that would disagree with that observation, male or female. And he is effortlessly hot. Some guys have to work for it by using their eyes to their advantage or compensating for their balding spot with a killer body, but he's all-over hot. Great body, epic tattoos, and a face photographers would drool over.

You can sense his dominance when you're near him. That, too, is effortless. It exudes from him, this power, for lack of a better word. It's loud if that makes sense. There's no mistaking him for anything else than a man used to being in charge.

He's completely different than Marshall, which is interesting because they're both Doms, and they're both hot. Attractive is such a lame term for men like them because they're not pretty. No McDreamy or McSteamy here.

But Marshall's dominance is much more dangerous. It's quiet, more subtle, which might make people overlook it sometimes. Harley has a major don't-fuck-with-me vibe, but Marshall's is more… I try to put my finger on it and let out a deep sigh.

"You done looking at me, boy?" Harley asks, humor lacing his voice.

"You're hot," I blurt out, and he grins.

"Why, thank you. So are you, though I suppose you'd fall more into the pretty or cute category."

I roll my eyes. "The joys of being a twink."

Harley's smile widens. "Don't pout. It doesn't fit you."

Ziggy

I shrug, but he's not wrong. "I was pondering the difference between you and Marshall."

"About an inch in his favor," Harley quips, and I almost spit out the sip of water I just took.

"Are you guys ready to order?" our server, a very cute boy named Neil, asks, looking at Harley.

"Yes, Neil, thank you. I'd like the T-bone steak please, medium rare, with grilled vegetables and broccoli on the side."

"I'll have the grilled salmon with a double side of green beans, please," I order, and Neil writes it all down.

"I'll put that right in for you guys," he says, then hurries off.

"I see you're limiting the carbs as well." Harley gestures at my club soda with lemon.

"First of all, I'm a pescatarian and only eat fish occasionally, so this is already an exception. But more important, a couple of days from now, I'm shooting a video that potentially millions of people could be watching. I have zero desire to show up with love handles."

Harley shrugs. "I wouldn't mind seeing more variety in body types. Besides, a little extra to hold on to can be super sexy."

"As long as they kneel for you, huh?"

"I can't deny I love seeing a sub on his knees for me. Speaking of which, Marshall told me he did a little experiment with you."

My cheeks flush. "Yeah. Not my proudest moment."

Harley leans forward. "He had the impression you weren't completely clear on what you'd agreed to."

"I'll admit I had some issues following his orders."

"That's okay. You're new to all this, so that was to be

expected. But you can't do this if you're not sure whether you want this or not."

"I do," I hurry to assure him. I don't need him reporting back to Daddy that I'm not motivated. I need this money. My first paycheck from Daddy is the only thing that will prevent me from having to terminate my lease.

He leans back again, then sips his beer. "You said you were pondering the difference between me and Marshall. Why?"

"I would've expected you to be more alike, considering you're both Doms."

"So is Hunter, and you didn't list him."

I frown. "Yeah, but he's different. He has Joey."

"He's still a Dom, and he has been for many years. He used to own a club in New York City called Balls to the Walls. One of the best clubs I've ever been in. It's where Marshall used to play."

That's news to me. I never knew that's where Daddy and Marshall knew each other from. "Yeah, but he still feels different. He's...softer."

Harley smiles. "Rank us from hardest to softest."

That's an easy one. "You're the hardest. Maybe that's what I was trying to put my finger on. Marshall is softer than you."

Harley nods. "He is. I'm far more hardcore than he is, both in my preferences and my approach. He's a very caring Dom."

Caring. That's not the first word I would've picked to describe Marshall, but it's fitting. He's strict but with softness and concern underneath. "You're colder," I say, then clamp my hand over my mouth. Holy shit, that didn't come out right.

But Harley chuckles. "Well spotted, boy. I am. I'm not

offended by you labeling me as such, because it's the truth. I'm a demanding Dom, one who can push my subs hard and derive great pleasure from their suffering. Marshall is much warmer. I suspect he likes the aftercare sometimes more than the scene itself."

Aftercare. Right. That was in the homework Marshall gave all of us subs to read up on. The care a Dom provides to his sub after a scene. The more intense the scene, the more important aftercare is. I have to admit that when I read through all the definitions and explanations, aftercare sounded pretty nice. I mean, being held for minutes and simply cuddling? Sign me up.

"Does that mean you're not gonna go easy on me?" I ask.

He's not smiling like I expected him to. "You should've asked these kinds of questions before signing that damn contract, boy."

His voice is stern now, and I don't like it at all. "I didn't know," I mumble.

He sighs. "So Marshall was right. You did sign a contract you didn't understand."

Neil stops by our table with our food, which gives me the opportunity to weigh my response. I don't want to deny it, but I also don't want to paint Hunter in a bad light.

"Can I explain?" I ask once Neil has wished us a pleasant meal and has taken off again.

"Please do."

"I did really read the employment contract. I'm not an idiot. A friend of mine who's a lawyer even read it for me to make sure I wasn't signing my life away."

"That's good to hear."

I take a deep breath. "But I did underestimate the kink aspect of it. I focused on the porn part, you know? If I had an issue with being fucked and having thousands of people watch it. I don't."

Well, I did, but that was before TJ took that choice from me, so now that my body is out there anyway, I may as well get money for it, right? Not that Harley needs to know all that.

"But you didn't think about the kink element?" Harley asks.

"Not as much as I should have. Hunter had called it kink for beginners, so I figured that it couldn't be that intense. Besides, I've seen the Fifty Shades moves—though not entirely out of my own free will, I must add—so I wasn't that worried."

Harley rolls his eyes so hard they about plop out of his sockets. "I swear to god, if I got money for every schmuck who thought they knew kink after reading those books or watching the movies..."

"I guess they're not very realistic, are they?" I ask sheepishly.

The salmon is delicious, which is about the only thing I'm happy about right now. What a clusterfuck. And I can't blame Harley for this. Or Marshall. He may have talked about me with Harley, but he's looking out for me. In a way, that makes me feel good, like he has my back.

"Kiddo, what those movies depict has little to do with the kink I love. And in itself, I have no problem with people experimenting in the bedroom and trying things like spanking or blindfolds or a pair of cuffs. I'm all for it. But call it playing around, then. Call it spicing things up in the bedroom. Don't call it BDSM or D/s play, because it's not. If people had read those books for what they are—fiction—it would've been fine, but they're treating it as a manual, and that's leading to some disastrous results."

"So I'm discovering." I feel very small. I'm such an idiot. I'm not usually one to cry because I have my pride, and it's not like I don't have my shit together most of the time, but for some reason, Harley's disapproval hits me hard. I push my plate back, suddenly not hungry anymore.

"Come here for a moment," Harley says, and his voice is much warmer now. Softer.

"What?"

He gestures me over. "Come sit with me for a bit."

Something in his tone invites me in, or maybe it's the kind look on his face, and I slide out of the booth and climb in next to him. Without paying attention to anyone around us, he maneuvers me on his lap, then holds me close against his chest. As soon as his arms tighten around me, I exhale and relax against him.

"That's better. Don't fret, boy. We'll work this out. I promise we'll go over every step, either me or Marshall, and we'll get you through this."

"You promise you'll go easy on me?" I ask, and much to my dismay, my voice is a little wobbly.

"I'll be as soft as my dark, tortured heart will allow me to be."

I'm glad when he lets me sit there for a while as he eats, just holding me tight. I never thought I'd be the type of guy to sit in someone's lap for a long time, since I'm usually way too energetic for that, and yet here we are. At least it's taken away my worries about the first scene.

5

ZIGGY

This is it. My stomach is rolling like the waves of the Pacific on a stormy day as I walk into the dressing room. Or rather, the undressing room. Harley is already there, casually dropping his pants, his back turned toward me. I'd already spotted the full-sleeve tattoo on his right arm, but he has one on his back as well. It's intricate and highly detailed in bold colors that contrast with his dark hair, as always pulled back into a ponytail.

"Hi," I say, not wanting to catch him by surprise.

He turns around, his flaccid dick slapping against his thigh. "Hey, kiddo. How are you feeling?"

His easy tone helps me relax a little. "Nervous as fuck."

He smiles as he folds his pants. "You'll be fine, I promise."

I watch as he takes his socks off and puts them with the rest of his clothes. Damn, he's so tall. That'll be a nice contrast with my petite build, I'm sure. He's completely naked now, but he doesn't seem fazed by that at all. He's probably used to it from the clubs he frequents. I, on the other hand, am not quite as blasé about the whole situation as I'd like to be.

I drop my bag on the wooden bench, then kick off my shoes. *Treat it like undressing at the gym.* Yeah, except at the gym, I'm not about to get tied up and fucked six ways to Sunday. Though there was that one time this spinning coach fucked me hard and fast in the shower after a session, and my god, talk about a guy who knew how to use his dick. I came hands-free, and that's not as common as rumors have it.

The thought of that encounter—the memories of it have been awesome jerk-off fodder for months now—helps me relax a little as I strip. As I move, the plug in my ass wiggles, pressing against spots in a way that otherwise would've had me moaning, but my dick barely takes an interest now. I guess it's true what they say about stress causing erectile problems.

Harley sits down on the bench right next to where I'm undressing. "What are you most nervous about?"

I let out an awkward laugh. "Take your pick from any of the following. That I won't be able to get hard, that I'll do something wrong, that I'll fail horribly at this whole submissive thing, that I won't be able to come or forget to tell them I'm coming so they can get the right shot…"

Daddy's stern instructions to "please, for the love of everything indicate when you're about to blow" have left an impression, to say the least.

Harley waits with answering until I've taken the last bit of clothing off, standing naked with a plug up my ass. "Come sit with me for a moment." He gently tugs my wrist.

I allow him to pull me on his lap because that's not awkward at all, considering we're both naked. But he settles me down, then wraps his arm around me and presses me against his chest. "Take a deep breath for me, boy."

His voice has dropped a little to a soothing timbre, and it hugs and calms me like a warm blanket. I fill my lungs with air, then slowly breathe out. Harley's warm hand caresses my back, making big circles. "Can you do one more for me?"

"You know what the great thing is about being a sub?" Harley asks. It doesn't sound like he expects me to answer, so I stay quiet, my heart rate slowing down and my stomach settling. "You don't have to worry about anything. That's my job. All you have to do is obey me. I'm in charge, Ziggy, not you. I'm responsible. There's nothing you can fail at other than obeying me."

Huh, when he puts it that way... "What happens if I'm not good at obeying?" I whisper.

"Hmm, you're a little worrywart, aren't you? You'll be fine, boy. I've been doing this for many years, so trust me when I say that if I do my part right, you'll *want* to obey me."

"I see you two have gotten a head start." Daddy sounds amused. He walks into the dressing room, Marshall on his heels. Whereas Daddy is smiling, Marshall frowns when he spots me on Harley's lap.

"Just calming the nerves of my sweet boy here," Harley says easily, then lets go of me. "Feel better?"

I nod as I slide off his lap. "I do. Thank you."

"You ready, Ziggy?" Daddy asks. This has got to be one of the most surreal situations ever. I'm standing naked in front of my fully dressed boss, with my naked coworker right next to me and another fully dressed guy looking at us with a scowl on his face.

"I will be as soon as I get over the strong high school nightmare freak-out that I'm standing here naked," I quip.

Ziggy

Daddy and Harley laugh, and that one even gets a hint of a smile from Marshall. Boom. Tip your waitress, people.

"You're all prepped?" Daddy asks.

I'm tempted to turn around and bend over so he can see the plug, but I'd better not. Not sure what the standard for professional behavior is in porn because bending over has to be in my job description, but probably not my boss's. Instead, I nod. "Cleaned, prepped, and ready for duty."

That gets another smile out of Daddy and Harley, but Marshall's mouth reverts to his previous tight line. Damn, tough crowd.

"Let's get started," Daddy says, and I follow him onto the set.

The setup is a sturdy four-poster bed, covered with dark blue satin sheets. It had to be esthetically pleasing, Daddy told me. Apparently, the sight of gorgeous me, bound and naked on a bed, wasn't pleasing enough all by itself.

The sound engineers are doing a last soundcheck, and Joey fiddles with one of the lights that beam down on the bed, then nods with satisfaction. I do a quick headcount. Daddy and Marshall, Joey and Silas as cameramen, a sound technician, and a production assistant, which seems to be a fancy name for everyone's assistant. All in all, six men will be watching me get fucked, and that's a situation I never thought I'd be in. Then again, I always did love to be the center of attention, so there's that.

"Whenever you guys are ready," Daddy says to me and Harley. Then he steps back, leaving the two of us standing there, naked.

"Before we start, I want to make one thing crystal clear," Harley says. Everyone in the room turns toward him, even Daddy and Marshall, proof of Harley's natural dominance.

"This may be a porn scene, but we're not acting here. I consider this a true scene with Ziggy, and I'll treat it as such. That means I'm responsible for him as his Dom, and if I see he's in distress, I'll stop everything right there and then. It also means that I'm in charge, so nobody talks to him directly while we're doing this. You have concerns, problems, need us to change position, whatever, you talk to me, not to him. For the next few hours, he's mine."

Everyone hums in agreement, even Marshall, who seems to look somewhat relieved. I'd have thought he had faith in Harley's abilities, considering they've been friends since forever, but maybe this little speech reassured him as much as it did me?

"You ready?" Harley asks me, and I nod.

He tilts my chin up, his eyes sharper now. "Lesson one. Use words whenever possible. It helps us communicate better."

"According to Marshall, lesson one was that I had to call my Dom Sir." I don't know why I said that. Must be that verbal diarrhea I sometimes get when I'm nervous.

Harley grins. "We'll make that lesson two. You ready, boy?"

"Yes, Sir."

Daddy gives a signal, so I assume we're rolling now. My hands instantly grow clammy, and I shiver.

"Kneel for me, boy," Harley says, and I do what I've been practicing for the last few days and sink to my knees. Those ballet lessons come in handy now, plus the fact that I'm flexible as fuck anyway.

Harley walks around me, then pulls my shoulders back. "Sit straight, shoulders and back aligned, head down."

I adjust my posture, and he purrs with approval. "Mmm, beautiful. Your body is exquisite, boy. So very, very pretty."

"Thank you, Sir."

He stands in front of me again, his cock hardening. "Nothing arouses me more than a pretty boy on his knees," Harley says, and I believe him.

"Your safewords?"

"Green when I'm good, yellow to slow down, and red to stop," I recite.

"If at any moment you can't use your voice, snap your fingers to get my attention. I'll make sure to check in with you."

God, things are getting serious, and my stomach rolls. "Yes, Sir."

He smiles at me, so apparently I'm doing well so far. "Since this is your very first scene, I'll tell you what we're going to do. This won't always be the case."

"Yes, Sir."

"I'm going to introduce you to bondage, which is nothing more than the practice of being tied down, restrained. Since you're new to this, we'll see how you react to that. Depending on how well you do, I may also blindfold you. Any questions so far?"

I shake my head, then remember what he told me. "No, Sir."

He rubs my hair affectionately. "Good boy."

The pleasure circuit in my brain lights up like a Christmas tree. Uh-oh. It feels like Harley has the secret passcode with those two words, the magic combination to make me do whatever. That was not the plan. This was supposed to be easy, fun, an experiment that would earn me some hard-needed cash. This wasn't meant to be real, but what I'm experiencing in my body at those two simple words is as real as it gets.

. . .

Marshall

I'M NOT proud of the momentary flare of jealousy I felt when Hunter and I walked in and found Byron on Harley's lap in the dressing room. It wasn't their nakedness or close proximity that hit me in the center of my chest. They were minutes away from fucking in front of a camera, for shit's sake. No, it was the soothing murmur of Harley's voice and the way he was rubbing calming circles on Byron's back.

Of course, seeing Harley as Byron's Dom, for today anyway, I wouldn't have expected anything less of him than comforting a nervous sub. But something about it still doesn't sit quite right. Maybe it's because *I've* been the one protecting and comforting Byron for the past week, slowly introducing him to the scene. And like I told Harley and Hunter at the coffee shop the other day, being responsible for all these boys' safety and well-being hits every Dom button I have.

My brain is confused, that's all. But Byron isn't *my* sub. I'm still not even sure he's *a* sub, which is why I study him closely as Harley starts the scene.

After putting Ziggy on his knees, Harley takes his time, running slow hands over his body, helping him relax until his breaths start to slow and his cock goes from soft to semi-hard. The boy squirms a little on his knees, and I make a mental note to check the cushioning on the floor once filming is done for today. If Harley notices the squirming, which I'm sure he does, he ignores it, continuing his gentle play for another few minutes.

I have no doubt they'll cut this slow start down a bit to move things along, but I appreciate that Harley doesn't rush, making sure Ziggy is relaxed before he orders him onto the bed.

Harley is considerably larger than Ziggy, and he uses that to his advantage, picking the boy up like he's nothing and arranging him exactly how he wants him. Ziggy seems to like that, his breath hitching and his cock jerking as it gets harder.

"Stay," Harley says with full authority in his voice.

"Yes, Sir," Ziggy answers, and the sound of those words on his lips strokes my cock to life as well. I'm watching porn being filmed. It's natural it would arouse me.

Harley grabs the multicolored ropes off the nightstand where they were laid out for him, and he takes a second to unwind them and run them through his hands, checking the softness and weight. Then he drags the end of the rope along Ziggy's chest and down his belly. Ziggy shivers at the sensation and lets out a quiet gasp.

"Color, boy?" Harley asks.

"Huh?" Ziggy blinks at him, confusion crossing his face for a second. Then understanding dawns in his eyes. "Oh, green." Harley arches an eyebrow at him. "Green, *Sir*."

"Good boy," he praises, and I catch Ziggy's cock jerking again. *Interesting*. "Hands over your head and lie still. If you squirm, I might tie you too loose or too tight."

Ziggy starts to nod but then catches himself and answers with a "yes, Sir" instead. *Good boy*. My body vibrates with the familiar thrill of a sub surrendering, even if it's not for me.

Harley takes his time tying Ziggy's hands. He and Hunter discussed this beforehand, and the camera should be zoomed in right now as Harley works, so viewers would be able to see exactly how he bounds him with a safe slipknot. There are a pair of safety shears on the nightstand as well, which Harley mentions as he works so viewers get a full idea of how to safely practice bondage. Hunter assured me that each video would start and end with a disclaimer that anything seen in the video should ideally be conducted under the supervision of a trained Dom if it's the viewer's first time. One of the goals of Kinky Boys studio is to teach about safe kink, but we don't want anyone to get the idea that just because they watch a couple of videos, they can run out there and start practicing any of the techniques shown.

Harley doesn't skimp on his soft skills, dragging the rope along Ziggy's skin as he ties his knots and continuing to touch and caress him as he works. Once the boy is restrained, he checks the tightness of the rope against Ziggy's skin, gives it a little tug to make sure he won't be pulling it free of the headboard, and then asks for colors again.

"Green, Sir," Ziggy answers promptly this time. After the time it took Harley to tie him, I half expected his voice would sound a little more peaceful, that relaxed, almost subspace, sleepy kind of voice that means he's giving in to it. But it's perfectly normal, if a little bored.

Harley stands over his bound boy, admiring his handiwork for a moment, stroking himself slowly, his cock hard and thick in his hand, precum glistening at his slit. It's a gorgeous sight and will look incredible on camera.

I sweep my eyes over Ziggy's body. His breathing appears even, and his cock is still hard, although it has flagged a little since Harley manhandled him onto the bed. His body language tells me he's calm. I glance at his fingers and am pleased to see they don't look overly red, which means the ropes aren't too tight or pressing on any pressure points. The urge to touch his fingers to check their temperature is almost overwhelming. I remind myself that Harley knows exactly what he's doing. Almost as soon as the thought crosses my mind, Harley checks Ziggy's fingers himself, and I relax.

Harley grabs the blindfold from the nightstand and holds it up. Ziggy gives an almost imperceptive nod, and I bite back a grin. He's still not getting what having a Dom means. Harley wasn't asking him. He was holding the blindfold up so Joey could get a good shot. A smile ghosts Harley's lips as well. Then he schools his features. I've seen him play with subs more times than I can count, and he's giving Ziggy a lot of latitude.

Harley puts the blindfold over the boy's eyes and then moves to the foot of the bed. Ziggy wiggles around a little again, but this time it seems more out of impatience than discomfort. If I had to guess, he's getting bored with this part and just wants to move on to the actual sex.

Without warning, Harley grabs Ziggy's calves and pushes his legs up to his chest. Ziggy gives a surprised squeak that turns into a moan as Harley slips one hand between his ass cheeks and touches the plug. But instead of removing it quickly and tossing it aside to be edited out later, he tugs at the base and then rocks it back in.

"Oh fuck," Ziggy groans, color rising on his skin, his cock coming fully to life now, resting hard against his stomach.

"No talking except your colors," Harley chastises, pulling the plug out a little farther and then fucking it back into him again.

"Green, green, green," Ziggy pants, tugging at the ropes and arching his back.

I put my hand over my mouth to cover the laugh that

nearly escapes. Technically he obeyed his Dom, but I don't think it was what Harley had in mind.

Finally, Harley removes the plug and drops it on the floor with a *thunk*. He grabs the condom that was laid out on the bed for him and quickly rolls it on.

"You're not allowed to come until I tell you to," Harley instructs gruffly.

Ziggy nods. "Green, Sir."

I cough to cover another chuckle. This fucking kid is too priceless. I have no idea how Harley is staying focused.

He enters Ziggy in one smooth stroke, the boy bowing up and moaning long and low, precum seeping from his cock and dripping on the skin of his belly. My cock pulses against my zipper, and heat pools low in my gut. I bet Ziggy feels incredible, all hot and tight and fucking perfect.

As clear as it was that Ziggy wasn't getting off on being bound, it's equally as obvious that he hadn't been lying when he said he loves sex. His whole body lights up as Harley pounds him. And I notice something else. Every time Harley strokes his fingers over any part of Ziggy's skin, he arches into the touch. Every time Harley utters praise, Ziggy whimpers and moans. Whether Ziggy is truly a sub is still up for debate, but whether *I* would enjoy playing with the boy, that's very much decided. And fuck if that isn't the last thing I need.

Harley's ass flexes with every thrust, and Ziggy quakes with the effort to hold back his orgasm. His cock is flushed red, and precum is leaking liberally from him now, his balls tight against his body.

"Please," he gasps, and Harley stills midthrust, drawing a frustrated cry from Ziggy.

"*Don't* speak, boy," Harley says again. "One more word that isn't your colors and you won't come at all."

Ziggy sobs, clenching his fingers and releasing them. He bites his bottom lip.

"Good boy," Harley murmurs, pulling back and slamming into him again.

Ziggy cries out again, and I see it coming a split second before it happens. His cock spasms, and the flush of his skin deepens, all his muscles tensing at once as his orgasm hits him without permission. Poor boy couldn't have held it back if his life depended on it. My cock throbs jealously as Ziggy is racked with pleasure, trembling as thick ropes of cum paint his stomach. Harley pulls out and tosses the condom aside, fisting his erection in his hand and jerking himself to completion, his mess joining Ziggy's.

Harley takes a few seconds to catch his breath and then quickly unties Ziggy and removes the blindfold before settling on the bed beside him and pulling him into his arms. We discussed this at the preproduction meetings and agreed that if we're showing D/s play, then it was only right to show at least a few minutes of aftercare at the end of each video as well. Part of the contracts I went over covered preferred aftercare for both the subs and the Doms. Aftercare for Doms can be too easily forgotten, but Top Drop is real. For me cuddling my sub is the best aftercare I could ask for.

Harley picks up the bottle of water that was also set out before the scene and offers it to Ziggy, holding it to his lips and helping him drink a little.

"Sorry I fucked up," Ziggy says shyly, pressing his face against Harley's chest to hide his embarrassment.

"It was your first time. We're still learning your limits. Next time I'll make sure to put a cockring on you to help now that I know what a hair trigger you have."

Ziggy laughs and nods, snuggling closer to Harley, a

blissful smile on his lips. He likes the cuddling a lot more than he liked the bondage.

They spend a few minutes like that. Then Hunter calls "Cut."

A bathrobe is waiting for both of them, and I grab Ziggy's without thinking and step onto the set.

Harley is talking to him in a quiet voice, both of them still lying on the bed. When he sees me coming, he gives me a smile and nods.

"You doing okay, sweetheart? How are you feeling?" he checks with Ziggy.

"I'm great." Ziggy pushes himself into a seated position and stretches. "Oh, a bathrobe, thank you." He reaches out, and I hand it to him.

"I'm going to go shower. Thank you, boy." Harley presses a kiss to Ziggy's lips and then gets out of the bed.

"Do you want to shower first, or do you want to have a quick talk to go over that scene first?" I ask.

"Um, both?" I arch an eyebrow at him. "You've already seen me naked. Can't you come with me to the shower so we can talk while I get cleaned up?"

"If that's what will make you the most comfortable." I hold out my hand and help him off the bed.

"Sorry about not warning you before I finished." He slows to a stop when we near Joey.

"You're all good. I saw it coming before it happened, so I still got the shot," Joey assures him, and Ziggy lets out a sigh of relief.

Hunter gives me a nod as I lead Ziggy back to the showers.

"Did I do okay for my first time?" he asks quietly when we reach the locker room. He drops his robe and walks straight for the nearest shower. "I'm not a very good sub, am I? That's what you're going to tell me, isn't it?"

I ignore his question because I don't think it's relevant right now. "How did you feel?"

He shrugs, pulling back the curtain and stepping into the shower, turning the knob instantly hot. "Good. The sex was great, obviously."

"I meant about the bondage and the blindfold."

"Oh, it was fine." He doesn't sound overly bothered one way or the other as he squirts soap into his hands and rubs them together to form a lather and then starts to soap himself up.

"That was a very light scene. Do you think you'll be ready when it becomes more intense?"

"I said it was fine. Honestly, the ropes and blindfold didn't do much for me, but they weren't unpleasant. It was just like when a guy wants to try a weird position or cover you in whipped cream or something. It didn't turn me on, but I'm not emotionally traumatized."

I watch as he runs his sudsy hands all over his body, washing away his release. The foam clings to his skin for a few seconds, then is washed away by the water. He wraps his soapy hand around his cock and strokes himself a few times, his shaft plumping under the motion. I lick my lips and tear my eyes away.

"Okay, good." I clear my throat. "Don't forget. We're taking a group trip to Ball and Chain this weekend."

"Yes, Sir," he purrs in a teasing tone, turning around so his sweet little ass is now in my line of sight instead of his cock.

"Watch it with that. You're playing with fire, boy," I warn before I can think better of it.

A few stalls down, a shower shuts off, and Harley steps out, giving me a curious look.

"If you need anything else, let me know." I turn away from Ziggy and give Harley a parting nod before taking off. I should sit down with Hunter and go over the scene, but I need to clear my head first.

6
ZIGGY

My body feels just like when I was a kid and we were about to leave for a field trip: all fluttery nervous and excited. It's stupid and somewhat childish, but I'm genuinely stoked to go back to the club Marshall took me to. Except this time, it won't be just him and me. Everyone is going.

It was either Harley's or Marshall's idea. No one knows for certain because they're both claiming they came up with it. I guess that's their version of whipping it out to see who has the biggest. Good thing Max—or Thunder, as I should start calling him—is not involved because otherwise, he'd win hands down.

I haven't seen his package yet, but I've heard rumors. They were enough to make me hope that once I'm done with this Experimenting with Kink series, I get paired up with him. I won't complain about Harley's dick, don't get me wrong, and he certainly hits all the right spots with it, but a ten-inch dick? Sign me up. Power bottom here and not apologizing for it.

I double-check the address to make sure I've got the

right place, then shoot off a quick text to Glam that I'm here. Seconds after it shows up as read, the door of the house opens, and he steps out, dressed in a pair of jeans so tight I'd be able to count his pubic hairs if he had any. He's wearing an equally tight sparkly top and a pair of heels, and my god, he looks amazing.

He slides into the passenger seat with ease, then bends toward me and kisses me on my mouth. "Thanks for picking me up, boo," he says, and I grin. He's so unapologetically fabulous that I already love him.

"My pleasure, sweetie. You don't drive?" I ask as I quickly type in the address of the club and turn on navigation again.

"No car. It got too expensive. I simply catch a ride with friends or take an Uber."

"Yeah, the insurance is killing me. But at least I'm not constantly bumper to bumper like in LA, so there's that."

"God, yes. Been to LA once, back when I contemplated a career in the movie business. God-awful city. Honestly, as horrific as the traffic was, it was the least of my issues with that city."

I smile at the horror in Glam's voice. "I didn't live in LA itself but to the east of it. I avoided it as much as possible, but we'd still hit the beach every once in a blue moon or do a Rodeo Drive drive-by."

"No shopping?" Glam asks.

I snort. "Not on my school teacher's salary."

"You were a teacher?"

The incredulity in Glam's voice makes me laugh. "Talk about a career change, huh?"

"The teacher-student scenarios are very popular in porn," Glam says with a smile, and I could kiss him for it.

"Not sure I wanna see myself in a school uniform, but

who knows? It may be a fetish I never knew I had. So what about you?"

"I'm a stripper. Or as my boss calls it, an exotic dancer. Which is just a fancy name for being on a stage and taking my clothes off. Most of them anyway. I have to leave on this teeny-tiny string that makes me happy I'm not packing an eight-inch tool, ya know?"

He's hilarious. He has a self-deprecating sense of humor that shows he's far more intelligent than most people probably give him credit for. He plays the role of flirty fuck boy well, but who's the real Glam? Every now and then, I catch glimpses of someone much deeper, much smarter than he allows others to see.

"My boss wasn't happy I requested tonight off," Glam says. "Apparently, we had some C-list celebrities coming in. It's not like I'm mad about it because they tip like shit."

"Ever met anyone famous?" Glam laughs. "All the time, but I'm not easily impressed. It's hard to be when they all stare at me as if they wanna eat me or have me ride their dick, you know? Some just look a little better being horny, is all."

I guess that's the stripper-version of the everyone-is-the-same-naked platitude, and I chuckle as I find a parking spot on the club's massive parking lot.

"Though I have to say, I did meet my big porn star crush once, and that was super cool. He used to work for Ballsy Boys, Rebel?"

I whip my head sideways. "You met Rebel?"

Glam nods. "He's as divine in person as he is on screen. I would've totally done a little extra for him, if you know what I mean, but I think his boyfriend was with him, so he blew me off. His loss, you know?"

I burst out in laughter. This is the funniest coincidence

ever. "His name is Troy. Rebel's boyfriend, I mean. I met both of them, and they're amazing."

"Get out of town!" Glam shouts, clasping my arm. "You met them too?"

"Even better, he's the one who got me the lead for this job. He recommended me to Hunter."

Glam's mouth drops open. "You're shitting me."

I laugh and shake my head. "Nope. Almost had a threesome with them, but Rebel was drunk off his ass when he offered, so Troy and I both agreed we'd better not. But they saved my ass."

I tell Glam about the bachelorette party and the paint and sip event, and by the time I'm done revealing Rebel's drunk antics, he's laughing so hard his mascara is running. "God, that's the funniest thing ever." He pulls down the visor and checks himself in the little mirror. He expertly cleans himself up, then blows a kiss at the mirror.

When we're out of the car and make our way toward the entrance, he links his arm through mine. "You and I are gonna be besties, boo."

He says it lightly, but for some reason, it hits me deep. After all the rejection and ridicule I've faced from coworkers, from people I thought were my friends, this matters. Maybe even more than I realized. "I could use a new bestie." I don't quite pull off matching his tone.

He stops me, his eyes suddenly sharp as he studies me. Then he pulls me in his slender arms with more force than I ever thought him capable of. "I've got you," he says softly, and this is the real Glam. His voice is warm and kind, all his flirtiness gone.

I hug him tight. "Thank you."

It's ironic that people always look down on strippers and

sex workers, yet he's given me more acceptance in a fifteen-minute car ride than all those so-called upstanding people who knew me for years but dropped me like a hot stone when they found out about my sex tape. And as we walk inside, I hold on tight to Glam's arm, beyond grateful that I've found a friend.

Marshall

FOR ONCE, I managed to be the first one to arrive somewhere. And not a little early either. I got to Ball and Chain an hour before the group was scheduled to meet. I was in desperate need of a little grounding, and as far as I'm concerned, there's no better place to get my head together than the kink club. Obviously, I'd never play with a sub when my head is this messy, but simply sitting here and watching the light scenes going on all around me is exactly what I needed.

I'm not sure how long I've been peacefully watching a Daddy with his little on his lap, the boy sucking a pacifier and seeming to nap while the Daddy chats with another Dom, when the sound of Byron's laughter draws my attention. Pulling my gaze away from the sweet scene almost feels like waking up from a dream, and the rest of the club comes into focus. I notice him the minute he walks in, arm in arm with Glam.

Byron is dressed in the same way I instructed him to the last time we came, while Glam is looking ten kinds of fabulous, turning the heads of every Dom within a five-foot radius and a couple of subs as well.

I stand up from my seat and stride over to greet them,

taking note of the way Byron blushes when he sees me, his laughter trailing off almost instantly.

"I have a table for us." I feel all sorts of strange inside my own skin. How should I greet them? With a hug? A handshake? Both options seem awkward and wrong. I'm not used to being so unsure of myself, and I don't like it at all. I have no use for *awkward* or *insecure*. I'm a Dom, for fuck's sake. Then I do what feels natural and press a quick kiss to Glam's cheek and then Byron's.

"Ooh, don't we feel special," Glam coos, wrapping his fingers around my forearm and fixing me with a flirty look.

"Don't cause any trouble. Harley, Hunter, and I had to vouch for all you boys tonight to bring you as guests, which means you'd better be on your best behavior."

"Yes, Sir," Glam purrs and glances around at the main lounge area. "Maybe I should look into getting my own membership after tonight. It's been ages since I've been in the scene properly. I miss it." He sighs wistfully and then fixes his smile back into place.

"The others should be here any minute," I tell them as I lead them over to our table.

"I can't believe you were the first one here," Byron says.

"Mm." I don't want to explain the strange feeling I've gotten since watching his first scene. I'm not even sure I *can* explain it. I came here to do a job and get over a messy breakup, not fall for some cute, vanilla twink.

"I'm going to get a bottle of water." Glam gestures toward the bar.

"Can you grab me one too?" Byron asks, and he nods.

Glam walks away, and Byron fidgets a little in his seat, scanning the room. I can't decide if he's purposefully avoiding looking at me or if he's genuinely fascinated by everything going on around him.

"Do I make you nervous?" I ask without thinking. He's relaxed considerably since we started spending some time together, but he still has that air of nervousness I can't seem to get past. I want him to be comfortable, laughing, joking, and letting his guard down around me like he does with the other guys.

"What?" Byron scrunches his eyebrows together and bites his bottom lip.

"I've noticed when you're around me, you tend to be quieter, a little clumsier. You definitely blush more," I explain.

"You noticed that?" He sounds embarrassed.

"I'm observant." I smirk. "So, do I?"

"I guess? I don't know, not really *nervous* per se. I know you wouldn't do anything to harm me or anything like that."

"Then what is it?" I press, more and more curious to know why he's so different around me than the rest of the Kinky Boys crew.

"It's silly, but you're sort of intimidating. You have this vibe that makes me want to stand up straight and make sure I'm behaving or something," he explains, tacking on that infectious giggle of his at the end. "It makes me feel flustered, I guess."

"Hm." I process his words, resisting the urge to lean into his personal space and test to see just how *flustered* I can make him.

"Like that." He waves his hand at me.

"What?"

"That *hm* you just did. I don't know if that means you're disappointed with my answer or if it was okay or what."

"What do you think will happen if I'm disappointed?"

"I don't know." He shrugs, his teeth worrying his bottom lip even more intensely now.

"I'm not disappointed."

"What then?"

"I was processing."

"Oh." He blows out a breath and slumps forward, putting his elbows on the table.

Before I can take any more time to consider his answer, Hunter and Joey approach the table, followed closely by the rest of the crew.

Byron jumps up and greets the other boys with hugs and animated welcomes, while Hunter pulls a chair out for Joey and then sits down next to him. Glam returns a moment later, and just like that, the whole gang is here. It's a surprisingly warm feeling, being surrounded by all the Kinky Boys, almost like we're family, which is silly, seeing as I've only known them for a few weeks.

"I have a scene scheduled in an hour. It's a hot wax play scene with an experienced sub I've gotten to know well over the years. You're all welcome to watch if you're interested," Harley says.

Ian sits forward, his eyes sharp and curious. "Hot wax? That seems like it would hurt."

"The kind of hurt this particular sub gets off on," Harley says, and Ian's eyes get wider, his pink tongue darting out to wet his lips.

"I might watch," he says softly, and Harley nods.

Byron bites his bottom lip, staring down at the table and then turning his head to look around again, which I'm now even more convinced is an avoidance tactic.

"Something wrong?" I ask him quietly so only he can hear me.

He darts a glance at the rest of the guys, then leans toward me a bit and says, his voice low, "I'm not sure if I want to see anything that's painful. I get that the sub likes it, but thinking about it makes me feel a little queasy. I've never been very good with a lot of pain."

"You don't have to if you're not comfortable. I'm sure we can find a scene you would enjoy watching."

"Okay," he agrees with a grateful smile.

"Real talk, though. Can we talk about how cute Tank and Brewer are on Instagram?" Glam pulls out his phone and brings up his Instagram. "I was bummed when they both cut way back on filming with Ballsy Boys, but their Insta gives me so much life." He scrolls through a few images of the two former costars going about their daily lives. From what I can tell, Brewer takes pictures in which Tank mostly scowls. Their scenes are legendary, and the story of how they got together is practically Gay Lore at this point.

"Not going to lie. Those two were definitely on my mind when I took this job," Ian confesses. "Not that I'm hoping to fall in love with any of you," he adds hastily.

"Okay, but if you were going to fall in love with one of us, who would it be?" Glam flirts, batting his eyelashes and drawing a laugh from Ian.

"Oh god, I don't know." He sweeps his eyes over everyone at the table, lingering for a few seconds on Harley, then jumping to me. "That's not fair. There aren't enough Doms here for me to choose from."

"Baby is right, Daddy. We need more Doms," Glam complains.

Hunter chuckles. "I'm running a porn studio, not a dating service."

"Boo." Glam sighs. "How about you, Thunder? Anyone here strikes your fancy?"

Thunder grimaces and runs a hand through his hair. "Uh...you guys are all great."

"Well, if that wasn't the nicest rejection I've ever gotten," Byron jokes, and everyone laughs.

We chat for a while longer until Harley declares it's time to get ready for his scene and lets us know which room he'll be in, in case anyone wants to watch. Everyone except for Byron eagerly gets up from the table. He bites his lip again and looks after the group uncertainly.

"If I'm the only one who doesn't want to watch, I can suck it up and just go," he says.

"I've witnessed plenty of wax play in my life and done a number of scenes myself. I'm fine to sit this one out. Why don't we go see if there's anything else going on you might like better?" I suggest.

"If you're sure?"

"Of course I'm sure."

We both stand up, and out of habit, my hand finds its way to the back of his neck to guide him through the lounge. He doesn't seem to mind the contact, so I leave it where it is, doing my best to ignore how warm and smooth his skin feels under my fingertips.

We head down the first hallway, and I smile at the scene in the first room. An inflatable pool is filled with plastic balls, and puppies are bounding all around, wrestling and playing.

Byron's breath catches, and wonder dances in his eyes. "Wow."

"What do you think? Want to watch some puppies play for a little while?"

"Puppies?" He tilts his head to one side, smiling at the sight before us.

"These subs like to let everything go by pretending to be puppies," I explain.

"Cool." He darts his gaze around the room like a kid on

Christmas who can't decide which new toy to play with first.

One of the puppies bounces over to us, skidding to a stop in front of Byron, his Master a few steps behind him.

Byron's eyes go wide, and a smile spreads across his lips as he stoops down. "Can I pet him?" he asks, looking up to the pup's Master. I breathe a sigh of relief at his manners.

"Sure you can. Taffy loves being petted."

Byron reaches out cautiously and brushes his fingers over the muzzle of the puppy hood. A sparkle of mischief lights up in the pup's eyes, telegraphing his intentions seconds before he pounces on Byron, knocking him onto his ass and then climbing on top of him to wrestle.

"Oh my gosh." Byron giggles as the puppy licks his face.

"Sorry, he's a little excited." The Master gives me an apologetic look.

"Doesn't seem like my boy minds," I assure him, biting my tongue as I realize the words that just slipped out. Byron isn't *my* boy. Correcting myself at this point would be more awkward than helpful, so I shake it off, but it stays stuck in the back of my mind as Byron runs his hands over the puppy's bare back and then give his ears a scratch.

"He loves to play fetch if you want to play." The Dom pulls a ball out of his pocket and offers it to Byron.

"Oh, can I?" He takes the ball and waves it in front of Taffy's face. "Go get it, boy." He tosses it only a few feet, but the puppy scrambles after it enthusiastically.

I lean against the wall as Byron plays with the puppy. A few more catch wind of the newcomer and make their way over to welcome him as well. He giggles and coos at each of them in turn, his cheeks flushed with excitement, his expression showing nothing but joy. I can't keep the smile off my face, my chest feeling almost too tight for the way my heart swells at the scene in front of me.

I swear I could watch Byron play all night long. What I can't figure out is if he just likes playing with the puppies or if it might be something he'd want to try for himself. And I don't just mean for the Kinky Boys.

Eventually, I get a text from Hunter, asking where we disappeared to. I'm guessing that means Harley's scene is finished and they're all gathering in the lounge again.

"Sweetheart." I put my hand on Byron's shoulder and squeeze gently. "Are you ready to go, or do you want to play longer?"

"Oh." He blinks as if remembering for the first time that the rest of the world exists. "Yeah, we can go." He gets to his feet and brushes his pants off. "This was fun, thank you," he says to no one in particular, and a few of the puppies bark as we leave the room to go in search of the rest of our group.

Even after we rejoin everyone, Byron's gaze snaps back to the hallway that leads to the puppy room every so often.

The puppies and Byron's excitement lingers with me the rest of the night, even long after I get home and tuck myself into bed. It's dangerous to think so much about a sweet boy I know I shouldn't have, but Byron isn't making it easy *not* to think about him.

7
ZIGGY

Round two. Daddy texted me this morning that there had been a change in plans for the second scene, but that he'd explain it to me beforehand. Nothing to worry about, he'd added because in the history of mankind, everyone has always been comforted by those words and stopped, you know, worrying. *Not.*

So yeah, my stomach is in knots as I walk in, and strangely enough, the only thing that prevents me from completely freaking out is the idea that Marshall will be there. Somehow, I trust him to look out for me. Even more after he so easily accepted my reluctance to watch the hot wax play and allowed me to hang out with the puppies instead. Now, *that* was fun.

"Good morning, Ziggy," Harley greets me as I enter the dressing room. It still jars me when someone calls me that. It's good that he does it, though, to prevent him from slipping up and using my real name.

He's dressed this time, a noticeable difference with usual. "Are we doing our shoot dressed today?" I quip as I put my bag down.

Harley grins. "Nope, though I can guarantee you I could make people jerk off to a scene of me undressing you."

I chuckle. "I bet you could."

"But no, that's not on the schedule for today. Come sit with me, boy."

As always, my belly does a little swirl at the word "boy." He grabs my wrist and pulls me down on the bench next to him.

"I've talked to Hunter and Marshall about the first scene, and we agreed to change the second scene so it'd better fit you."

I swallow, uneasiness rolling in my stomach. "Did I do something wrong?"

Harley puts his hand on my knee, and even that little touch helps me. "No, boy, you didn't. You're an inexperienced sub. No one expects you to be perfect after one scene. If we showed that, we wouldn't portray kink as realistically as Hunter intends to."

Relief fills me, and I breathe a little easier. "Okay. You had me worried there for a moment."

Harley's eyes are kind as he affectionately rubs my knee. "You really are a little worrywart. Try to remember that all you have to do is obey me. You have nothing else to worry about but that, okay?"

I nod. "So, what are we doing today?"

Harley's kind smile turns into something a little more wicked. *Uh-oh.* "Edging."

"Edging?" Isn't that where you don't get to come for, like, hours?

"You are easily aroused, my boy, so we need to teach you how to hold back your orgasm for your Dom."

Oh god. That doesn't sound like fun at all. In fact, that seems like an absolute nightmare. I may be the lousiest sub to ever walk the face of the earth, but I've learned by now that this is not my call. If the three Doms have decided this is what's gonna happen, then that's what's gonna happen.

"In all honesty, I think that's, like, a whole lot of awful, but more important, I'll fail spectacularly at it. I've never been good at denying myself in that sense."

Harley's grin only grows wider. "You don't say... No worries, boy. I brought some helpful tools."

"I'm not gonna like them, am I?"

"Probably not, but keep this in mind. When I will allow you to come, you're gonna have an orgasm that will make you kiss the face of god."

Okay, I have to admit that part does appeal to me. But how long is he going to make me suffer to get there? I have a sneaky suspicion that I don't want to know. Not that he'd even tell me. "It better be." I sigh.

"I promise. Now, let's go."

As soon as I step onto the set, Marshall walks over to me. "Are you okay?" The genuine concern in his voice warms my heart.

"Yeah. Yes, Sir," I catch myself. I'd better get used to uttering those two words.

"Harley explained to you what he's gonna do?" I nod. "And you're on board with that?"

I shrug. "I can't really complain, can I? I mean, it's not like it's hardcore kink."

Marshall studies me for a moment. "He'll make you suffer. Make no mistake."

I let out a deep sigh. "Yeah, I figured as much." I straighten my shoulders. "It's okay. I can take it."

Marshall shoots me a look I can't interpret, then leans in and kisses me right next to my mouth. "Make me proud, boy," he says.

My stomach flutters as he walks away.

Half an hour later, I can say with absolute certainty that I've never hated a man as much as I hate Harley right now. It started all out fine, with him kissing me—yummy, for the record—and then doing what he called mapping my body to see where I was most sensitive. Dude found that spot behind my ear that drives me crazy when you suck on it, discovered that my nipples are not that stimulating for me, and ascertained that both my holes are very, very hungry.

For minutes, he fucked my mouth with two fingers, making me drool all over him, desperate for more. When he finally fed me his cock—I was damn close to begging for it. The only thing holding me back was his stern admonishment that if I spoke another word, he'd not let me come at all—I almost came on the spot.

Except as soon as I trembled, he pulled his cock out again, then waited until I'd cooled off, those evil eyes of his gleaming. And then he did it again. And again. And again until I wanted to fucking kill him. So I love the sensation of a cock in my mouth. Sue me. But to feed me a cock and then pull it back out after a minute? That's plain cruel.

And that was only the beginning. He tied my hands above my head to the headboard, immobilizing me again except for my legs. He controlled those himself by folding them back or over his shoulder when he started the next part of his torture: fucking me.

Not with his cock, mind you, because that would've been too easy. No, he's using anal beads, a long string of smooth anal beads, increasing in size. He pushes them in, one by one, and I squirm and moan. Holy shit, it feels so good to be this full. And then he pulls them out again, my body making obscene noises as they plop out.

I'm about to die from not being allowed to come. My

body is aching everywhere, my muscles cramping from holding back, my balls throbbing. But every. Single. Time. I'm close to the edge, he stops everything. Just drops his hands and lets my body crawl back from the ledge. It takes longer every time to recover, and I'm losing my mind.

"Please, Sir," I beg, unable to stay quiet anymore. "Please..."

His eyes sparkle. He takes perverse pleasure in my suffering, proving that what he said at the steakhouse is true. He's a demanding Dom, and this is heaven for him. His cock—which looks spectacular with a silver cockring he slipped on before we even started, making it stand as hard as I've ever seen a cock—is dripping. Literally. Hell, Joey moves in for a super closeup shot as it dribbles a thick trail of precum onto me.

"What did I tell you what would happen if you spoke again without my permission, boy?"

Shit, shit, shit. He's not really gonna...? Oh god, he is. I swallow. "You said you'd gag me, Sir."

"I did, didn't I?"

"Yes, Sir."

"Do you want to be gagged, boy?"

"Not particularly, Sir. It's just... It's hard to stay quiet, Sir."

"Mmm. And yet you don't think you need help with it."

I open my mouth, then realize at the last moment he didn't actually ask me a question, and close it again.

He smiles, a happy gleam in his eyes. "Good boy," he says, and bam, here we go again, my whole body responding to those two simple words. I hate him. Absolutely fucking hate him.

"You know, I'm feeling benevolent today. I'm not going to

gag you, but I am going to help you in fighting back your orgasm. How's that sound?"

There's only one correct answer, even I am not that stupid, but holy shit, I'm not gonna like this, am I? "Good, Sir. Thank you."

I have to force the last two words out, and judging by the smirk on Harley's face, he knows it too. Fucker.

He holds up a leather strap to the camera. "I'm going to tie this around your balls and pull them away from your body, which will help you to not come. Actually, it will prevent you from coming. Even better."

Even better? That was some lame joke, right? I clamp down on my bottom lip to keep myself from protesting.

Harley turns toward the camera. "This is not something to do at home if you've never done it before. If you want to experiment with a cockring or a cock and balls ring, start with slipping one on before you're hard, like I did."

He strokes himself and holds up his cock for a closeup shot. Joey moves in so close Harley's gotta feel his breath on his balls. When Joey signals he's got the shot, Harley reverts his attention back to me. "As you can see, that's too late for my boy here, so I'll help him in a different way."

He expertly wraps the leather straps around my balls, pulling them back and away from my body. It doesn't hurt as much as I expected, though it's anything but pleasurable.

"Keep in mind that you can't use a method like this for a prolonged time. If you're new, maybe start with fifteen to twenty minutes. As soon as it gets too red or tingles or you experience a loss of sensation, take it off immediately."

Loss of sensation? Is he kidding? My alarm must've shown on my face because Harley chuckles and presses a quick kiss on my lips. "No worries, boy. Your package is way too pretty to let anything happen to it."

I can't help it. My head drops to the side, and my eyes seek out Marshall. I know he's there, watching. It takes me a moment to find him, and when I do, I'm almost shocked by the fierce expression on his face, like he's watching Harley's every move to make sure he treats me right. But then he catches my stare, and he nods at me, his face softening. I want to make him proud. Be his good boy.

And so I say nothing as Harley finishes wrapping up my balls, then leans back to admire his handiwork. "Oh, aren't you gorgeous, boy? Your pretty balls snug and wrapped up. Let's have some fun."

By fun, he means that for the next half hour or so—though I admit I lose track of time, so it may have been longer—he fucks the living daylights out of me, taking my ass in every position he can manage with my hands bound like that. Including me kneeling on all fours because the ropes on my hands are long enough for me to turn around. Imagine that.

It's...amazing. So fucking good. Like the single best dicking I've ever had...except for the tiny little fact that I. Can't. Come. Oh, my body tries. My balls pull against the leather straps, but they got nowhere to go. It's like I'm tiptoeing on the ledge of a deep ravine. I want to jump in so badly, but I can't. And every time I feel like I might just tip over and fall anyway, Harley yanks me right back.

At some point, I lose it. I'm babbling. Incoherent pleas for mercy. To let me come. I only vaguely register when Harley pulls out and jerks himself off fiercely, then sprays me with his cum as I lay quivering on my belly. He rubs his cum into my skin, into my hole, and by now, I'm convinced I'm never gonna come.

I'm weak as jelly when he flips me over, then positions

me so the camera can get a good shot. "Now it's your time. You did good, boy. Now, come for your Sir."

He unwraps the straps from my balls, and I'm screaming. It slams into me, robbing me of my breath as every muscle in my body clenches at the same time. It hurts, a powerful agony that packs a punch of pleasure at the same time. My orgasm is so violent I black out. I wake up on Harley's lap with him holding me, cuddling me, and whispering sweet words. When he sees I'm up, he feeds me a straw, and I greedily empty half a water bottle.

"And cut!" Joey calls in the background.

"You did good, boy. That was spectacular."

I stay silent as I lean into him, needing the comfort of his embrace a little longer. Harley calls it spectacular, and I'm sure the video will look amazing, but I don't know how I feel. Yes, that orgasm was the single most intense orgasm I've ever had in my life. But was it worth it? I don't know.

Harley is a good guy, and I genuinely like him. He's experienced, that much is clear, and I trust him not to go past my boundaries. But everything I've learned so far about this D/s dynamic says I should want to please him, want to obey him. Harley said it himself. If he did his job right, I'd want to obey him.

What does it mean that I don't? Not really. Not to this degree. He takes great pleasure in making his subs suffer for him, as today showed once again, but I don't want to suffer *for him*. I want to be a good boy, I really do, and I love it when he holds me like this, but I hate that I have to go through that whole suffering part before we get to the good stuff.

I let out a sad sigh. Maybe I'm really not cut out to be a submissive.

. . .

Marshall

An array of emotions flash across Byron's face while Harley cuddles and cares for him after the scene. Everything inside me is urging me to go over to him and make sure he's okay, but I don't want to step on Harley's toes either. Until Harley is satisfied that he's finished with aftercare, Byron belongs to him, and I have to respect that, even if my skin is crawling with impatience.

"Good scene." Hunter sidles up next to me and nods toward the two men still lying in bed together.

"Yeah," I grunt, then clear my throat. "Seemed to be more Ziggy's speed, but there was still something missing."

"Hmm. Are you going to talk to him?"

"Of course. I take my job seriously."

"Your *job*, right." Hunter claps me on the shoulder and walks away before I can process what he just said or form a response.

I shuffle impatiently, breathing a quiet sigh of relief when Harley finally gets up and helps Byron to his feet. Like last time, I grab one of the soft bathrobes and rush over to the boy's side. Harley gives me an amused look.

"What, no bathrobe for me? The service around here sucks," he jokes as I hand Byron's over.

"Bite me, Harley."

"With pleasure." He shows me his teeth threateningly, and I shake my head with a smirk on my lips.

"Quick talk while you shower again?" I ask Byron, and he nods.

"Damn, my legs are still like Jell-o." He takes a step, wobbling a little.

"Here." I put an arm around him, pulling his small, slender body against mine to support his weight.

"Thank you."

I hold off asking any questions while I focus on helping him to the showers. By the time we reach them, he seems a lot sturdier on his feet, but I'm still reluctant to let him go. Like last time, he takes off his robe, pushes the curtain back, and steps inside the shower. *Unlike* last time, I follow him without thought, stripping my shirt over my head and reaching for my pants.

"What are you doing?" he asks, and I look down at myself with embarrassment.

"Sorry, I was on autopilot, I think." I grimace, pulling my shirt back on and leaning against the wall just outside the shower stall.

"How are you feeling?"

"Good, kind of drained. That was more intense than I expected. I think I need a nap now." He chuckles, but the truth is right there on his face, his blinks slow and his eyelids drooping a little. My mind drifts to the puppies he had so much fun playing with last week and then conjures the image of a sweet little Ziggy puppy, orgasm drunk and sleepy, curling up with his head in my lap, looking for cuddles and pets while he sleeps for a few hours. My heart somersaults in my chest at the image, and my throat tightens.

"Aside from physically, how are you feeling?" I press. I spent the entire two hours of the filming observing his expression closely, keeping an eye out for any signs of distress he might not voice for fear of ruining the shoot, and it was curious at times. It was obvious he liked a lot of it, but there were moments when he seemed to grow anxious or impatient. During those times, he looked over at me and seemed to relax. I can't deny that each time it made my dick harder and my heart beat faster, but I'm not entirely sure he was aware he was doing it.

He bites his lip, seeming to consider his words carefully as he washes himself, cleaning away all the sweat and cum and lube coating his skin. "I want to tell you something, but I'm afraid you'll tell Daddy and I'll get fired," he confesses in nearly a whisper.

I frown and shuffle a little closer, stray droplets of water splashing against my clothes and shoes, but that's the least of my concerns right now. "Tell me, boy," I command in a gentle but firm voice.

"I know I'm supposed to *want* to obey him, but it really doesn't feel that way when we're doing a scene." He meets my eyes for a fraction of a second, then glances away again. "At the club the other night, when I was playing with the puppies, you looked really proud of me. It made me warm and happy inside, and I *think* that's what I'm supposed to feel when Harley is Domming me. Is that the right word even? Anyway, I feel it a little bit sometimes, like at the end when we cuddle, but not for the rest of it."

"You're worried that you don't have a submissive reaction like you should and that it'll make more intense scenes even more difficult to do?"

He nods, turning around to rinse the suds off his back and then shutting off the water. I grab a clean, dry towel and hand it to him. The urge to step closer and dry him myself is almost overwhelming.

"I want to ask you something, but I'm afraid it'll be over the line." He chews on his bottom lip as he dries himself off.

"You can ask me anything."

"Well, I thought maybe the problem is that I can't fully relax in front of the cameras. You can totally say no, but I was wondering if maybe we could try a scene, just you and me, no pressure, no one watching, so I can see if it feels any different?"

My breath catches. Of all the questions I thought he might ask, that was *not* on my list. "What kind of scene did you have in mind?"

He shrugs, running the towel through his hair. "You're the Dom."

I grin and shake my head. "*Now* you're the perfect little submissive?" I tease.

"I don't mean sex or anything.

"I understand. You want to see if I can make you let go fully." Excitement dances across my skin at the idea. I shouldn't cross this line, especially when I'm already far too obsessed with his well-being as it is, but how can I say no when he's looking at me with those sweet, hopeful eyes?

"Please?" That one word is all it takes to break me.

"Okay," I agree with a sigh. "I want you to come to my place tomorrow night."

"Tomorrow night, got it," he says with a resolute nod.

"I'll text you my address. Be there at seven."

"Yes, Sir."

"And wear something comfortable."

"Okay. What are we going to do?"

"Oh no, boy. I'm the Dom, remember? Don't you worry your pretty little head about what I've planned. Just be good and do as you're told."

His eyes widen, and his pink tongue darts out and wets his perfect bow-shaped lips as he gives a shaky nod of agreement. My cock twitches. It's safe to say I'm completely fucked.

8

ZIGGY

Marshall's apartment is not what I expected. It's nice and got a bit of a view, but inside, it's cold. He's got furniture, but the fake leather and chrome doesn't match his personality at all. The glass coffee table comes straight from the nineties, and the patterned curtains you usually see in cheap hotel rooms.

"I'm renting this furnished, so everything here isn't mine," Marshall says. That explains a lot.

"Where's your own stuff?"

"Back in New York. I agreed to six months with Kinky Boys, so I didn't want to pay for an expensive cross-country move and then have to haul it all back."

He's only here temporarily? That's news to me. "So, you just drove here with your essentials?"

He smiles. "I didn't own a car in New York. Didn't need one. So I flew in with two suitcases. God bless Southwest. And I'm leasing a car here."

He's done everything to be able to leave again easily, hasn't he? I mean, it makes sense if he has a life there worth returning to. He's not a porn star but a consultant, and I assume that six months in, there won't be much for him to consult on anymore. Still, it makes me sad in a way I don't quite understand.

"Anyway." I change the subject. "What do you want me to do? Strip? Kneel? Kiss your feet?"

His smile is like that of a predator luring in his prey. "You'd look very pretty naked and kneeling at my feet, but that's not what I had in mind. I want you to go into the guest bedroom, strip down to your underwear, and then sit there kneeling until I come get you. Do you think you can do that?"

It sounds easy enough, so I nod.

"Words, Ziggy," Marshall admonishes me, and my belly does a little flip at the way he says my new name.

"Sorry, Sir. I'm supposed to call you Sir, right?"

"Yes. Sir or Master, whichever you prefer."

I taste them both on my tongue. Funnily enough, I actually like Master better, but I can't explain why. "Yes, Master," I say. His eyes widen in surprise. Then he catches himself.

I go into the bedroom he pointed at and strip. Why did he want me to leave my underwear on? I bite my lip. Is he saying something with that? Like, does it mean something? I lay out my clothes on the bed so they don't wrinkle, then do a self-check in the big mirror attached to the wall. At least I'm wearing a nice pair of black, snug boxer briefs.

He didn't tell me where to kneel, but I'm assuming the idea is to wait for him and not peek, so I sit back on my heels right next to the bed. The carpet is soft, though I don't want to think about what others have done in here if the place is rented out often. Ew. I'd better take a long, hot shower when I get back home.

Two minutes or so in, and I'm already bored. What's up with this kneeling thing? I saw it in the club as well, all these subs on their knees, sitting patiently. How do they do that? I can't sit still if my life depends on it. Not even when Marshall asked so nicely, though I do try to keep the fidgeting and shifting to a minimum.

Finally, Marshall walks in. He didn't tell me I couldn't look at him, so I take him in. Hot damn, he's hot in a pair of leather pants, his chest bare except for a harness, showcasing his tattoos and...oh my god, he has nipple piercings. Mmm, I'd love to play with those. Would he let me if I ask him nicely? And more important, does he have piercings anywhere else?

"If you're done staring, let's work on your posture," Marshall says, and I drag my eyes off him, my cheeks heating.

"Yes, Master."

He walks behind me, grabs my shoulders, and pulls them back. It's the first time he touches me, and my skin breaks out in goose bumps. "Sit straight, head down, eyes on the floor."

I do as he says, tightening my core to keep my back straight while slightly pushing out my ass. Gotta showcase my best features, right?

"Beautiful, boy," Marshall says as he walks in front of me. I'm focusing on his bare feet. Dammit, even the man's feet are sexy. It's not fair.

He lifts my chin up with his index finger, and I meet his eyes. "Are you ready, boy?"

I nod, then remember that won't work, and say, "Yes, Master."

"Good. No more talking unless I ask you a direct question. Remind me of your safewords."

"Green to keep going, yellow to slow down, red to stop immediately."

"Perfect. I'm counting on you to use them when necessary."

"Yes, Master."

He lets go of my chin. "Ordinarily, I'd have you crawl back to the living room, but I don't know the history of this carpet, so let's not."

I grin. A man after my own heart. I follow him into the living room, frowning when I see what he's set up. He's pushed all the furniture to the sides, and a large white sheet covers the floor. He's put some weight on the corners to keep it in place. On the couch is a small crate, but I can't see what's in it.

Marshall sits down on the couch, then points at the spot on the floor between his legs. "Come here, boy."

Okay, that's weird. Why do my insides go all funny and twirly when he says something like that? They never do that when Harley tells me to do something. Well, a little when he praises me, but even that feels different.

I obey his command, and his downward finger makes it pretty clear what I'm supposed to do, so I kneel at his feet the way he showed me.

"Good boy," Marshall says. "No allergies, right?"

Why is he asking? "No. I'm a vegetarian, though."

He smiles. "That, I knew."

When he holds out his hand to me, I automatically open my mouth. It's a Hershey's Kiss. The man is feeding me chocolate. That's some serious bribery. I open my mouth to crack a joke along those lines, but Marshall snaps his fingers at me. Right, no talking. I should probably have an opinion on him using a signal like that, but I don't mind. Weird.

"Put your hands on my knees," Marshall tells me.

Why is it so easy for me to obey him and do I struggle so much with Harley? I don't get it. I place both my hands flat on his knees, letting out a happy sigh at the contact. I like touching him.

"Good boy," Marshall says again, and he gives me another Hershey's Kiss that I eat with a smile. I'm loving this.

"Can you sit on your hands and knees for me?" Marshall asks.

Of course I can, and I quickly put my hands on the floor and push myself up until my back is straight. Well, until I remember that it's much more attractive if I push my ass back a little, and so I do.

Marshall laughs. "Shake that butt for me, Ziggy."

I grin as I oblige, waggling my butt. Then it hits me. He's treating me like a... I freeze.

Marshall's hand is immediately on my back, gently stroking me. "It's okay, puppy," he croons. "You were such a good boy for me." I arch my back and lean into his touch. "Such a sweet puppy."

A puppy. That's what we're doing, puppy play. It feels so natural that I don't even have to think about it. Marshall is studying me, waiting for my reaction, and I inch closer to him and nuzzle his hand. When I look up again, he's beaming with pride, and it makes my insides go all weak.

He lifts his hand from my back, and I immediately miss the contact. I bump against his leg with my head, wordlessly asking for more. I like it when he touches me. It makes me feel safe. The kneeling in itself does nothing for me, but I could sit at his feet for hours as long as he touches me, strokes my hair, scratches my neck, or pets me like he did just now.

He holds something out that he took from the crate next to him. Ears. Puppy ears. I swallow. This will make it real. I'll be his puppy. Do I want to be? He's holding the ears in his hand, not forcing them on me or even asking me to take them. How would a puppy react?

I inch a little closer, curiously studying them. They're cute, soft and furry, the ones that you can attach to your head with a headband. I nudge Marshall with my head. These will look adorable on me, and I can't wait to have them on.

"Do you want to try on your ears?" Marshall asks, and his tone has shifted subtly. It's more playful and affectionate, like someone would talk to a dog.

I nod, hoping that in this case, that's sufficient because I don't want to talk. I like the headspace I'm in right now, all eager to please him.

He smiles at me as he puts the ears on. As soon as he's done, I shake my head, giggling when the ears move. They're perfect. I wish I could see myself, though. Marshall must've read my mind because he grabs his phone. "Look at me." I immediately sit up straight and smile at the camera.

The picture he shows me makes my heart skip a beat. That's me? That adorable puppy with the sparkle in his eyes, the red cheeks, and the big smile is me? I barely recognize myself.

"You're such a cute puppy, Ziggy."

I shake my butt, then look at him questioningly. "I don't have a tail for you, pup. We'll do that next time."

There will be a next time? I'm in. Then Marshall takes out a tennis ball from the crate and throws it for me to fetch, and I'm in heaven.

Marshall

. . .

CUTE IS an understatement when it comes to Ziggy happily bounding after the ball. His ass wiggles as he leans forward and studies the ball like he's trying to figure out how he's supposed to pick it up. After a few seconds, he seems to give up overthinking it, grabbing it in his mouth and trotting back over to me.

I hold out my hand. "Give," I command. But he doesn't drop it. Of course he doesn't. He's Ziggy. His eyes gleam with mischief, and he wiggles his butt again. Fuck, he'd look good with a tail. Next time we play, I'll make sure to tell him to wear a jockstrap, and I'll have a brand-new tail ready for him. I imagine the fluffy tail peeking out from between his adorable, round ass cheeks, and my cock perks up to take notice of the situation. I shift around a little so it's not noticeable, and do my best to ignore it.

If there is a next time. There's no guarantee, of course. I agreed to help Ziggy explore a little light kink tonight. We didn't talk of anything after this. Which means I have to enjoy tonight for what it is.

Ziggy drops down so his chest is on the ground, the ball clutched between his teeth, his ass in the air, still slowly moving back and forth.

"Give," I repeat, putting as much authority into my tone as I can summon, and for a second, it looks like he'll obey, but then the naughty spark comes back, and he scoots back. "Ziggy," I warn, sitting forward and fighting the smile that desperately wants to make an appearance.

How long has it been since I've played with a sub like this? So light and carefree without worrying so much about expectations? Too damn long.

He jumps back. I lunge after him and chase him around the room as he dodges and scrambles with the ball in his mouth. Obviously, I could catch him easily, as I'm on two feet, and he's awkwardly darting around on his hands and knees, but the chase is fun, and so is his playful bark when he thinks he's besting me.

I reach into my pocket, grab another chocolate, and hold it out so he can see it.

"Be a good boy, and you can have another treat," I tempt, and he cocks his head to one side as he considers the offer. My heart beats heavily, the feeling in my chest so big I can hardly breathe. This is too much and definitely too dangerous, considering the circumstances, but it's been so long since I've felt this way, and a big part of me wants to dive into the feeling head first and drown in it.

He sets the ball down and prances over to me. I smile, plopping myself back down on the floor and unwrapping the treat to give to him. When he reaches me, I give him a stern look.

"Sit," I command, and he eagerly puts his butt on the floor. "Good boy," I praise, holding the chocolate out on my hand. He swipes it with his tongue, catching my fingers in the crossfire and sending a slither of lust down my spine, right down to my still hard cock. "Want to keep playing or cuddle a bit?"

Ziggy looks back at the ball lying abandoned a few feet away, and then back at me. He makes a small circle and curls up beside me on the floor. He rests his head on my lap, and I slowly drag my fingers along his soft, warm skin. He sighs and arches up into my touch.

"Such a good, sweet boy, aren't you?" I coo. "We found what my boy likes, didn't we?" As soon as the words are out, my heart skips a beat. I hold my breath, waiting to see if he caught my slip. He whines in what seems to be agreement. Maybe he didn't catch the *my* part. He might be too far into puppy space to be paying much attention to my words. He's reacting to my soothing tone, that's all.

After a few minutes, he rolls onto his back, pulling his arms up to his chest, his eyes closed and a peaceful expression on his face. My eyes flicker to the bulge in his tight briefs, an undeniable erection tenting the fabric. I swallow hard, my cock throbbing against my thigh as I stroke over Ziggy's belly.

"Such a sweet pup you are," I praise in a low, calm voice, and Ziggy nuzzles his face against my thigh. Fuck, he's so perfect. My whole body aches with longing.

We sit like that, me murmuring soft praise as I pet him, his head growing heavy against my thigh as he relaxes more and more as the minutes wear on.

I'm not sure how long we spent that way, but when he finally sits up and blinks sleepily, tugging the puppy ears off his head and clutching them in his hand, it feels like it wasn't long enough.

"How are you feeling, pup?" I run my fingers through his hair with the excuse of taming it when really all I want is one more touch before it's over.

"Mmm." He hums happily, almost like he's a little drunk. "So relaxed. That was amazing and so much fun."

"I'm glad you enjoyed it. If you want to get dressed, you can." He glances down, and a surprised laugh tumbles from his lips as if he's just now remembering he's nearly naked. "I guess I'd better." He rises to his feet. I get up too and follow him down the hallway to the bedroom, not bothering to fight the overwhelming urge to stay near him until he leaves and I'm left to confront the situation in my own head.

He doesn't seem to mind, and I sit down on the bed and, leaning against the headboard, watch him get dressed at a languid pace.

Once his clothes are on, I expect him to make his excuses and leave. Instead, he stands at the foot of the bed, biting his lip, clutching the ears between his hands.

"Come here." I pat the spot on the bed beside me. A relieved smile spreads over his lips, and he climbs onto the bed and crawls up next to me.

"Why don't I hang on to these for you, and then if you want to play again another day, they'll be here for you?" I suggest, running a finger along one of the soft ears.

His fingers tighten on the headband part, and he looks at me with a mixture of emotions.

"Are these yours? Like, do you use them with other pups who you play with?"

"I don't play with any other pups here in Vegas. But no, these are yours. I bought them after you asked to come over, so if you'd rather keep them with you instead of leaving them here, that's okay."

He stops clutching them so hard, shakes his head a little as if he's scolding himself for something, then hands them over. "Leaving them here sounds good."

I take the ears and set them on top of my nightstand.

"Can I ask you a question?" He wiggles a little closer on the bed and rests his head on my pillow.

"Shoot."

"Why don't you have a sub of your own?"

Damn, this boy knows how to ask the hard questions. "I did, before I moved out here."

"What happened?" He sits back down next to me, close enough that I feel the warmth radiating off his body. We spent the last hour cuddling while he was half-naked. Surely it'll be okay if I put my arms around him now? Fuck it. I throw caution to the wind and tug him closer, wrap him in my arms and rest my chin on the top of his head to cuddle him properly.

"It's embarrassing," I say quietly. It's certainly not the kind of thing I'm eager to tell a sub I'm admittedly developing an interest in. But if he pushes for an answer, I won't lie to him.

"More embarrassing than having your ex put a home video on Pornhub?" he challenges.

"There's a story there." My eyebrows go up.

"Yeah, not one I want to talk about right now. It would ruin all this zen I have going on."

"Fair enough. I had a boy, and I loved him a lot. He was a rambunctious, bratty sub and a lot of fun to play with. We were together just over a year when he broke it off. He said I was too soft for a Dom, that he wanted someone with a *firmer hand*." Shame claws at my throat as I confess. What kind of Dom can't please his boy?

Ziggy pushes against me, forcing me to loosen my grip on him, and my heart beats harder. Obviously, he thinks I'm pathetic now. Will he even trust me to keep him safe on set now, knowing what an inadequate Dom I've been in the past?

"Sir," he says softly, and I chance a glance at him, bracing myself for a pitying expression on his face. "I think you're a great Dom. Look how much you've gone out of your way to take care of me and keep me safe, even when it was way above and beyond your job description."

"Thank you, sweetheart." I tug him close again and press a kiss to the top of his head.

I take a peek at the clock on my dresser and cringe at the time.

"It's late. We'd better get you home."

He follows my gaze and sighs. "Yeah, it is late. And I

suppose I'd better go…" He leaves it hanging like a question, looking up at me through his eyelashes with that perfect, heart-melting, begging sub expression.

"None of that," I scold gently. "You need to go home and clear your head tonight. This was a lot, and you need to process it."

"I guess you're right. You said we can play again, right?"

"Let's talk about it in a few days." I don't want to make any concrete plans. He may very well go home and decide that rather than play with me again, he wants to go back to the club and find a master who doesn't have the complication of *technically* being his sort of boss.

"Okay. Thank you again. Tonight was…amazing," he says. "Master," he tacks on at the last second. He leans forward and brushes the barest kiss against my lips. It can hardly even be called a kiss, just a touch of the lips that's over so quickly it doesn't fully register.

He gets out of bed, and I follow him to the door and watch as he heads down the hallway. When he reaches the stairs, he pauses and turns, a sweet smile still on his lips. Our eyes meet. A blush rises on his cheeks, and his grin widens.

I stand in my doorway, staring after him long after he's disappeared.

I am so utterly fucked.

9
ZIGGY

Both Daddy and Marshall keep stressing the importance of team building, and so Ian—Baby—suggested we'd all see Glam stripping. Truth be told, I've never been to a strip club, so I was instantly on board, but even more when Glam's face lit up as if he'd won a prize.

Besides, I'm in for anything to take my mind off my worries over the next scene. That puppy play with Marshall was amazing, but it's made things only more confusing. What does it mean that I have no trouble obeying him but that it's such a struggle with Harley? I don't understand it.

And being a puppy was so much fun, but I know my next scene with Harley won't be. I'm dreading it, so I'll take all the distraction I can get. Then Max asked if he could come too, even though the rest of us are all subs, and that's how we ended up with an Uber full of boys.

Max is sitting in the front, chatting with the driver who he seems to know well, judging by their conversation, and Baby and I are in the back. I point at the cup the driver has that says "Tip a bitch," and Baby and I both snicker.

"So guys, this is my best friend, Benton," Max says over his shoulder, and Benton raises a hand in acknowledgment. "He's the one who told Hunter about me and got me into this whole mess."

"Mess?" Benton sounds indignant. "This whole opportunity, you mean. You and your monster cock are destined for fame and fortune, my friend."

Baby and I look at each other, and then we burst out laughing. Max chuckles sheepishly while Benton bumps him with his elbow. A car honks his horn, and Benton pulls sharply to the left. "Sheesh asshole, I was only, like, an inch over the line," he mutters.

"Keep your eyes on the road, Ben." Max sighs. "It would be really bad for my career if you killed the two in the back seat, you know?"

Benton huffs. "I've never had an accident."

"I swear your guardian angels must all retire after a year or so because they're getting more action with you in a year than with others in a lifetime," Max mumbles.

Watching these two is hilarious, and Baby and I share another smile.

"I'll pick you guys back up when you're done," Benton says a few minutes later.

I frown. He doesn't have his app on like Uber drivers always have. "Erm, did you forget to start the ride?"

Benton waves his hand dismissively, then hits the breaks as he nearly misses a stop sign. My heart skips a few beats, then settles back into my chest. "I don't charge Max. Or friends of Max. Oh, I guess I should start calling you Thunder now, won't I? You should ask Hunter if he can make that song by Imagine Dragons your signature song. Like, have it play at the beginning of each of your scenes."

I hold my hand in front of my mouth to keep my

laughter in. He's a riot, that one. Also, gay as a basket in a way that instantly endears him to me.

"Pretty sure Hunter wouldn't be able to afford the royalties for that," Max says, "but I'll be sure to ask him. But please, for the love of everything holy, don't call me Thunder. I still can't believe I listened to you when you suggested that stupid name."

"You could've easily gone with your own name," Baby suggests. "I mean, Max covers the idea pretty well, right?'

Max shrugs, but I'm watching him from the side, and he's not quite as indifferent as he pretends. "It certainly makes clear what my unique selling point is."

"We're here." Benton whips the car into a pull-up lane at the last moment. God, if he drives us back, I'm gonna need to get life insurance. "Text me when you're done, and I'll pick you up."

Max reaches for the door, then stops and looks back at Benton. "Why don't you come with us? You're not working, are you?"

Benton clicks his tongue. "Hell to the fucking no. I can barely feel my ass anymore after spending ten hours in this damn car today...which is a shame because it's such a pretty ass. Men have literally kneeled to kiss this ass."

Max rolls his eyes at him. "Focus please, would you? You can join us if you want."

Benton glances over his shoulder at me and Baby. "Are you sure you'd be okay with that?"

He sounds more vulnerable now, losing some of that sassy outer veneer.

"Absolutely," Baby says almost at the same time as I do.

"Okay, let me park the car real quick," Benton says with a big smile.

My hand is instantly on the door. "We'll wait for you

here." I get out as fast as I can. Baby does the same on the other side, and even Max gets out. Benton drives off as Max is still slamming the door shut.

"Was he joking that he'd never had an accident?" Baby asks.

Max laughs sheepishly. "I know it's hard to believe, but the gods are on his side or something. He's never had so much as a scratch."

I shake my head. "That's a fucking miracle, man. He should play the lottery."

Max grins. "He does. Every week."

"So...Thunder." I wiggle my eyebrows. "Dare I ask how Benton knows about the size of your dick?"

Max shuffles his feet. "We've been friends for a long time, so... It's not like it's a secret or anything. And he's driven me home with hookups a few times who were...mentioning my features."

I frown. "You don't have a car?"

He shakes his head. "No."

His voice holds enough finality that I don't press any further. Benton comes sauntering over in a pair of tight leggings, rainbow-colored sneakers, and a sequined top. "If I'd known I'd be going out, I would've dressed up," he complains, quickly checking himself in a compact mirror. He's fabulous, and I love him already—aside from his kamikaze style of driving.

"You should apply with Daddy for a job as well. You'd fit right in."

Max's mouth drops open, but Benton puts his mirror away and winks at me. "Honey, I don't do submissive. If I were ever to do porn, I'd be calling the shots."

How can he say that with such ease? God, I wish I had

his confidence, his self-reflection. After two shoots and a scene with Marshall, I still don't know what I am or where I stand. But nobody here needs to know my issues, so I plaster a smile on my face and wink back at Benton. "You do you, boo, as Glam would say. Now let's go. His show starts in ten minutes."

Glam has reserved seats for us, we discover when we go in, and we have a prime spot with a perfect view of the stage. We'd better tip him good because he'll be losing out on money otherwise by giving us these seats. A waitress brings Ian and me our drinks—after checking our IDs, of course—but Max didn't order something alcoholic. Neither did Benton, but he's driving. I shudder at the thought of him driving with alcohol in his system. That would surely be too much, even for his guardian angels.

A few minutes later, Glam is announced, and the lights dim except for a single spotlight.

"Are you feeling patriotic?" a booming voice calls out.

The crowd cheers, and the occasional "USA!" chant goes up.

The one spotlight dims, and then Bruce Springsteen's "Born in the USA" bursts through the loudspeakers. Seconds later, the lights come back to life in red, white, and blue, illuminating Glam, who's standing motionless, his back toward us. He's dressed in a pair of impossibly tight jeans with a star-spangled-banner bandana stuck in his back pocket. The top of a red G-string peeps from under the low waistband. His upper body is covered in a red tank top that leaves his midriff bare, and he's wearing a white cowboy hat.

As soon as Bruce starts his second line, Glam swivels around, tipping his hat as he beams at the crowd, and we all go wild. Our cheers drown amid the whooping and yelling of the packed room. Saturday night in Vegas. Welcome to Sin City.

His jeans have holes in strategic places, and as he dips low on his heels, I hold my breath, as does everyone else in the room, hoping to catch a little more of what he's teasing at. He's good, moving his body so fluidly to the beat of the music.

He swings and sways, shakes and stretches, as limber as a dancer. I'm sure that if the jeans would've been able to withstand it, he could've sunk down into a split. After a good two minutes, he takes off his top, revealing his upper body covered in glitter. That'll be a bitch to get off.

He's getting the first tips already, shamelessly flirting with every man in the first few rows. Loud catcalls rise as he grabs his crotch and makes suggestive movements with his hips. That earns him a few more tips. He throws his legs up high, then turns his back to us again and shimmies out of those jeans inch by inch.

The red glittery G-string barely covers his dick, and it's so tight, everybody can see he's circumcised. Not that I'm checking, obviously. He winks at me as he sinks low to his knees right in front of me, and I hold out a ten-dollar bill. For that show, it'll be well worth eating peanut butter and jelly sandwiches for a week.

He turns around, looking at me over his shoulder, and shakes his ass. I grin as I get up and shove the bill in his waistband. I want to slap his ass something bad, just because I can, but I don't want to give others the impression they can touch him as well, so I don't.

The song transitions into "Party in the USA," and Glam brings it, using every inch of his body to flirt and flaunt, seducing us to keep our eyes glued to him as he makes that little bit of fabric stretch as far as it will go.

Near the end of the song, he slides off the stage, dressed in nothing but that G string, and he gives a few men a lap dance they won't soon forget. One guy is wearing a "Last Night Single" sign around his neck, and Glam rubs himself against the poor guys as his friends let the tips rain down. He's smart, knowing exactly who to go for.

He climbs back onto the stage, ending on the last beat of the song with his back toward us, his legs slightly spread and straight and his hands on the floor, offering us a perfect view of that single line of fabric covering his... Well, modesty is pushing it here. His hole, and even that I can see. He's amazing, and if he moves like that onstage, he'll have no issue doing porn.

Unlike me. My happy mood disappears as Glam saunters off, his hands full of bills. Baby appears to adjust well, Glam is obviously gonna kill it, and Max seems a little embarrassed but exudes enough confidence that I know he'll be just fine. But me? I still haven't figured out how to get myself to obey, how to make myself like what Harley is doing with me.

Being a puppy with Marshall? That was easy, effortless. Hell, that was fun. Amazing. The most relaxed I felt in months. But two days from now, it's showtime again, and Hunter and the others will expect me to be a good, obedient submissive. That means I have two days to determine how to make it work. I can only hope it'll be enough.

Marshall

. . .

I SPENT several days considering my current situation—namely that I'm falling hard and fast for someone I should *not* be falling for. It occurred to me that maybe it's not so much that I'm falling for Byron, but more that I haven't done a proper scene in ages and he's the one I've been pouring all my Dommy urges onto. It's no surprise that my feelings have gotten confused when I frame it that way. And the only solution to that kind of problem is more than obvious.

I lean back in my seat, letting my eyes roam through the lounge of Ball and Chain. This is the first time I've stopped by the club here in Vegas without Byron in tow, the first time I've been to a kink club without a sub of my own in...years. Picking someone up to play with should be like riding a bike, but I'm having a hard time remembering how to even start.

I take a sip from the bottle of water I bought when I walked in and watch a sub with his master just like I did last time. As far as finding a sub to play with, it's not the most efficient use of my time, but it's peaceful as hell to see the relaxed bliss on his face as he rests his cheek against his Dom's thigh, the other man's fingers combing through his hair absently.

My fingers twitch with the memory of touching Byron the other night, and I curse under my breath. This is getting out of hand.

I tear my attention away from the sub and his Dom and force myself to start looking for a sub who appears available instead. What is Byron up to tonight? The boys have been whispering about a trip to the strip club, and I'm almost positive that was supposed to be tonight. It's all too easy to imagine Byron blushing as a half-naked Glam gives him a lap dance. I smile to myself, just picturing it.

"Excuse me, Sir." A soft voice draws my attention. In front of me stands a petite man, dressed in a black mesh top and a pair of tight black leggings, his eyes downcast, bleach blond hair falling over his forehead, and a small smile on his pretty pink lips.

"Can I help you, boy?"

"Yes, Sir." A blush spreads over his cheeks. "I hate to be forward, but I was wondering if I could sit with you and maybe cuddle a little. And then I was hoping we could talk about you giving me a spanking?" He bites his lip, and I grin. He's shy but knows what he wants. It's endearing.

"Yes, you may." I pat the seat beside me, and he slides into the booth, scooting close until I feel the warmth radiating off his body. I lift my arm so he can nestle against me and then wrap it around his shoulders. "What's your name, boy?"

"Gregory," he answers. "Thank you, this is nice." He rests his head on my shoulder and lets out a little sigh.

"What brings you out to Ball and Chain tonight? Just looking for a spanking?"

He blushes. "My Daddy and I broke up last week. I was feeling lonely sitting at home all by myself. Even my bunny stuffy, Clyde, wasn't much company."

I squeeze him a little tighter, my heart hurting for the sweet, lonely boy.

"Breakups stink."

"Yes, they do." He nods emphatically against my shoulder. "Is that why you're here too?"

"Not exactly. I met a boy I was hoping to get out of my head tonight, but we didn't break up. We've never been together, so we can't break up."

"Life is complicated," Gregory complains with a huff. He

sticks his thumb into his mouth and wiggles against me until I hold him tighter again.

"That it is. But it doesn't have to be tonight. Why don't we sit here and enjoy each other's company for a while? You can relax, and I'll watch over you. How does that sound?"

He hums happily, nodding and closing his eyes. The comforting weight of him in my arms is even more soothing than watching the other sub, but it doesn't come close to the butterflies I had playing with Byron. Come to think of it. I never got those butterflies when playing with my ex either.

We sit for about an hour, his breaths deep and slow as if he's fallen asleep, the bustle of the club lounge falling away as I get lost in my head about Byron all over again. Would it be the absolute worst thing in the world if I *did* fall for him? I'd have to disclose the relationship to Hunter so he wouldn't feel that there was a conflict of interest, but maybe...

I shake my head. I moved out here to get *away* from the relationship drama in New York, not start it fresh with someone else. Maybe I'm just not cut out to be anyone's full-time Dom.

Eventually, Gregory takes his thumb out of his mouth and sits up, blinking at me with a sleepy expression. "Sir, do you mind if we do the spanking another time? I think I want to go home now."

"No problem, baby." I brush a kiss to the top of his head. "Can I give you my number in case you ever need anything?"

He grins and nods quickly, pulling his phone out of seemingly nowhere and handing it over to me. Butterflies or no, he's a sub in need, and I've never been able to ignore that. I type in my number and then hand his phone back to him.

"Are you okay to get home, or do you need a ride?"

"I'm okay, thank you, Sir."

He slides out of the booth and leaves, drawing a few gazes from other interested parties. I finish my water and get up as well. It's clearly going to take a hell of a lot more than another sweet sub to get my mind off Byron.

When I get back to my apartment, I strip out of my clothes and crawl into bed. Without thinking, I reach over toward the nightstand and grab the puppy ears, clutching them close and rubbing my thumbs over the soft fur.

And then, because apparently my hands have a mind of their own tonight, I pick up my phone and open it to a fresh message screen, choose Byron's number from the drop-down, and type out a message.

Marshall: Hey, pup, you home?

THE MESSAGE SHOWS as read almost immediately, and after a few seconds, the little dots appear, indicating he's typing a response.

Byron: Just got in. We went to see Glam strip tonight. It was a blast

Marshall: I thought that was tonight. I'm glad you had fun. Did you get a lap dance?

Byron: Lol. No! Why would I pay to have Glam grind all over me when I can get PAID to do it on camera together later?

I BARK out a laugh at his reasoning.

Marshall: Shrewd thinking. Good pup.

Byron: What did you do tonight?

. . .

I HESITATE FOR A FEW SECONDS. Would it be weird to tell him how I spent the evening? I'm already crossing the professional line by texting him to chat in the middle of the night.

Marshall: I went to the club

Byron: Oh. Did you have fun?

I PONDER HIS QUESTION. I certainly didn't have the kind of fun I'd intended on having, but I did enjoy being there for that sweet sub in need.

Marshall: Some. Not as fun as I had with you the other night, though

AS SOON AS I hit Send, I close my eyes and utter a curse. Byron doesn't respond for a long time. So long, I consider sending an apology and then turning off my phone and going to bed. In fact, I type out a "sorry for making it weird" message three times and deleting it each time. Then his reply finally pops up.

Byron: Sorry. I was in the shower. Glitter, yuck.

Byron: I had fun too. Maybe we can play again soon?

A SMILE CURVES the corners of my lips, and those damn butterflies are back.

Marshall: We can talk about it. You should get some sleep now. It's late.

Byron: yes, Sir ;) Good night.

Marshall: sleep well

. . .

Once I send the message, I put my phone away, set the puppy ears on the nightstand, and settle into bed with that damn smile still on my face.

10

ZIGGY

Scene three. One would think I wouldn't be as nervous after two scenes and my scene with Marshall, but it's actually worse. My hands are shaking as I undress in the dressing room. Harley's voice is coming from the studio, so he must already be on set. He's laughing with Daddy because, of course, Harley is not nervous.

Why would he be? He's done this millions of times. It may be boring for him at the most, an inexperienced sub like me, but at least he gets a good fuck out of it. Me? Not so much. Well, the good fuck part, yeah. Hopefully. That part I can't complain about.

But it's what has to come first that scares the crap out of me. The pain part. I swallow as a wave of nausea rolls through me again, and with shaky legs, I sit down on the bench, bare-assed, save the plug in my hole, that is.

Harley is gonna introduce me to pain this week, and while he's assured me up and down it'll be very mild, I'm terrified. When he was talking about hot wax play in the club, my balls shrunk to the size of raisins, and I don't think my poor dick has ever been that small except for that one time I went on a skiing trip and thought I didn't need ski pants. I thought it was never gonna show back up from having retreated somewhere near my bladder.

My mouth tastes bitter, like iron. I've bitten my lip so hard it's bleeding. Great. That'll look cute on film. I bury my face in my hands. Why the hell did I ever agree to do this? And why haven't I suggested other forms of kink?

Those cute puppies in the club were adorable, and what I did with Marshall would be fun to do again. Be a gorgeous puppy, all decked out in a mask and with leather mitts on and kneepads. I bet my ass would look delicious with a furry tail. And I'd love playing fetch. Or getting groomed. Going for a walk with my handler, my Master. I could do that.

The funny thing, though, is that when I picture myself as a puppy, all happy and carefree, it's not Harley who's holding my leash, but Marshall. Marshall who's petting me, who's training me, praising me every time I get it right. Where is this coming from? Is this because I've already been a puppy with him?

Not that I don't like Harley or have issues trusting him. I like Harley just fine, and I'm convinced he would never hurt me on purpose. He'll respect my boundaries. I'm certain of it, and yet I'm still scared to death. It's gonna hurt, and I can almost guarantee I'll hate every second of it. How can I possibly pretend I'm into this?

"Are you okay?"

My head jerks up at the sound of Marshall's voice. I haven't even heard him come in. "Yeah, I'm fine," I say automatically.

"If you were Pinocchio, your nose would've just grown by an inch."

I cast my eyes down, unable to face him. "Okay, so I'm not entirely fine. No big deal. I can do this."

He sits down next to me, leaving a few inches of space between us. "If you have to assure me you can do this, don't you think that's a good sign you shouldn't be doing this?"

I shrug, still stubbornly staring at the floor. "What's that saying again? Life begins at the end of your comfort zone? Isn't that what I'm doing, pushing myself outside my comfort zone?"

"Boy, this is not pushing yourself out of your comfort zone. This is jumping out of an airplane without a parachute. You're terrified, and that's not how it's supposed to be."

I finally look sideways and meet a pair of very concerned eyes. "I don't have a choice," I whisper. "I signed the contract. I agreed to this."

"Bullshit," Marshall snaps. "Hunter will release you from your contract in a second if you tell him no. He'd never prioritize his business over your well-being. He's too honorable a man for that and too good a Dom. You say red, boy, and everything stops."

I swallow. "But if he releases me, then what? If I'm not good enough for this, what's left?"

His eyes drill into mine. "Are you that eager for the money?"

I debate lying to him, but only for a second. What's the use? Daddy already knows, so it's not like it's the world's biggest secret. "I'm one paycheck away from being utterly and completely broke."

Marshall's expression changes. "Come sit with me, sweetheart." He taps his legs.

"I'm naked," I point out, and he smiles.

"I'd noticed. I'm not blind, boy. And your point is?"

Yeah, what was my point with that? He's already seen me naked. Hell, he's seen me get fucked—not that that makes him special after that sex video, but at least he's one of the few who's watched me get fucked live. In person. What does it even matter anymore?

With a sigh, I get up and sit down on his lap. He immediately pulls me close and gently pushes my head against his chest. "We're gonna sit here for a bit until you've stopped shaking and until your heartbeat has dropped down to a normal level. Once it has, you can start at the beginning."

It only takes about a minute for my body to relax, for the crazy avalanche of thoughts and emotions to slow down, to stop. This man centers me, and he does it by simply holding me tight, his arms clamping around me with just a little more force than in a normal hug. I feel him everywhere, like a wall around me to protect me from the outside world.

But I don't start talking yet. I want to enjoy this a little longer, this sensation of being safe and at peace. Of being sheltered and taken care of. Like nothing can hurt me.

"Talk to me, boy," Marshall says softly.

I let out a deep sigh. "I was a full-time first-grade teacher. Graduated from college last year, and I was so proud to get promoted from teacher assistant to teacher. I didn't make a lot, especially with how expensive California is and paying off my student loans, but I was doing okay. Had a roommate, a boyfriend, no debts other than my student loans. But I also had no savings."

Marshall hums as a sign he's listening, and I love how that sounds rumbles through his chest. He's still holding me tight, and I don't ever want to leave. "My boyfriend, TJ, was very different from me. We'd only been dating for three months, and in hindsight, I already had spotted some warning signs, but I was ignoring them. I wanted it to work because I was ready to settle down, or so I thought. He was a party animal, hitting the clubs every weekend, doing the occasional popper. Look, I've never been a stranger to Grindr dates and random hookups, but I don't do drugs. To each his own, but it's not my thing, if only because my school could do random drug tests."

Now it gets hard, and I bite my lip. How could I have been so stupid? I've always prided myself on being street smart, on using my brain. I'd never thought I'd find myself in this situation.

"What happened?" Marshall asks, his voice warm and understanding.

"He was great in bed. That part, I didn't have to pretend. He was adventurous, he gave as good as he got, and he knew how to make me fly. So when he suggested we'd make a little video of him fucking me so we could watch it together and jerk off to it, I agreed. He said we'd better use his phone because his was new, whereas I had an older iPhone. Again, I agreed. God, I was so fucking stupid..."

Marshall sighs. "I'm gonna take a wild guess and say that video ended up somewhere where it shouldn't have?"

"Yeah. Ten points for you."

"Where did he post it?"

"Pornhub. The guy had his own fucking channel with a few of his friends where they posted videos of their hookups, including ones he scored while he was with me."

"How did you find out?"

"Their channel was popular, and the video he posted of him and me did really well." I winced. "I'm...I'm quite vocal when I'm enjoying myself."

"I noticed that in your scenes," Marshall says dryly. Can I get even more embarrassed?

"So did viewers, and apparently, they appreciated it. It's

still one of the highest-rated videos of this year. Go figure. Anyway, Pornhub started recommending it, and a parent recognized me. And of course no one questioned the hypocrisy of her reporting me for making gay porn while she was watching it herself, never mind the fact that I hadn't agreed to it. School board got involved, things got ugly, and I was fired."

"Oh, baby," Marshall says, and the genuine care in his voice makes me tear up.

"I feel so stupid that I trusted him. I should've known better. It cost me everything. You need a background check to work in schools, so I could forget about working as a teacher again. I worked retail for a bit in a high-end clothing store, but I barely could make rent, so I had to move out, and everything came crashing down. I'd met Rebel once, Ballsy Boys Rebel, and he recommended me to Daddy. I'm looking for another job here so that between those two, I can get back on my feet."

His arms never moved an inch, and I breathe out the tension that had seeped back into my body as I recounted the whole sordid story. It's such a fucking mess, and I still can't believe how naïve I was with TJ.

"So I found a shitty apartment here and an even shittier roommate, and I'm doing what I can to make ends meet…"

"I'm so sorry, sweetheart. You were taken advantage of, and that must've left a bad taste in your mouth. I now understand why you think this is your only chance to make enough money, but, Byron, you can't do kink for money. I'm already unhappy with people doing porn just for the money, but kink goes even a layer deeper. It's…" He's quiet for a little, apparently searching for words. "Kink is special. It's almost sacred to me, this trust between a Dom and his sub.

It feels all kind of wrong that you'd subject yourself to it when you hate it so much."

He's right, and an intense sense of shame overwhelms me. "I don't hate all of it," I whisper. "At least, I don't think so."

Just then, the door to the dressing room opens, and Daddy and Harley are standing there, sporting almost identical confused expressions. "We were wondering where you were," Daddy says slowly. "Is there a problem?"

Oh god. Now what? Is there a way out of this? I'm inhaling to answer him, but Marshall's arms tighten around me for a moment, then ease again, and I stay silent.

"Yes, we have a problem. Byron is not doing a scene today. At least, not with Harley."

11

MARSHALL

Hunter looks stunned, and rightly so. Harley frowns, his eyes darting between Byron and me.

"What's wrong exactly?" Harley asks, directing the question to me as I hold Byron closer.

"He's not feeling comfortable. Impact play is more than he's ready for."

"Okay. We can change the scene," Hunter offers. "Would it be better if—"

"I'm going to do the scene with him," I blurt before he can finish his sentence, my firm tone leaving no room for argument. Byron gasps, pulling back enough to look at me with surprise.

"You are?" he asks quietly, and I nod.

"We're going to do a light puppy scene and a spanking." Byron's expression turns from weary to excited.

"Huh." Hunter strokes his chin, considering the idea. "Okay, that works. Must be kismet because I just got a puppy hood in a couple of days ago. We should have a leather leash and harness too."

Byron perks up, wiggling a little on my lap like the excited puppy he is.

"Can I see the hood?" he asks.

"Of course. I take it you're comfortable with all this?" Hunter checks.

He nods rapidly, climbing off my lap. His cock, which was so soft when I came into the locker room it was nearly crawling up inside his body, is now half-hard, plump, and hanging against his leg. His butt is eye level now that he's standing while I'm still sitting, and when he wiggles it again, I can't resist a quick slap just to watch it jiggle.

Byron yelps, color rising in his cheeks, followed by a surprised smile. My cock perks up too as it hits me for the first time that I just volunteered to fuck this boy, on camera...

He follows Hunter out of the locker room so he can see the hood, but Harley stays behind, still eyeing me with his arms crossed over his chest.

"What exactly happened here? Ziggy could've come to me if he wasn't feeling comfortable with the scene."

"I know, and I'm sure he would've. I just happened to come in here first and find him practically shaking he was so scared."

He frowns. "We can't have that," he agrees. "I could do the puppy play scene with him. It's not my usual style, but I can make it work."

"It's okay. I don't mind," I hurry to assure him, and his frown turns into a grin of understanding.

"Ah, okay."

"No, it's not..."

"I get it. I've seen you two, and I've been wondering if there might be some sparks flying."

"No sparks," I insist, but his smile stays in place.

"Uh-huh."

Before I can argue further, Byron comes bouncing back into the locker room with a leather puppy hood in hand. It's not a full-coverage one. Instead, there are large eye holes and big floppy ears on top, as well as plenty of space on the underside for licks or treats.

"Look how cute it is, Master," he says excitedly, holding it up to show me. Harley's eyebrows shoot up, and he shakes his head at me. I glare at him and turn my attention back to Byron.

"It's very cute. You're okay wearing this for the scene today?"

"Yes, Sir."

"And a spanking?"

"Not too hard?"

"Not too hard," I assure him, and he nods. "And sex."

He shrugs. "Sex is the easy part."

Right, of course. He's never been worried about the sex, only the kink. Unfortunately, the opposite is true for me. I could play puppy with him all day, but knowing that I'm going to have to fuck him on camera in a few minutes is making my heart flap wildly in my chest.

I'll be fine. It's not like I haven't had sex with an audience. It's something I grew used to at the club years ago. And sex with Byron isn't the problem. It's the *opposite* of a problem, and maybe *that's* the problem. I've never been good at separating sex from emotions. The little flicker of a crush I've been harboring on him is about to be fanned into a full-on flame. Then what?

"Are you ready, Marshall?" Hunter asks. I square my shoulders and nod. I can do this.

"Wait, do you have an on-screen name that I should call you?" Byron asks.

A slow grin spreads over my lips. "Just stick to Master, puppy."

The set was organized for an impact scene, so it's fairly minimalist with just a spanking bench on the nice thick carpet. After Ziggy was uncomfortable kneeling, I'd made sure extra padding was added under the carpet, and now I'm extra glad for that fact, since we'll be on the floor for today's whole scene.

"If we move the bench out of the way, this should be fine," I tell one of the stagehands, and he nods, lifting the bench. I take in the rest of the scene not just the set but also the crew standing around, the position of the cameras and the lights. I take a deep breath, letting it center me as I settle into that calm, commanding place inside myself.

I put a hand on the back of Ziggy's neck and give it a gentle squeeze. He relaxes instantly under my touch. He wears the harness Hunter found for him, so I take the leash out of his hand and clip it on. Then I take the puppy hood from him as well. He looks a little panicked, reaching for it as I pull it away.

"Calm, pup, I'm going to put it on you at the start of the scene, that's all."

"Okay. Sorry." He gives me an apologetic smile, and I ruffle his hair to let him know there's no harm done.

Cameras or no cameras, this is no different than any other scene I've done, and something about the metallic click of the leash on his harness reminds me of that fact. I'm not a porn star; I'll never be a porn star. What I am is a Dom taking care of the sub who needs me.

"Come, Ziggy," I say firmly, giving the leash a gentle tug and leading him onto the center of the set. I sit down on the plush carpet, and Ziggy drops to his knees in front of me. I'm assuming the camera is rolling. If anyone called "action," I'm too far in the zone to have heard it. I'm completely focused on my boy now.

"Red if you need to stop," I remind him.

"Yes, Master," he answers obediently, licking his lips. His posture in his kneel is better this time, just like I showed him at my apartment—back straight, hands on his thighs. He's a beautiful sight.

"My perfect pup. Come here and let Master get you ready to play."

He leans forward without hesitation, the palms of his hands meeting the floor. I slip the hood over his head and tighten the strap on the back enough that it won't fall off while we play. Then I tilt his head up so I can get a proper look at him. The joy shining in his eyes is undeniable.

"Are you my good puppy, Ziggy?" I scratch the top of his head. He lets out a happy bark and wiggles his bare ass. "I don't have any treats for you this time, but if you're a good boy, I'll give you a bone," I joke, and someone off-camera snorts a laugh. Ziggy barks again, and I'm pretty sure that if he wasn't a puppy right now, he'd be laughing too, based on the humor dancing in his expression.

"Let's run through a few tricks." I got to my feet, my hand clenched around his leash. "Sit," I command, and Ziggy plops his butt down, still wiggling it happily. "Down." He lies forward, his cute ass up in the air as he puts his chest down on the carpet. "Roll over."

As he obeys, it's obvious he's enjoying himself. His cock is already hard, flopping against his stomach as he rolls over, and then swinging between his legs when he rights himself. We do a few more tricks while I praise and pet him. But then he starts to get bored.

I ask him to sit again, and he huffs in annoyance, a flair of mischief passing behind his eyes a second before he grabs the leash between his teeth and tries to tug it out of my hand.

"Ziggy, drop it," I say firmly. Instead of obeying, he growls playfully, sticking his butt higher in the air and wagging it faster as he tries to wrestle the leash away from me. "Be a good puppy."

He looks a little contrite, easing his grip on the leash, but as soon as I relax mine, I realize my mistake. He bites down again, wrenches it from my grasp, and darts away. There's no question about how Ziggy enjoys his puppy time. As I chase him around the set, laughing each time he wiggles his butt or barks at me, I imagine how much fun it would be to take him to a puppy play event at Ball and Chain so he could play chase with other puppies as well. I bet he'd like that.

I let him have his fun for a little while. Then I finally catch him and give him a stern look. "You've been a very bad puppy. And bad puppies deserve a spanking."

I don't need anything as formal as the spanking bench. I wrap one hand around the harness to keep him in place and then raise my hand and bring it down against the nice round globe of Ziggy's ass. I'm careful not to do it too hard, just enough to make his skin rosy where I made contact, the imprint fading within seconds. He gasps, and I hold still for a few seconds, waiting to see if he's going to safeword. When he doesn't, I give him another slap, and this time he tilts his ass up for it.

A smile tugs on my lips. He likes it.

I give him a couple of more swats, enough to warm his skin but not enough to make it so he'll be sore sitting down later. My cock is hard and aching now inside my pants. It never occurred to me to strip before the scene started. I've always loved being fully clothed while my sub is bare for me, and I have to think that'll be appealing to viewers as well. But that does leave me with the awkward moment of needing to undress on camera.

"Kneel for me," I command Ziggy, and he scrambles to do as I say. While he kneels, I get undressed and toss each item of clothing off-camera as I go. I assume they'll do some kind of jump cut so viewers don't have to watch three minutes of me getting naked, but that's way above my pay grade.

Ziggy's eyes go wide as he rakes them over my body. The naked lust in his expression sends a thrill of heat through me. I started working out for my health, but it never hurts to know someone finds you attractive too. I'm sure my tattoos and piercings only help matters. His gaze lands on my hard, thick erection, dangling between my legs, my PA piercing glistening with precum, and he lets out a low whine.

"Does Ziggy want his bone?" I ask in a deep, teasing tone, grabbing the base of my cock and stroking slowly. He holds his kneel, but his entire body looks like it's vibrating with impatience.

I playfully bounce my cock against his puppy snout, eliciting another desperate whimper from my cute boy.

Ziggy

THE MAN HAS a Prince Albert piercing. I've only seen them in pictures, but I've never looked at one in real life, let alone this close. It's practically in my face, and true to my puppy nature, I'm drooling.

How will it feel in my mouth? Will it bring Marshall pleasure if I play with it? I stick out my tongue, making a motion to lick it, but Marshall pulls it back. "Uh-uh. You gotta be a good puppy for me and wait until I tell you you can have your treat."

Another shudder travels down my spine. Best. Treat. Ever. I've always loved giving head—well, with the right guys anyway—but this is the single most drool-worthy cock I've ever seen. It's fat and straight, not even that long, but just stunning with that piercing. I want to swallow it whole. Hell, I want to ride it until it fills that emptiness inside me that aches almost painfully now.

I whimper softly in disappointment that I can't have it yet and look up at Marshall with pleading eyes.

"Are you going to be a good puppy for Master, Ziggy?"

I nod and let out a little bark.

"Good boy," Marshall says, and those words reach deep inside me. I want to be his good boy. I want to earn his treats, his praise...his bone. "Hold out your tongue."

I stick out my tongue as far as I can. He drags his cockhead over it, wiping off that thick bead of precum. More than anything, I want to taste it, to swallow it, but Marshall's eyes are drilling into mine. He hasn't told me yet I can. So I wait, my body quivering with need.

He pulls back his cock an inch or so. "Swallow."

I close my mouth and taste him, the saltiness filling my mouth, making me moan. I smack my lips, then immediately open up again for more.

Marshall smiles. "Such an eager puppy," he coos, and I hear the pleasure in his voice. He's happy with me, and that's all that matters. "Open your mouth wide, pup. You've earned your treat."

As soon as I tilt my head and drop my jaw as low as it will go, he slides into my mouth. He's careful, testing my gag reflex, but when I'm not reacting, he goes in deeper. His piercing hits my throat, and it startles me for a moment.

Usually, I don't have much of a gag reflex, but I have to concentrate to stay relaxed at the sensation of the metal in my mouth.

"Mmm, look at you, taking all of my cock," Marshall says as he sinks in all the way. My mouth has never been this full. He's so thick it closes off everything else, and my eyes water. He's staring at me intently, but I have no intention of safewording. Over a blow job? With the most perfect dick ever in my mouth? Hell no.

"My beautiful puppy." Marshall pulls back a little to let me breathe. He wipes a tear off my right eye. "I like seeing you with drool on your chin, Ziggy."

I've been so concentrated on Marshall that I forgot for a moment we were being filmed, so when Joey moves in for a close-up, I jerk in surprise. Marshall's hand wraps around my neck, and that simple touch steadies me.

With his other thumb, he taps on my chin, and I open up again. When he slides back in, I close my eyes, drowning out everything else but the sensation of his cock in my mouth. It's strange, but he takes over my whole mind like that. My head stops worrying about everything and fills with calmness, with peace. Being Marshall's puppy makes me happy in a way I've never experienced before.

When he pulls back, I flick his piercing with my tongue, and he lets out a low moan. I explore it further, swirling around it, licking it, and even gently tugging it with my teeth. That last move makes his cock jerk in my mouth, so I do it again. Mmm, he likes that. I get another thick drop of precum as a reward.

He chuckles. "Looks like we're both having some fun with my piercing, hmm?"

I play a little more with it, but then he sets a rhythm, sliding his cock deep into my throat, holding it there until my eyes water, and then retreating. He keeps fucking my mouth until my jaw starts to ache. He must've sensed it because he takes his cock out with a satisfied grunt. "You did so good, pup."

I move my jaw left and right to get the soreness out, then nuzzle Marshall's leg. I love the way his hand holds me with this tight grip. It makes me feel so safe when he does that, like he's my protector and nothing can hurt me.

"Mmm, such a good puppy for your Master," Marshall praises me.

He rises, and I whimper at the loss of contact. We're not done yet, right? We can't be done. I need... I need more. I need to feel him, to feel safe just a little longer.

"Hush, I'm not going anywhere," Marshall says and simply lifts me to my feet. He takes me in, smiling with a pride that warms me on the inside. "You're beautiful, Ziggy. Absolutely perfect."

It's a scene. This is part of the scene. My heart has a hard time believing that, though, the traitorous bastard. It soaks up Marshall's words like a precious gift, and I don't know how to stop it.

He unfastens the straps of my mask and gently pulls it off my head. "I want to see your face when I kiss you, pup...and when you ride me."

I swallow. My head feels strangely empty and light without the mask, but he's right. He can't kiss me when I'm wearing it, not the way I want to anyway. And did he say *ride* him? He wants me to... Hell, yes. Absolutely, sign-me-up, where-do-I-sign yes.

He chuckles. "I thought that might get your attention." He lays the puppy mask on the floor, then eyes me and strokes himself proudly. "Tell me you want this."

He looks confident. Cocky even. And yet I can't shake

the feeling he has a reason for asking me this. Consent? An extra opportunity for me to indicate I'm getting close to my boundaries? Or does he need the confirmation because he's insecure himself? The man is a trained Dom, but as far as I know, he's never done porn, so this is new to him.

Whatever his reason, I'm on board with this. With him. With all of it. "Yes, Master," I say softly, and his eyes go dark with want.

He grabs my chin between his thumb and index finger, tilting it upward so I meet his eyes. "Taking you doggy style might be more appropriate, but I'd hate not to see your beautiful face when I bring you pleasure."

And then he presses his mouth to mine and kisses me. He's more tender than I expected. The first touch is careful, probing, a light pressure of his lips on mine. But when I open up for him, he surges in with his tongue, taking full control of the kiss.

He employs his tongue the same way he did his cock before, claiming my mouth and using it for his pleasure. All I can do is hold on, my fingers digging into his biceps as he fucks my mouth. My knees go weak, my belly flip-flops, and my heart rate triples.

Joey steps in for another close-up, but I barely register it, too busy trying to stay standing and not collapse on the spot from an acute overload of feelings, of sensations. Marshall's hands roam my back now, caressing me with firm strokes, traveling lower and lower.

His fingers dip between my ass cheeks, and for a moment, I'm startled by that bold move until he gently tugs on my plug. Right. Now is the perfect time to remove that inconspicuously. I widen my legs a little and relax so he can pull it out.

As soon as it's out, Joey walks around me, zooming in on

Marshall's hands cupping my ass, then dipping his middle finger inside me. Damn, the man can multitask, kissing me breathless while caressing my ass at the same time.

My knees buckle, and he holds on to me as he breaks off the kiss. "Time to get horizontal, puppy."

My head is spinning, but I allow him to pull me to the floor. The original scene was for Harley to fuck me on the spanking bench, but Marshall has other plans, it seems because he stretches out on the floor on his back, all six-foot-something of him on delicious display. I run my hands over his colorful tattoos.

He suddenly has a condom in his hand—no idea where that materialized from—and after rolling it on, he squirts out some lube and coats himself. I'm watching with hungry eyes, my body aching for him in a way I've never felt before. Like I'm not complete without him, though that thought scares me a little.

He grabs my wrist, then yanks me on top of him, spreading my legs wide. His hard dick slides between my ass cheeks, his cockhead finding my hole all by itself. I'm so slick from prepping well and the plug I'd been wearing until minutes ago that he's already pressing slightly into me.

Joey drops on the floor beside us, and Marshall waits for him to be in position, running his hands over my ass and spreading my cheeks wide. "It's gonna feel so good, pup, my fat cock in your hole."

Ah, right. The porn talk. Daddy briefed us on that, giving us the top twenty phrases viewers love to hear. I bet the guy who did market research was really proud to use his degree in statistics like that. "Mmm, I can't wait for you to stretch me wide," I moan, fervently hoping it's not too over the top. Then again, it's porn. If I had any serious acting skills, I wouldn't be doing this job. Just saying. Cheesy kind of comes with the territory here.

Marshall's mouth pulls up in a slight grin, and I'm pretty sure we're both thinking the same thing. Joey gives a signal that I only see from the corner of my eyes, but Marshall has caught it, and he grabs his cock with his left hand and holds it upright.

"Take me in." His voice is low and commanding, and my belly swirls in response. How can this man make those three simple words sound so sexy? So...bossy?

I rise on my knees, then lean back and spread my ass cheeks wide. When I sink down, he's right there. I bite my lip as he slips in, testimony to how well I prepped. The gasp that falls off my lips is real this time, and I whimper as I take him in all the way. He is splitting me wide open, burning through me in the best way possible. His piercing creates an electric zing deep inside me as it hits my prostate. Oh god, that's gonna feel so good...

When he's inside me all the way, my ass resting on his neatly trimmed pubic hairs, I take a moment to breathe, waiting for my body to relax. Marshall grabs my hips, and his eyes are full of lust. He doesn't speak a word, but his look says everything, and I lick my lips.

When I relax, he lifts his hips up and grinds into me with a slow, circling motion that sets off fireworks inside me. I can't wait anymore, and I raise my ass, then lower it again.

"Ah, pup, that feels good," Marshall groans, and that's the last word he utters for a while as we find a rhythm. His grunts mingle with my gasps and whimpers as he rocks up every time I slide down, thrusting deep inside me with a wet sound that should make viewers happy. I throw my head back and close my eyes, riding him, driven by instinct.

I find the perfect angle at which his piercing hits my

happy spot full on, and soon my cock drips long, sloppy trails down onto Marshall's stomach. He swipes it up, then licks off his fingers and moans at the taste. Damn, he's good at this. Or is that real? I can't tell anymore.

Within minutes, I'm close to the edge already, but I'm not sure if I need permission to come. One look at Marshall shows he's aware of this too, and he's grinning at me expectantly. The fucker knows I need to ask him, and I hate and love it at the same time. But my hate isn't strong enough to become more important than the urge building inside me that makes my balls throb and my muscles tense in anticipation.

"Please, Master..." I beg, strangely proud that I remembered to call him by his title even now.

He makes a sound of approval. "I love it when you call me that," he says, his voice low and full of passion. "And you beg so prettily."

I'll beg all fucking day long if it gets me my orgasm. No kidding. "I'm so close, Master. Please, can I come?"

"Yes, puppy, you may."

Thank god because I'm not sure how much longer I could've held off. My hand curls around my cock, but Marshall slaps it away. "Hands-free." His eyes are gleaming.

If he thinks that's gonna make it impossible, he's wrong. I lean back and angle my body until he hits me full on. And then I increase the tempo, slamming down on him at a brutal speed.

I won't be able to keep this up for long, but I don't have to. I feel the telltale signs, my muscles quivering, my cock tensing up, and my balls so tight against my body they have nowhere else to go.

It hits me like a punch, knocking the breath right out of my lungs as my body jerks. My hands seek purchase, and

Marshall takes them, lacing our fingers together as I ride out my release, rocking myself back and forth on him as my cock spurts out rope after rope. When I'm finally done, I collapse on top of him, and he holds me, murmuring soft words until I come down from my high.

Only then do I realize that he hasn't come yet. Shit. Now what?

Marshall pulls my head close to his and whispers into my ear, "Pup, under normal circumstances, your pleasure would've been all the satisfaction I need. Do you understand? But this is porn, and Hunter needs more."

I melt, my body all pliant against his. He smiles as he slowly pulls out of me, then flips us over. He takes the condom off, throws it aside, and kneels over me. His eyes never leave mine as he jerks himself off, fast and hard until he sprays me all over, including on my face. I lick my lips. Joey is close, so he must've gotten a good shot of that.

"Cut!" Joey calls, but Marshall doesn't get up. Instead, he sits down and pulls me between his legs. I lean back against him and put my head against his shoulder. His arms are warm and tight around me as he nuzzles my neck.

And as he holds me for minutes after, allowing me to process and recover, I'm not sure which part I liked more: the puppy play, the sex, or him cuddling me like that.

12

ZIGGY

Daddy asked me to come by for a talk, and since anything that starts like that is usually bad news, my stomach is all in knots and twists as I knock on his office door.

"One moment," Daddy calls out, sounding agitated. Is he okay?

Some shuffling noises inside. What the hell is going on? The door opens, and a sheepish-looking Joey steps out, his cheeks red and his hair disheveled. Ah. Now I understand.

"I'm, erm..." Joey says, then jerks his head in the direction of the studio. "I'm just gonna go and, erm...do stuff. Right."

I laugh as he hurries off, his cheeks so red they must hurt.

"Sorry," Daddy says as he straightens his shirt. "We lost track of time."

"Clearly." I'm still laughing.

When I step into the office, the scent of sex is heavy in the air, so I hope one of them at least got to come. Daddy, if I had to hazard a guess, and I think Joey was on his knees, judging by his hair and the slight dust prints on his jeans.

An image of me on my knees for Marshall fills my head, and I swallow. He would like that, me on his knees for him. He'd call me his good boy, his pretty pup. And I would be because he makes me feel good. He'd hold my hair, strong enough to be aware of him but not enough it really hurts. And his cock would stretch my mouth wide open, leaving me at his mercy. He'd take care of me afterward. I know he would.

A gaspy sound escapes my lips, and Daddy's eyes twinkle as he sits down on his desk chair, stretching his legs in front of him. "Pleasant association?"

I can't even be embarrassed about it, not when I just caught him and his boy engaging in a little office nookie. "Very pleasant."

"Dare I speculate as to the object of that particular daydream?" Daddy gestures for me to sit down, and I lower myself in the comfortable chair across from his desk.

I bite my lip. Is this what he wants to talk to me about? "I didn't ask Marshall to stop or take over the scene."

His mouth pulls up into a smile. "I find it telling that you immediately know who I was referring to. I'm not imagining the sparks between the two of you, am I?"

How the hell do I answer that? "Did Marshall say anything?"

Daddy chuckles. "No, but if you want, I can pass him a note in study hall."

I barely resist the urge to stick out my tongue. Instead, I cram my hands into my pockets, avoiding Daddy's scrutinizing look. "So what if we have chemistry?"

"It's not wrong, Byron. Whatever is happening between

the two of you is not a problem. Not unless either of you makes it one."

I shoot a careful glance in his direction. "Then why are we talking about this?"

Daddy leans forward on his desk, and his eyes are firm but kind. "Because this does affect my business, and as such, I need to know where we stand. Can you still continue the series we're shooting with you? Will you be doing all the shoots with Marshall now, or are you still open to doing scenes with Harley as well? Do you need to go over your limits again, and if so, is Marshall the one to help you with that, considering he'll be playing with you, one way or another? Help me out here, kid. What is happening here?"

"I don't know," I whisper. "I was a little lost, I guess, and Marshall helped me find my footing. He's..."

I don't know how to describe it. It's not easy to put all these jumbled thoughts inside my head into words. Besides, Marshall and I haven't talked about any of this, so how do I know what he thinks? All I know is that he was open to playing with me again, but we never said anything beyond that.

"He makes me feel safe," I say quietly. "You know what happened to me, how my ex-boyfriend violated my trust. I stopped feeling safe, but with Marshall, I do. He's got me."

"The core characteristic of a good Dom/sub relationship is trust. I'm glad Marshall is able to provide that sense of safety. Is it different than with Harley?"

I nod. "Harley is really nice, and it's not like he'd ever hurt me." I think of the impact scene he'd originally planned and winced. "Not beyond what he was supposed to do anyway."

"Was Marshall right? Were you scared of doing impact play?"

I hesitate. What will happen if I tell him the truth? I signed a contract, so if I can't do my job, will he fire me? This is all that stands between me surviving and getting homeless.

"You can tell me the truth, sweetheart," Daddy says, his voice so full of concern that it takes away any fear that this man would let me become homeless.

"I was terrified," I say softly. "Absolutely terrified."

"Oh, boy, why didn't you say something sooner?"

I bite my lip. "I don't know. At times, I wondered if I'm even submissive, but Marshall seems to think I am, at least in some areas. I didn't want to displease you or Harley, and I didn't want to risk losing my job here. I need the money. I hate to be all desperate, but if you'd fire me, I would—"

"I'm not gonna fire you," Daddy interrupts me, his voice wonderfully strong and confident. "Worst-case scenario, I'd shoot some vanilla porn scenes with you and sell them to Bear for the Ballsy Boys."

My ears perk up. Vanilla porn? That actually sounds hella attractive right now, and if someone had told me that a few weeks ago, I wouldn't have believed them.

Daddy smiles. "You're relieved now, aren't you? That's not how it's supposed to be, boy. Being submissive doesn't mean you have to like all kink, including impact play. Joey is submissive to me, but we don't engage in anything more than a pleasure spanking at times."

I sigh. "Rationally, I know that. It's just that... I hate disappointing you or Harley...or Marshall. I have this deep urge inside me to get your approval, which probably speaks volumes about how fucked up I am."

Daddy shakes his head. "That's your submissive side, your need to please. The fact that you don't want to suffer pain for your Dom doesn't mean you don't want to please him. I think you do, but it depends on what he's asking you to do. I understand you had a puppy scene with Marshall in his apartment?"

The memory makes me smile, my insides warming after the cold fear that had held me. "I really like being a puppy. It's freeing. I get to play, to be without a care in the world, knowing that Marshall..."

I stop talking. Why did I automatically fill in Marshall's name there? Technically, I could do puppy play with any Dom willing to engage in that with me. Harley had indicated he wanted it, but even when I try, I have trouble imagining him as my master. He's not. It doesn't fit him, but more important, he doesn't fit me. He's not what I need...and I'm not what he needs either.

"I don't think Harley and I are a good fit."

Daddy's mouth curls up again, and I see not only acceptance in his eyes but also understanding and pride. "I agree. He's a great Dom...and I think you're a better sub than you give yourself credit for. But you and Harley are not a good match."

"But what about the series?"

Daddy shrugs. "The first two scenes with the two of you were super hot, so we can use those. I haven't looked at yesterday's scene yet, but Joey was happy and said the chemistry between you and Marshall translated well to the screen. We'll talk about how to move forward, whether he's willing to do more scenes with you and if you want that. But take your time to think about that. The whole idea of that series was to show someone completely new to the scene exploring things, and that's exactly what you have done. That means concluding that some things are not for you even before trying is also fine."

I wanna hug him, but I think that's crossing a line in our

already complicated boss-employee relationship. I mean, a boss who sees you naked and being fucked on a regular basis is not exactly standard, let alone one who rates you on said performance.

"Thank you," I say instead. "Knowing that you're not angry with me is a big relief."

"Of course I'm not angry. We'll work things out. But may I suggest that the first conversation that needs to take place is one between you and Marshall? The two of you need to make clear what your expectations are."

I know he's right, but god, that is one conversation I do not look forward to.

Marshall

I WAS UP HALF the night, thinking about my scene with Ziggy. What did it look like from the outside? Was it as explosive and incredible as it felt? Or was that part all in my head? Even my morning run did nothing to center me.

And now I'm heading to the editing room. For the first time since being in the business. I have no idea why this part of the process would interest me, but here I am.

"Hey, Marshall, are you looking for Daddy?" Joey asks when I peek my head inside the room.

"Oh, uh..." I consider lying and saying I was trying to find Hunter. Then I could turn around and walk away with my dignity intact.

Understanding dawns on Joey's face, and he gives me a warm smile. "It's not finished yet, but if you want to see a little bit, I can show you," he offers.

"Only if it's no trouble."

"It's no trouble. Come on in."

I'm not sure what I expected the editing room would look like, but not this. It's barely more than a closet with different recording equipment taking up most of the space, along with a single desk with a large computer monitor on top. I was picturing something more high tech.

"They were just working on the money shot." He clicks on the Play button.

Ziggy's face fills the screen. I had already taken the puppy hood off, so none of it's obscured. The sight of the blush on all the exposed bits of his skin has my heart thundering. On-screen, his eyes flutter closed. The clip has no sound, but the memory of the little whimpers and moans he was making reverberate in my bones, stroking my cock to life in no time. It's an awkward predicament to be in, standing in a small room with the boss's boy, my cock hard enough to pound nails, but I can't tear my eyes away from the screen.

I lick my lips. The camera pans out, including me in the shot. My face is glistening with a sheen of sweat, an intense expression in my eyes as I push into my pup. My cock throbs, and I drag in a deep breath, discreetly adjusting myself and then taking a step back.

"Great, that looks great," I say, my voice coming out huskier than I intended.

Joey glances back over his shoulder with a grin. "You two have a lot of chemistry. This is a fantastic scene. I haven't seen on-screen chemistry like this since Tank and Brewer's first scene. This baby is going to break the Internet, so make sure you ask Daddy for a bonus check."

I'm not about to say out loud that getting to do the scene with Ziggy was all the bonus I need, so I smile and nod instead. "Thanks for letting me have a peek. I was worried I might've made a strange face or something," I lie.

The look Joey gives me tells me he's not buying it, but bless him, he doesn't call me out.

"He's here, by the way."

"Who?"

"Ziggy. He had a meeting with Daddy. They'll probably be finishing up soon."

"Oh, okay. Thanks. And thanks again." I nod toward the computer and then slip out of the office.

Without the conscious decision to do so, I walk toward Hunter's office. I'm halfway down the hallway when Ziggy steps out. He startles when he sees me.

"Are you here to meet with Daddy too?" he asks.

"No, I was looking for you."

"Right, we should talk, I guess," he agrees with an unsteady smile.

"There's a coffee shop at the end of the block. Why don't we go there? I'll buy you a double chocolate cookie."

His eyes light up, and his smile turns more genuine. "Thank you, that sounds good."

The sun beats down on us like the fires of hell, making me sweat all over from the short walk. Whoever thought the middle of the desert was any place for civilization was out of their mind.

"Grab us a seat, and I'll order for us."

"Okay. Can I have an iced mocha too?" He bats his eyelashes at me. I chuckle and shake my head.

"That's way too much sugar. You can have one or the other."

Byron sighs. "Fine, the mocha, but with whipped cream and sprinkles."

"All right, pup. Go sit." I point at an empty table, and he beelines for it.

I order myself an iced green tea and the mocha for Byron and then join him at the table.

"So, you had a meeting with Hunter?" I ask, figuring that's a safe place to start.

"He wanted to make sure I knew that I don't have to film any scenes I'm uncomfortable with."

"Good, I'm glad he reminded you of that." I take a sip of my tea and wait for him to add anything else. When he doesn't, I decide the ball is in my court. "Where does that leave you? Are you going to go forward with this series? Are you going to stay with the studio?"

Byron shifts in his seat, using his straw to scoop up some of the whipped cream and then wrapping his tongue around it to lick it off. Holy hell, that boy could make anything look pornographic.

"I want to stay with Kinky Boys. I have to."

"You don't *have* to do anything, least of all film porn you aren't comfortable filming." I'm nearly ready to gather the boy up and save him from himself if I have to.

"No, I know that. But I feel like I haven't seen this thing all the way through yet. I know I won't do porn forever, but I want to be here right now."

"And what about the rest of this discovering kink series you're supposed to do with Harley?" I try to keep my tone as neutral as possible. If it was only sex, I don't think I would mind. It's a job. Even if Byron *was* mine, I'd understand that part of it. But the thought of another Dom playing with my sub... And yes, I know he's not *mine,* but my inner Dom isn't buying that.

He wrinkles his nose and takes another scoop of whipped cream. "Part of being a porn star means filming with different people," he says almost to himself. "And Harley is great. He's nice and really hot. The sex with him was fun..."

"But?" I prompt.

"But I only really like it when *you're* my Dom."

It feels like a helium balloon has been shoved inside my chest. "You want to do more scenes with me?"

"I don't know." He shrugs, his eyes fixed on his drink, but a slight pink blossoms on his cheeks. "Would you even want to? You didn't come here to be a porn star."

"In the abstract, no, I wouldn't want to. If you're asking me to do this with you..." I leave it hanging between us, not wanting to come across as overeager.

Byron finally looks up, meeting my eyes, his cheeks pinker than ever. "Would you do the rest of the scenes with me, Master?" he asks so quietly I almost can't hear him over the din of the cafe.

"Of course I will, sweetheart," I agree.

13

ZIGGY

Z iggy

SHOOT FOUR. I feel like a pro by now as I step into the dressing room. Or maybe the fact that I'm actually looking forward to this scene rather than dreading it has more to do with the man who's already standing there in a pair of tight black briefs that hug his prominent bulge. If my eyes linger a little too long on Marshall's dick, it's because I'm trying to spot his piercing through the fabric. When I finally manage to tear my eyes off his package, I find him looking at me with an amused glance.

"Good morning to you as well," he says dryly, and my cheeks heat up.

Great start, idiot. I almost trip over my own feet and plop down on the bench with more force than I intended.

"Good morning," I say, ignoring him now. "Thank you for doing this."

I'm untying my shoes when his bare feet show up very close to mine. When I straighten, his crotch is right at eye level, and of course, I look again because I really am that much of an idiot. Or that obsessed with his dick, which is crazy because it's just a dick. I've seen plenty.

Not this perfect, though, and certainly not with a piercing that makes me want to... Right. Focus. Marshall is watching me, his eyes sparkling. "I see we're having some issues focusing?"

"It's right in front of me," I say defensively, but then roll my eyes at myself because, really, who am I kidding?

He crouches in front of me. "Are you nervous?"

"Not about the scene."

We're shooting a Daddy care scene today, and the script sounded mighty good to me. I don't think it's gonna be as much fun as puppy play, but it's not gonna bother me in any way either. Now that impact play is off the table, I'm a lot more relaxed. Or maybe it has to do with this weird connection I have with Marshall that I don't share with Harley.

"What are you nervous about, then?" Marshall frowns a little.

I shrug. "It's still public sex. It may be the fourth time, but it's still somewhat surreal. Plus—" I stop talking, unsure if I should voice my next thought out loud.

"Plus, what?" Marshall's voice holds enough of an edge that I obey the unspoken command.

"You always make me a little nervous," I admit.

I expected him to frown even more or something, but instead, his face lights up into a cheeky grin. "You know, I consider that a compliment. It's not a good thing when subs are completely at ease around their Dom. A little fear goes a long way into making sure you obey me."

I swallow. It's easy to forget who Marshall is at his very

core when he's being so sweet and allowing me to be a puppy with him. But he's still a Dom, and in moments like this, I feel that into my core. "Yes, Sir," I say almost automatically, and the way his smile widens tells me he likes that.

I quickly get changed into the clothes Daddy has put out for me. My Andrew Christian underwear comes off, and in its place, I'm putting on a pair of soft cotton superhero briefs that are surprisingly comfy. They're a little baggy on me, but then I remember what will come later in the scene, and I understand why.

The rest of my outfit consists of cute red coveralls, a blue Superman T-shirt, and white socks with dragons on them, plus a pair of red Converse. Okay then. That whole ensemble will take ten years off my age, but I guess that's the whole idea. At least I can pull the combination off, I think, as I check myself out in the mirror.

"It's cute on you." Marshall studies me from the bench he's sitting on. "Adorable."

He's dressed in a pair of simple jeans and a black T-shirt that says "Baby Daddy." We're going for the obvious here, apparently.

"Thank you." I turn around and check out my ass. Hmm, it doesn't really pop in these baggy pants, but whatever. It's not like I'll wear them the entire scene anyway.

"Ready?" Marshall steps up behind me.

I love the way he towers over me. Makes me feel small and safe. Or is that thought inspired by the outfit I'm wearing? I can't deny it does something to me. "Yeah."

He smiles at me in the mirror, then messes up my hair. "Littles don't wear their hair as stylish as you do."

He has a point, and I have to admit that the messy look doesn't look bad on me.

My stomach does a funny little roll as Marshall holds

out his hand, then laces our fingers together as I take it. As soon as he touches me, my shoulders relax, and that tight ball in my belly disappears.

We walk onto the set, holding hands. Daddy's eyes linger on our joined hands for a moment. Then he greets us. He runs through the scene real quick with us, but it's nothing more than a one-minute convo since Marshall and I are both fully on board.

"It's gonna be weird calling you Daddy," I muse as I position myself onto the couch we'll be using today.

"I know it's not a term you're used to, but it's okay if you slip up and call me Sir," Marshall says.

"No, it's more that Daddy to me is Daddy. Hunter, I mean. In my head, he's Daddy, and you're..."

"What am I?"

I bite my lip, suddenly unsure how to finish that sentence. He's not so easy to capture in one word. Daddy's name fits because his whole essence is being a Daddy figure. Most of all to Joey, but Hunter shows that same mix of care, kindness, and strict discipline to all of us. Harley is very much a Dom at the core.

But Marshall is... He's more. He's my Master when I'm a puppy. He's Sir when I'm not. He's like a safe place, like someone I can lean on and go to, someone I can ask for advice. Someone who will catch me if I fall.

And with blinding clarity, I realize that I *am* falling. For him.

I am so fucking stupid. God, I feel like such an idiot. Falling for the first man who respects me, who takes me and my boundaries seriously, who shows me kindness and concern. It's such a classic mistake to misread kindness for more.

Marshall isn't into me. Why would he be? He's

concerned for me because that's who he is. He cares. But it's a professional care, something he provides to everyone. Sure, he likes playing with me...but he's a Dom. That's what they do. It doesn't mean anything.

"Pup, are you okay?" Marshall asks, looking concerned as if to prove my whole point. "You went all quiet and into your head."

I steel myself. Marshall doesn't need to know about this. The last thing I need from him is pity. "Yes, I'm fine. Let's do this...Daddy."

Marshall's eyes widen slightly at that last word, and I can't blame him. It sounds all kinds of wrong. But my personal feelings have no bearing here, and neither do his, for that matter. We're here to do a job, and if that includes calling this man Daddy, then that's what I'll do. I'm gonna hold on to that last shred of professionalism, even if it kills me.

"Have you been my good baby boy today?" Marshall croons a few minutes later as the scene has started and I'm on his lap on the couch, my head cradles against his chest. I can't believe I'm getting paid to do this. Seriously, I'd do this all day for free if I could.

"Yes, Daddy," I say, and much to my own surprise, my pitch is a tad higher than normal.

"Mmm, I'm so proud of you, baby boy. You're such a good boy for Daddy."

It doesn't feel as weird as I expected, calling him Daddy. Maybe it's because the way he talks to me now isn't that different from how he treats me when I'm a puppy. Then again, a puppy and a little have a lot in common, so it would make sense.

"Did I earn a reward, Daddy?" I ask, following the script. After this, we play it by ear.

"You sure did," Marshall says. "And I think I know what my boy wants..."

I don't have to pretend to look a little shy and excited at the same time because that part is all natural. After the way I felt the last time when he gave me a few swats, I can't wait to feel this. "You do, Daddy?"

He grabs my ass and squeezes, laughing. "Daddy's hand on your bare bottom, how does that sound?"

Really fucking hot, but I'll have to censor that sentiment for this scene. Littles don't curse—or so I was told. "Yes, please, Daddy."

If I sound a little breathless when I say that, it's because I am. Hell, my cock is already hardening in my pants at the thought. Impact play may scare the living daylights out of me, but after last time, the words bare bottom spanking light a fire in me like nothing else. Well, being fucked while in puppy gear maybe, but that's a different story.

"Mmm, Daddy can't wait to make your pale skin all red and hot... Give me a kiss, baby boy."

Marshall lets me straddle him, then takes my mouth in a passionate kiss that makes me forget about everything else. I dimly register Joey stepping in for a close-up, but it's right there near the bottom of the list of things I care about at the moment. I'm inching closer to Marshall, moving my hips to seek friction.

He chuckles into my mouth. "Uh-uh, you don't set the pace here, baby boy. Who's in charge here?"

I flutter my eyelashes. "You, Daddy."

His grin widens as he cups my hard dick through the layers of clothing. "And who's in charge of your pretty little cock?"

I mentally sigh. "You are, Daddy."

He squeezes it, and a rush of heat shoots through my

dick into my balls, then further into my body. "Good. Glad we have that cleared up."

With one final kiss, he lifts me off his lap and sets me on my feet. He wipes off my wet lips with his thumb, and his eyes soften. "You're beautiful," he tells me, and for a moment, I'm not sure if it's him or the script. It has to be the script, the scene. I can't allow myself to believe anything else. It will only end with me getting hurt.

He starts to undress me, untying my shoelaces first, then taking off my shoes. My coveralls are next, and I feel weird, standing there dressed in what are basically kids' clothes, until he boldly grabs my ass and kneads it. Who the hell cares what I'm wearing as long as he keeps touching me?

He leaves my shirt on and pulls my underwear to my ankles. With one quick yank, I'm across his lap, my bare ass sticking in the air. "Your bottom is so perfect, baby boy... And it's all Daddy's, isn't it?"

Okay, that layer of possessiveness is totally doing it for me. "Yes, Daddy. I'm yours," I say quietly, and how I wish it were true.

Marshall

MY THROAT TIGHTENS at his soft, sweet words. Fuck, I want them to be true. There are a million reasons I shouldn't want Byron, but the only thing that really seems significant right now is the man draped over my lap, ass in the air. Unlike the last time, he's not tense or nervous. He's lying across my lap as peaceful as can be, waiting for me to do with him as I please.

I grab his ass cheek in one hand and knead it, enjoying

the way his body goes all nice and pliant for me. His cheeks part as I continue to massage them, and I get a little peek at the base of the plug, snugged up in his hole. My cock throbs in response to the enticing sight. But I won't be getting in there today. In fact...why is he wearing the plug at all? Beforehand, we discussed the scene, which Hunter planned as a spanking and making him come.

After the last scene, I talked with Hunter about wanting to showcase the side of care that's not always about a sexual release for the Dom, and I thought this scene would be perfect for that, since it's age play.

"What's this about, baby?" I stroke down the crease of his ass, over the plug while I continue to grip his cheek with the other. He shivers, tilting his hips up higher.

"I...I like it," he admits, barely above a whisper. Fuck, he sounds cute and innocent. He's making it extremely difficult to remember this is only a job.

"Such a dirty boy," I murmur, tugging the plug a little ways out and then thrusting it back in. Ziggy gasps, his cock twitching against my thigh, a trickle of precum wetting my skin. I let go of the plug and stop kneading his ass, draw my hand back and land the first satisfying smack against the round spot, watching as it jiggles, the red imprint from my palm fading quickly.

With Ziggy's aversion to pain in mind, I hold back from going too hard, gauging his reaction with each blow, his skin glowing redder and redder, getting warm to the touch. He's being such a good boy, staying still for me, even though his body is trembling, his cock hot and throbbing against my thigh, precum dripping onto my skin.

"You're such a good boy. Look how perfect you are for your Master," I praise. I realize few seconds too late that I slipped up and said Master instead of Daddy, but it doesn't seem worth correcting myself, so I just roll with it.

"Daddy," he gasps, the sound going straight to my dick, tightening my balls and making my entire body feel hot.

"My good boy likes that, doesn't he?" My hand connects with his upper thigh.

"Yes," Ziggy pants. "Please, Daddy. Please."

"You beg so prettily," I hum, slowing my strikes and rubbing my hand over his heated skin, kneading his ass cheek again, drawing a hiss from him. For a second, I'm worried it's more pain than he can take, but then his cock throbs against my leg. He's right at his limit. It still feels good, but much more and it'll be too much, and he's put all his trust in me knowing where that line is. If there's a better feeling in the world, I can't imagine what it would be. I'd happily take this moment over a hundred orgasms. Well, a hundred orgasms for myself because there's nothing I wouldn't trade in favor of making my boy fly.

"You're going to come when Daddy tells you to, aren't you?" I squeeze his ass again, more gently this time, and Ziggy gasps. I slip my fingers back into his crease, dragging them along the soft silicone of the plug. He cries out.

"Yes, Daddy, yes, yes, yes," he babbles.

With one hand reminding him of the sting from the spanking, I tug the plug out until only the tip is still stretching his pretty hole. My cock aches, making my underwear damp and sticky with precum. But this scene is about pleasing my boy. My own pleasure is a very distant priority in my mind.

I thrust the plug in and out, angling it down so I peg his prostate each time. My other hand strays from his ass, petting all along his back and dragging through his hair a few times. He gasps and pants and whimpers, his body shaking with his effort to hold back his orgasm. He wants to be good for me so badly. That thought rocks through me, nearly making me spill in my pants on the spot.

"Come, Ziggy," I say in a deep, commanding voice, and my boy makes me proud. He cries out with a sharp sob, tensing as his hot, wet release spills over my lap.

I keep fucking him with the plug, watching with satisfaction as his hole twitches and clenches through his orgasm. When his cries taper off and he sags on my lap, I push the plug back inside him and pull him into a seated position.

"Stand," I command, and he gets shakily to his feet. I take Ziggy's hands and place them on my shoulders so he can support himself while he recovers. I lean forward and drag my tongue over his softening cock, cleaning off the cum still clinging to him.

He hisses through his teeth, jerking away from me to protect his oversensitive cock. I put my hands on his hips to steady him.

"I have you," I assure him. "Lie down for me."

He does as I say, lying on the floor exactly where he's supposed to so I can do the diapering part of the scene like Hunter wanted.

Diapers generally aren't my thing, but I manage to get Ziggy powdered and diapered without looking like I have no clue what I'm doing. Then I pull him back up onto the couch next to me, gathering him into my arms for our aftercare cuddle session. I'm willing to admit to myself, and *only* to myself, that I've been looking forward to this part all day.

Ziggy is all loose and relaxed as he burrows into my arms, resting his head against my chest and sighing happily. I place gentle kisses on the top of his head and rock him a little without thinking about it. We are in a Daddy/little scene after all. My cock is rock hard, tenting my underwear, but it can wait until later. Having Ziggy, spent and happy, in my arms is more than worth a little delayed gratification.

I barely register someone calling "cut." Ziggy seems to be having the same problem, blinking with confusion.

"Come on, pup, why don't we get you cleaned up?" I suggest, standing and then helping him to his feet.

"Good idea. No offense to anyone who likes them, but diapers are definitely not my thing." He wrinkles his nose and immediately undoes the diaper, letting it fall at his feet. Chuckling, I bend down to pick it up and toss it into the nearest trash can.

He doesn't seem to give a second thought to walking stark naked through the studio. He must be used to it by now, but for me, taking care of him post scene when I'm still fully in Dom mode is different. After our last scene, I was trying hard to keep my emotions in check after fucking him. This time all I can think about is stepping into the shower with him and covering him in soap.

"Would it be weird if I asked you to shower with me?" he asks, almost echoing my thoughts.

I clear my throat and do my best to keep a neutral expression. "You want me to shower with you?"

"My legs are still a little shaky." He seems sturdy enough on his feet to me, but who am I to argue?

"Sure." I put a hand on his ass and squeeze, drawing another moan from him. His spent cock gives a weak twitch.

I strip out of my underwear, toss them in the direction of the lockers as we pass, and follow Byron through to the showers. He claims the same one he's used before, and this time I don't hesitate to follow him inside. I draw the curtain closed behind us, creating the very distinct and intimate feeling of being alone together.

He turns on the water, which heats up instantly. Bless Hunter for making sure his boys have a tankless water heater at the studio.

I stick my hand under the soap dispenser attached to the wall and pump some into my hands.

"Turn around for me, sweetheart." I rub my hands together to get a good lather going. Byron does as I say, putting his back to me. I gently run my hands over him, mesmerized by the way the bubbles gather on his body before the water whisks them away.

"That feels nice," he says softly, leaning into my touch like the sweet puppy he is. I'm beyond tempted to bend forward and press my lips against the back of his neck, taste his clean, wet skin against my tongue.

My still hard cock throbs at the thought, jerking and bumping against the curve of Byron's ass. He giggles and peeks over his shoulder at me.

"Sorry about that."

"I'm not complaining." He shrugs. "I could take care of it for you if you want."

"You don't have to."

"I know I don't *have* to. I'm going to blame the orgasm endorphins for making me say this if you ever try to hold it against me, but I've kind of been dying to have you in my mouth again."

"Jesus," I mutter, wrapping my fingers around the base of my cock. Now that I'm touching it, I'm suddenly hyper-aware of how close to the edge I already am. My balls are sore from how long I've been hard, my tip slick with precum.

"Please, Master," he begs. He swivels around and puts his hands on my chest. His fingers graze over my pierced nipples, and I shudder. *We've already had sex. What could it hurt?* A faint warning bell goes off somewhere in my brain, but I can hardly hear it over the sound of my heart thundering in my ears.

"On your knees, pup," I command. A slow, sexy smile spreads over his lips as he hits the floor. He winces when his knees connect with the hard tile, but he doesn't let that stop him, and he leans forward eagerly with open mouth. "Wait," I bark, and Byron freezes midmotion. "Tongue out."

He obediently sticks his tongue out, holding still as I give myself a few slow strokes until a fresh drop of precum glistens at my slit, clinging to my PA piercing. I drag my cockhead over the flat of his tongue, and a bolt of electricity dances along my spine. Byron glances up at me with the most alluring expression I've ever seen. I swear he looks like he'll crumble and die if I don't stuff his mouth with my cock.

I slide my cock back and forth against his tongue, then push into his mouth. As soon as his lips stretch around my shaft, he moans, the sound vibrating down my length.

"Such a good boy," I groan. I thread my fingers through his hair and push deeper into his mouth. He takes me easily...no, greedily— sucking and licking and moaning as if my cock is the best thing he's ever had in his mouth.

His hands stay on his thighs like a good sub who has been told he can't touch. But this may be the one time I can have him off-camera, and I want to feel his hands on me.

"Touch me, sweetheart." I draw my hips back and thrust into his mouth again. He snaps out of his still posture and paws at me eagerly.

I fuck his mouth while he gropes at my thighs, my ass. He runs his hands up and down my torso, grazing his fingers over my nipple rings. In my life, I've had plenty of partners: men, women, and nonbinary. I've played with newbies to the scene, experienced subs, and even had a fair few vanilla encounters here and there. I can say without a shadow of a doubt that none of them have sucked dick like Byron.

"Here it comes, sweetheart. Swallow," I groan as my balls draw tight against my body, heat flaring over my skin, pleasure rolling through me like a wave.

Byron whimpers and moans, swallowing as fast as he can as I fill the back of his throat with my cum, his tongue lapping greedily at my cockhead, his lips still wrapped around me. When my orgasm slows and tapers off, he continues to tongue my slit like he's desperately trying to coax more out. He tugs at my piercing, and a jolt goes through me, one last spurt of cum hitting his mouth. He makes a happy noise and finally releases my softening cock with a pop.

"I mean this as the utmost compliment. You give new meaning to the word cumslut."

He beams at me, licking his lips like he's worried he might've missed a drop. No danger of that, that's for sure. I reach down and help him to his feet, then turn off the shower.

I pull back the curtain. Hunter stands on the other side, his arms crossed over his chest, with an expression on his face that's a mixture of amusement and irritation.

"Good shower?" He arches an eyebrow at me.

"Listen, I'd say this isn't what it looks like, but I'm not about to insult your intelligence." I grab a towel off the rack just outside the shower stall and hand it to Byron. He's blushing from head to toe at being caught by his boss. If anyone fucked up here, it's me. "Go get dressed. Don't worry about this."

Byron looks between Hunter and me for a few seconds, then wraps the towel around himself and scurries away.

Once he's gone, I square my shoulders and face my boss. I wouldn't blame him if he fired me for doing something so unprofessional, but the thought of walking away from this job, from Byron, right now isn't appealing.

"Relax." He chuckles. "Based on the muffled moans I heard, it sounded like there was pretty enthusiastic consent for whatever just happened in there."

"Absolutely."

"Okay, then we don't have a problem. I'm the last person to tell you that you can't fall for someone you work with. Besides, this is porn. With this much sex going on, it's bound to happen from time to time."

"It's not like that," I lie. "I was still worked up after the shoot, and he offered to help. We got a little caught up, that's all."

Hunter grins at me and shakes his head. "Whatever you say."

He walks away, and I grab a towel for myself, drying off as I make my way over to the lockers. By the time I get there, Byron is already long gone. I do my best to ignore the pang of disappointment in my chest at his absence.

14

MARSHALL

"Where are we going?" Byron asks, bouncing in his seat, his nose practically pressed to the car window as he watches buildings pass, trying to guess our destination. It's been over a week since our last shoot and the very *interesting* shower we shared afterward. I haven't been able to stop thinking about him. I picked up my phone to call him at least three times a day until I finally had a stroke of inspiration this morning. Weeks ago, I promised Byron I'd take him to look at puppy stuff, and what kind of a man would I be if I didn't follow through on that promise?

"You'll see. We're almost there," I answer, unable to keep a smile off my face at his enthusiasm.

I want to kiss him so badly it's almost a physical need, but off-screen is very different than filming a scene. And I don't think a blow job when we're still in a post scene high counts. We haven't talked about crossing that line off-set, even though we've played together a couple more times at my apartment in the past several weeks. Ignoring his hard-on while he's in nothing but a pair of tight briefs and puppy ears should make me eligible for sainthood.

I pull into the parking lot of the shop, and he makes an excited noise that's almost a yip. Fuck, he's cute.

"Are we going into the sex shop?"

"We are. It's not just any sex shop. The man who owns it is a Daddy Dom, and he stocks all kinds of kink gear."

His smile gets even brighter. "Are we looking at puppy stuff? Can I get a hood of my own?" He wiggles, reaching for his seat belt and fumbling with the buckle, too excited to manage to unlatch it.

"Be still, pup," I say in a deep, calm tone, and he freezes. I press the little button on the seat belt to release it. "Stay," I command, getting out of the car and going around to open his door. "That's my good pup."

He preens under my praise, his whole body vibrating happily. Without giving it a second thought, I put my hand on the back of his neck and squeeze gently. He melts into my touch, letting me lead him into the store.

The man standing behind the sales counter is a mountain of a man, all muscles. At first glance, he looks a bit intimidating until you know he's basically a giant teddy bear. He goes by Daddy Titus at the club and is known as one of the gentlest Daddies in the city.

"Hey there. Marshall, right?" he greets me.

"That's right." I shake his hand. "And this is Ziggy."

"Nice to meet you, Ziggy. What are you two in the market for today?"

"Some puppy stuff for my...for Ziggy," I answer, nearly calling him *my* puppy. In so many ways, he is mine, but most of them are just in my head and not at all official.

Daddy Titus's grin widens. "I bet you're a cute puppy," he says, and Byron blushes. "Along the far back wall, we should have everything you're looking for. If you have something specific in mind that you don't see, let me know. I might be able to do a special order."

"Thank you, Sir," Byron says politely, and I nearly burst with pride.

We head in the direction Titus indicated and find a whole corner dedicated to hoods, ears, tails, leashes, toys...just about anything a pup could want.

Byron's eyes go wide. "I had no idea there were so many kinds of hoods." He touches the nearest one.

"That's right. There are varying degrees of coverage and then of course different styles and designs for different dog breeds."

"I don't think I want one of the plastic-y ones," he declares.

"No? How about leather? That would probably be more fitting for you anyway." I gesture toward some of the more expensive options. The price doesn't matter to me. I just want him to leave happy with his very own hood.

He nods and moves closer, checking out all the variations. "This one is like the one I wore during our first shoot together." He points at one of the more open ones with cute floppy ears and nice big eye holes.

"It is. Did you like that one?"

"Yes, it felt comfortable."

I take the one he's looking at off the rack and hold it up. "Why don't we try it on and see what you think?"

He ducks his head, and I slip the hood into place, fiddling with the straps until it sits right.

Byron rolls his head this way and that like he's getting a feel for the hood, the ears flopping around. He gives a happy little yip. I chuckle at his silly antics.

"I take it this is the one?" In answer, he leans forward

and licks a wet stripe along my cheek. "Okay, let's take this off so you can pick out some more stuff."

Byron huffs but lets me remove the hood. "What else can I get?" he asks.

"Whatever you want. How about your own leash and harness? Some toys to play with? A tail?" I point at a few different items, and his gaze darts around to all of them.

"I can really pick whatever I want?"

"Anything, puppy. Let me hold on to your hood while you pick what you want."

He hands the hood over and goes to town, browsing through all the different options. Before long, he has his arms full and a huge grin on his face.

"Okay, I'm done."

"Are you sure? I think there might be a toy you haven't grabbed yet," I tease.

"This should hold me over for now," he says seriously, and I chuckle.

"Okay, let's go, then."

"Find everything you were looking for?" Titus asks.

"I think so, at least to get us started."

"I can't believe all the fun puppy toys you have," Byron says.

"We have a few regular puppy customers, so I always make sure to get their input on anything I might be lacking."

"That's so cool."

Titus rings everything up, and we leave the store with several bags nearly bursting at the seams.

"Master," Byron asks in a small voice as I load all the bags into the back seat of my car.

"What's up, pup?"

"Could we go home and try my new stuff? I mean, your apartment."

"Sure thing." I give in to the urge to press a kiss to the top of his head and ruffle his hair. Then I open the car door for him.

Ziggy

We're in the car when it hits me. Marshall has paid for all this. And not only that, but I expected him to. It's a sobering thought for someone who's always prided himself on being financially independent. I can't afford to spend money on puppy gear right now, so if he hadn't paid for it, I couldn't have bought it.

But I never even considered who would pay for it. Somewhere deep down, I knew it would be Marshall. And that doesn't sit right with me. He's not my boyfriend. We're not in any kind of relationship, so why would he have to pay for all this? And god knows we spent a lot of money there.

"Marshall?" I ask, my stomach lurching with stress.

He takes a quick look at me, then puts a hand on my thigh. "What's wrong, pup?"

How can one touch and those few words already calm me down? He hasn't even said anything. Hell, he doesn't even know what my worries are, and yet he manages to communicate with that simple gesture that he's got me. He's like the safety net around a trampoline that assures you you can't fall off, no matter how crazy you jump.

"I don't know if I can pay you back anytime soon," I say softly, all my happiness over the gear gone.

"Did I say you had to pay it back?"

I bite my lip. "No, but you spent a lot of money on me."

"That was my choice, pup. That's not for you to worry about."

I chew on that for a bit. It sounds a lot like what he told me before we did the scene, that I shouldn't worry my pretty little head about it. Is that condescending? Should I object to him saying things like that? But how can I object when it doesn't bother me? It's not like he's taking over in areas of my life where I didn't invite him in.

Should I give him more say? Is that how this works? I see it in how Daddy and Joey interact. In his work, Joey is completely confident and in charge, but as soon as the cameras are off, he defers to Daddy in everything...and he's happy to do it. And Joey is not some young twink who doesn't have his shit together either. He's Daddy's age, if I had to guess, and clearly he's accomplished in what he does.

"How does Daddy kink in real life differ from puppy play?" I ask. "I mean, aside from what you do in playing together, obviously."

"That depends on how far you take both, but usually, puppy play is something you do at specific times, in a scene. It's rare to do it as a 24/7 lifestyle. For Daddy kink, it can be either or some middle ground. For some people, it's enough to keep the Daddy kink to the bedroom. They get a sexual thrill out of it but nothing more. And that's fine."

"But Daddy and Joey are much more than that."

Marshall nods. "Yes. Daddy is a full-time Daddy for Joey, with the exception when Joey is at work."

"How does that work? I mean, what does Daddy decide for him?"

"I'm not privy to all the details, but generally speaking, they both like it when Daddy makes the decisions for him. So he sets their routine, decides what's for dinner, maybe tells Joey what to wear, things like that. He's in charge of everything, and Joey likes it that way."

"But that's not the case with puppy play."

"It can be, but it's usually not."

"Is that something you would want?"

Marshall glances sideways. "With you or in general?"

"Both."

"Not particularly. I've played with Daddy kink before, and it does turn me on sexually speaking, but I don't need to be a full-time Daddy. It's too…" He sighs as if searching for a word. "It's too dependent for me, if that makes sense. I know that full dependency and vulnerability is like catnip for true Daddy Doms, but I'm not a huge fan."

A massive wave of relief washes over me. It seems I'm not into full-time Daddy kink either. "So, you're okay with not being in charge outside the bedroom?"

"Of you? Yes. I like to be your Master in scenes or shoots we do or anything relating to sex and kink, but outside of that? Nah. I like you the way you are, and I have zero desire to boss you around the whole time. Besides, I think that if you tried to be a full-time boy, you'd give the word bratty a whole new definition."

I laugh, some of the tightness uncoiling in my stomach. "You may be right about that."

"I *may* be right? Boy, I can spot a brat a mile away…and Hunter sure picked a few. Harley is gonna have his hands full with the other ones."

I giggle. "I bet he's glad to be rid of me."

Marshall squeezes my leg. "No, he's not, pup. He really likes you. You two just weren't a good fit."

"Do you think we could do more Daddy kink for the next scene but without the age play? Maybe do some role play with it?"

Listen to me, sounding like I actually know what I'm talking about.

"Sure. It was on Hunter's list anyway, and it fits you well. I could give you another spanking. Hunter said the last one was incredibly hot when he watched the footage."

My cheeks heat up, and I remember how it felt when he swatted my bare ass. Damn, that set me on fire. More of that would be... "I'd be down with that."

"If I remember correctly, you were *up* for that," Marshall quips, and it's such an unexpected double entendre from him that I burst out laughing.

"True. I would definitely like to do that again."

We've reached my apartment complex, and Marshall parks in an empty spot in the shade, leaving the engine running. "If you want, we can do some role play in private first," he offers. "Maybe do a school boy-principal scene? Or a pretend dad with his real son?"

I frown. "Why would I want to do that in private first?"

"Because not all your first experiences should be on camera. Our first kiss was in a scene, and so was the first time I fucked you. Don't you want to leave something private?"

He makes it sound like what we have is special, and it confuses me all over again. It's not a relationship, so why does he treat it like it is? "I don't mind. I'm barely aware of the cameras anyway with the way you make me feel. All I see is you."

It comes out huskier and far more cheesy than I intended, but I guess Marshall doesn't mind because his eyes darken the way they do when he's turned on by me. "Do you now?" he asks, his voice a low grumble that shoots straight to my cock.

"You make it impossible to see anything else..." I whisper.

"Pup, I'm about two seconds away from kissing you, so if that's not what you want, I suggest you either get out of the car now or use your safeword."

He's joking, right? He can kiss me anytime he wants, and so I unbuckle and turn toward him. "Please, Master." The words fall from my lips breathlessly all by themselves.

He yanks his seat back, then hauls me over the middle console and plants me onto his lap. I squeal in shock as I straddle him, and he swallows my protest in a fierce kiss. I close my eyes and give in to the need to be dominated by him. I don't know what we are, but as long as he keeps kissing me like that, I don't really care.

15
ZIGGY

It's a brutally hot afternoon, and the sweat is dripping down my face from the short walk from where the Uber dropped me off to the entrance of the Kinky Boys studio.

"I don't understand how you guys can live in this heat," Marshall is grumbling to Harley as I walk inside. He's patting his forehead with a handkerchief, which I find strangely amusing for some reason.

"New York is blistering hot in the summer," Harley counters.

Marshall scoffs. "Yeah, for three months max. And it's a different kind of heat."

"Yes. This is dry heat, not humid. Everyone says this is far easier to tolerate."

"Then everyone is wrong because I can't breathe here. I'd kill for some humidity right now," Marshall says, his face radiating his frustration. I can't say I understand his issue with the weather, but I'm from California, so it's not like the heat is new to me.

Our eyes meet, and I hesitate. The other day, we kissed

for a long time in the car, but Marshall did send me home afterward. We've texted since, but I haven't seen him. Do I kiss him? No, that's weird. Besides, I'm not sure either of us is ready to let the others know what we've been doing.

"Ziggy is here, so if you guys could stop your bitchfest about the weather, we can get started," Daddy says. I hadn't even seen him, but he's leaning against the wall, holding Joey tight against his chest. The man has his eyes closed, and his face shows pure bliss. No wonder, when he's being held like that. My stomach aches a little with want.

Daddy kisses Joey on the top of his head, and Joey opens his eyes and lets go of him with a smile, as if he's recharged. Marshall sends me a wink, then starts walking.

I follow everyone into a small meeting room, where a large flat-screen TV is set up at the head of a conference table. Someone has put out some bottled water, the outside still wet with condensation. Thank fuck for whoever did that. I grab a bottle as well as a mini bag of chips, then find a chair way in the back and sit down.

Marshall takes a seat to my right and Harley right next to him, while Daddy and Joey install themselves on my left. "Okay," Daddy says. "The scene we're about to see is the first shoot with Harley and Ziggy. Obviously, I've seen this already, and I think it turned out amazing, but if you guys spot any errors or anything you'd like to see changed, let us know. This video is scheduled to go live next week."

The idea of watching myself in a room packed with others is somehow way more terrifying than getting fucked in front of them...or by them, in Harley's case. Why is that?

I take a few big gulps of the ice-cold water as Daddy starts the laptop that's hooked up to the TV. "We haven't done the intro yet, so it's just the scene."

An image of me and Harley fills the screen. And when I

say fills the screen, I mean that I can count the hairs on my ass as the camera moves downward, showing me on my knees for Harley. Okay, I have to admit my butt has never been more spectacular, but holy shit, this is awkward.

My cheeks burn with embarrassment as the scene unfolds. Daddy was right. The scene is incredible once I get over the utterly surreal experience of watching myself on a screen that size. Naked. Kneeling. Getting fucked.

It's hot, I guess, though I really try to focus on Harley and not on myself. Technically, I can't see anything wrong with it. The quality is certainly a hell of a lot better than that video TJ shot of us with his iPhone. I don't care how much Apple wants to convince us it's a high-quality camera. It doesn't even come close to the studio's equipment. Then again, they also have professional lighting and audio equipment and everything.

God, the audio... Does it really make such a wet shlick when someone fucks me? And do I create all these little sounds so much in real life? They're positively slutty. All these gasps and moans, the way I smack my lips, even the way I whimper is like a concert, mixing in with bodies slapping against each other and Harley's much lower grunts.

My cheeks burn even hotter. No one will ever believe this is authentic. I'm too over the top. I can't believe Daddy wants to broadcast this. Reviews are gonna kill him.

A knee bumps against my leg. Marshall presses his leg against mine in a silent show of...of what? Support? Pity? I bury my face in my hands, watching the screen from between my fingers. As a kid, I wholeheartedly believed it made scary movies far less frightening, so maybe it will work here as well? But even from that angle, I'm still a horny slut who's getting ravished.

Why the fuck did I do this? When this is over, I won't

dare to look the men here in the eyes, let alone anyone else once they know. And then it hits me. This will be uploaded. To the Internet. For thousands of people to see, to buy, to watch, to jerk off to. Tens of thousands. How many views did Daddy say he was hoping for?

The blood drains from my face. What the fuck did I do? Oh god, oh god, oh god.

I made *porn*. I let myself get filmed while being fucked by different men. And everyone will see it, including my parents, my family, my former colleagues. They'll all know how desperate I was. They were right to judge me after TJ leaked our video after all. Everyone will know how cock-hungry I am.

"Ziggy?" Marshall says, and I shove my chair back, my lungs feeling too constricted to breathe, even as my head is reeling. Literally. "Puppy, what's wrong?"

"Can't breathe…" I whisper. "I can't fucking breathe."

After that, everything becomes hazy. Marshall pulls me down on his lap. He sits on the floor and drags me between his legs until I'm leaning back against his chest, his strong arms around me.

"Sshh, sweet puppy," he says softly. "Focus on your breathing."

I don't know how long it takes before that horrifying sensation finally ebbs away and my body unclenches, but when I feel like I have a solid grip on reality again, the room is empty except for Marshall and me.

"What happened?" Marshall rubs my arm with one hand and holds the other tight around my waist.

I can't tell him. It's too late now. I signed a contract, and no matter how much I regret it now, I have to live with the choices I made.

Daddy has already paid me, and I used the money for

rent. I can't pay him back, and even if I could, he spent much more on that video than just my check. There's Harley and Joey and all the other technical guys. The editor. Himself. We're talking thousands of dollars that would be all wasted if I told the truth.

"Puppy, I can see the emotions flash over your face, and I don't like it one bit. Talk to me. Let me help you."

"You can't tell Daddy," I whisper. "I don't want him to know."

Marshall lets out a sigh. "I promise that for now, I won't tell him, but that doesn't mean I won't lean on you hard later to inform him if I think he needs to know."

That's as good a promise as I'm gonna get. "I think I made the biggest mistake of my life by signing the contract with Kinky Boys."

Marshall

THE INSTINCT TO wrap him up in my arms and find a way to protect him from the world went into overdrive as soon as he started freaking out. I had no idea when everyone else filed out of the room because I was solely focused on calming Byron down.

Now that his breathing is returning to normal and he's talking to me, I rearrange him on my lap so I can see his face while we talk. It doesn't take a genius to figure out what upset him. It's one thing to be cavalier while getting fucked in front of a dozen people or so. It's another to face reality that your naked body, your "come" expression, every intimate and private thing about you is about to be splashed across the Internet for the entire world to have access to.

"So we'll break the contract." Yes, *we*. It's officially my job to fix anything that upsets him this much, whether he's aware of it at this point or not. Whatever line of bullshit I've been telling myself about keeping my distance emotionally went out the window as soon as he started hyperventilating.

"I can't," he whispers.

"Listen to me, Byron." The use of his real name seems to snap him out of a bit of his haze. He blinks at me in surprise, his eyebrows scrunching together. "If you don't want anyone else to see that video, then I can promise you no one else will ever see it."

Despite his still pale skin and anxious expression, he snorts. I arch an eyebrow at him in question, and that only makes him laugh harder. "I'm sorry. I'm picturing you all *Mission Impossible*-style dropping into Daddy's office on some kind of wire to steal the footage out of a safe." He laughs harder, his body shaking until the laughter turns to tears, and not the fun kind. A sob escapes his lips, and he buries his face in the crook of my neck as he cries.

I hold him tighter, running my hand up and down his back and murmuring sweet nothings until eventually the tears ebb, and he sniffles.

"I'm sorry. Fuck, I'm such a mess right now." He wipes the back of his hands across his cheeks and tries to move off my lap.

"Stay, pup," I say, putting a bit of that deep authority into my voice.

He settles again, and I press a kiss to the top of his head.

"One shaky, poorly filmed home video destroyed my career as a teacher. What will a bunch of high-quality porn videos do?" he asks in nearly a whisper. "I thought it didn't matter because that other stupid video is already out there, but this feels so different."

"I agree. It is different. And I'm not going to sit here and lie to you that this won't possibly take you out of the running for some jobs in the future." He nods miserably, and I tilt his chin up so he's looking at me while I say this next part. "But *none* of this, not that bullshit video your ex posted or any of the scenes you've filmed for this studio, change one single thing about who *you* are."

He sniffles again. "I look like such a slut in that scene." He jerks his head toward the now blank screen.

"You looked hot as fuck in that scene," I counter, and a ghost of a smile graces his lips. "Honestly, I'm kind of glad you got freaked out because I was two seconds away from having to excuse myself to deal with the hard-on you were giving me."

He makes a sound that's somewhere between a tsk and a laugh, wiping his eyes again and shaking his head at me. "You're just trying to make me feel better."

"Yes, but it's also completely true. I was hard as hell, watching that scene being filmed too."

"You were?" He bites his bottom lip, a light blush creeping into his cheeks.

"You have no fucking clue what you do to me, do you, pup?" I use my thumb to catch a stray tear that drips off his eyelash and rolls down his cheek.

He squirms a little in my lap, the pink in his cheeks darkening. "I probably shouldn't say this because we work together and all, but I think I really like you."

His words hit me like a bolt of lightning right in the chest, jolting me and sending a tingle of electricity skittering all along my skin. There are a million reasons this is a bad idea, but none of them seem like they matter anymore.

I cup Byron's face in both hands, pressing my lips against his in a kiss that's somehow hard and sweet all at once.

We've kissed before, but this is different. I swear I can taste his confession on his lips, feel his words making a home somewhere inside me.

I break the kiss and rest my forehead against his, matching his smile with my own. "I think I really like you too," I admit, parroting his phrasing just to make him laugh.

"This is crazy, though, right?" When I go in for another kiss, he puts a hand on my chest and leans back.

"Crazy how?"

"You're a Dom, and I'm..." He seems to struggle with his words, fidgeting in my lap. "Not a very good sub," he concludes with a self-deprecating laugh.

"Do you enjoy submitting? I mean, do you get something physically or emotionally out of letting go and trusting the Dom to take care of you?" I already have a hunch of what his answer will be. After he melted so beautifully in my hands the other night, I have no doubt that he truly has submissive tendencies.

"When it's you."

"Then you're a good sub," I say, putting a firm air of finality into my tone so he won't question them. "Do you think anyone's idea of the ideal Dom includes a chronic inability to keep time or a general skew toward disorganized?"

He giggles and shakes his head. "No, I guess not."

"But do you think I'm a good Dom?"

His eyes go a little hazy, a sweet smile tilting the corners of his lips. I'd kill to get a peek at the images I'm sure are playing through his mind right now. He squirms again, his cock tenting the front of his jeans, and it's all I can do not to puff up my chest and preen.

"Yes, you're a good Dom," he answers finally.

"I'm glad you think so. There's no right or wrong way to

be a Dom or a sub. There are safe and unsafe ways, and there are right and wrong for certain scenes. But there's no right or wrong way for you to be submissive. Understand?"

He nods resolutely. "Yes, I understand."

"Good boy."

He gives a happy sigh and leans into me, nestling his head under my chin so I can hold him close.

"What does all this mean?" he asks after a few more minutes.

"First things first. Do we need to call George Clooney and Brad Pitt to assemble a heist crew to get that footage back?" He giggles. The sound is enough to light me up inside.

"I think it's okay. I don't know what I want to do after this, but I definitely don't want another job where I have to worry about being judged for what I do in my private time. This will narrow down my options, but maybe in a good way."

"You're sure?"

"I'm sure."

"Okay, if we don't have to Ocean's Eleven this shit, then we have time for a date."

"A date?"

"Yeah. What do you say? Will you let me take you out for dinner tonight?"

"Yes."

"Perfect." I press a kiss to the top of his head. He tries to get up, but I tighten my arms around him. "Give me a few more minutes of cuddling."

"Mmmm, green," he says happily, melting against me.

16

ZIGGY

A date with Marshall. If I say the words in my head, they sound ridiculous. I would never have thought I'd be on a date with him, and at the same time, it feels completely natural. Inevitable. He's been my rock from day one, and we've been gravitating toward each other from the moment we met.

He likes me. I may have insecurities in some areas, but this, I believe. Marshall really likes me. I could see it in his eyes when he told me, on his face, but I've also seen it in the way he treats me. He's so protective of me, so caring. No way is he doing that only because he's getting paid for it.

I glance at him sideways as he navigates his car through the evening traffic. He's taking me to a hotel on the outskirts of the city that has a renowned vegetarian restaurant, and the fact that he specifically chose a vegetarian option for me speaks volumes. He really likes me.

I feel like I'm back in high school, discovering that Cody, the boy I had such a crush on, liked me too. He was my first kiss, and it was about as perfect as you can imagine. Sweet, romantic, clumsy as fuck, but I've never forgotten it.

"Why are you looking at me like that?" Marshall asks, and I realize I've been staring at him.

"I was thinking of Cody Bergstrom, my first crush back in high school. We shared our first kiss after a homecoming game, and it was perfect."

Marshall smiles. "I never pegged you as a late bloomer."

I raise an eyebrow. "Late bloomer? I was sixteen."

"That's what I'm saying. Late bloomer. I had my first kiss at thirteen."

I grin. "I was out and proud at thirteen, but I wasn't ready for that yet. I did make up for my late start afterward, though."

Marshall chuckles, and I'm happy he doesn't show even a trace of condemnation. "How were your parents when you came out?"

I shrug. "I think they knew pretty early on. They were simply waiting for me to be ready. When I was ten, they got divorced, and both remarried, but they've been great, supportive parents. They're pretty liberal, though they weren't amused when TJ leaked that video."

"They did get the part where you didn't give permission for that, I hope?"

I love Marshall's indignant tone. "They reasoned that I never should've trusted him to even shoot it in the first place...and it was hard to argue with that because I should've known better. They didn't like him, my dad especially. I figured it was classic dad behavior, you know? My dad can be a tad overprotective. But he caught some weird vibes from TJ, and in hindsight, he was completely right, of course."

I let out a deep sigh, and Marshall lays his hand on my thigh. "We all make mistakes, pup. Unfortunately, that's how we learn. Wanting to trust people is a good habit. You see the best in people, want to believe the good about them."

That's one way to look at it, and I love that he tries to cheer me up. "So, thirteen? You were pretty young." I change the topic back to him.

Marshall shrugs, his hand still resting on my leg. "I grew up in Queens in a neighborhood where at thirteen, you were pretty much considered an adult. My mom was on her own with four kids from when I was seven years old, so we took care of ourselves. I'm the oldest, so I grew up fast."

"What about your dad?"

His face tightens, and his fingers tense for a moment as well. "He's in prison for armed robbery and manslaughter. He killed a cop when they were trying to flee the scene after a robbery gone wrong. He was the driver of the getaway car, and he hit a cop who was trying to stop them. He claims he never saw him, but that doesn't change what he did."

Wow. I didn't see that coming. Something tells me Marshall doesn't like to share this story. "That must've been so hard on you all," I say softly. "Do you still go see him?"

"No. I never did. He was an asshole, even before this happened. Drunk or high half the time and zero sense of responsibility. I was glad when he got locked up, to be honest. My mom was heartbroken for a while, but after that, things got much better. She found another man, and my stepdad was amazing. He was a real dad to me, and I'll always strive to be the man he was. Unfortunately, he passed away really young of a heart attack."

What do I say to that? Aside from my parents' divorce—which I saw coming months before it happened—I had a pretty perfect childhood. Both my parents remarried, and my stepmom and stepdad are great, as are my halfsiblings. We're the classic example of a postmodern blended family, but my parents stayed friendly with each other, so it never really negatively affected me. They were always at every school function or important event, first alone, later with their new partners.

"It's a completely different childhood than I had."

"I'd like to think I turned out okay."

I frown. "What do you even do for a living? I can't imagine this is a full-time job."

"I owned a private security business, but I'd just sold it when Hunter called, so it was the perfect moment to take some time off to think about what I want to do next. I needed to step away from it all for a bit."

We've arrived at the restaurant, and he shuts off the engine. One gesture from him keeps me glued to my seat until he gets out and walks around to open the door for me. "Thank you." I flutter my eyelashes at him. "You're such a gentleman."

He smiles, the tightness from before leaving his face. "You deserve to be treated well, puppy."

He holds my hands as we walk inside, and my stomach does a happy dance.

This is not a cheap place, I notice with one look at the menu once we're seated, but when I open my mouth to say something, Marshall shoots me a warning glance, and I close it again. Messaged received. I am not to complain about the prices. Got it. I hope to god he'll be paying. If I have to cough up the money for this myself, I won't be able to make rent.

The food is amazing, though, and conversation is surprisingly relaxed. Marshall shares some fun stories about all the crazy stuff he's experienced and witnessed as a dungeon master in his club in New York, and I entertain him with my own adventures in dating. It's refreshing to be with someone who doesn't want me to pretend I'm a virgin.

So many guys either get jealous when you talk about past boyfriends or hookups, or get all weird and call you a slut. I'll happily admit I was for a long time, and I don't apologize for it. I've always been safe, it's always been consensual, and I've always been sober enough to remember it.

Granted, I lost count along the way, and if asked for names, I'd probably remember ten percent, but whatever. I don't need someone's full name and background to get fucked real good in a bathroom stall. And I've had some fun and weird experiences. When I tell him about the time a condom got lost somewhere in my ass, Marshall laughs so hard he has to stop eating.

"You're shitting me." He wipes tears from his eyes.

"True story. It took the guy five minutes to get it back out...not my sexiest moment. I mean, getting fingered is amazing, but not when the guy has a full-blown panic attack because he thinks you're gonna get a bowel obstruction from a condom that's stuck somewhere. He was a medical student, by the way."

"How did that even happen?"

I roll my eyes. "Because mister six-inch dick had bought a magnum-sized condom, convinced he had much more than six inches. And his aim was a little off, and he was half-drunk and clumsy, so at some point, it rolled off his dick, and he didn't realize it and pushed it in."

"I can't even. God, my jaw is hurting from laughing so much. I haven't laughed this hard in forever."

My belly fills with warmth at that indirect compliment. I love seeing him carefree and so much lighter. He's often so serious, a little sad even. Like me, and I cringe at the thought. I'm not who I was before. Will I ever be again?

"I used to be a carefree guy who trusted everyone and more or less breezed through life." A cloud of sadness rolls over me. "He took that from me. I have issues trusting people now, and I suffer from insecurity and self-doubt, something I never did before."

I let out a deep sigh. "I never understood how something like that could affect you so intensely until it happened to me. It's such a violation of your trust, of your privacy. It should've been my decision whether or not I wanted others to see that, and he didn't respect that. I thought I'd feel angry for a while but just at him, or maybe need some time to start trusting people again. But he took so much more. He cost me my job, which he did feel horrible about, to be fair. He apologized multiple times, stating that he'd never realized it would endanger my position at school. But it also cost me friends who didn't believe me that I never gave permission...or who thought I was a whore for agreeing to that video being shot in the first place."

Marshall takes my hand and holds it, squeezing gently. "It will get better. Easier. I know that's a cliché, but it's true. You're grieving something you lost. Your innocence, maybe. Your trust. But over time, it will get less and less, and your faith in people will come back. You'll come back stronger."

He's only eleven years older than me, but he's so much wiser. He's mature, for lack of a better word. It's a far cry from the party boy TJ was and probably still is. I can see myself with Marshall in the long term. On his arm. At his feet. In his bed.

"Can I come home with you tonight?" I ask, and Marshall's eyes widen for a moment. "Not because I want to do a scene or because I need you to assure me everything will be okay, but because I want to. I want to be with you, be in your bed."

Marshall's expression grows intense. "Yes, puppy. You can be in my bed tonight."

Marshall

IT's safe to say this has been the best first date I remember having. Sure, we've covered some heavy topics, but it's impossible to deny the genuine connection growing between us. It feels like we've been building something this whole time without even realizing it, something real and sturdy.

I lead Byron up to my apartment, my entire body already aching for him. As much as I love playing with him, tonight, all I want is to worship his body. It's almost embarrassing how badly I want him, considering that this isn't exactly our first time together. This feels different, though. No cameras, no script, nothing except for the two of us exploring this attachment that's been developing between us since the first moment we met.

My heart thunders as we step into my apartment. We both kick off our shoes, leaving them by the door. He looks at me with a smile that holds all kinds of dirty promises. My whole body prickles with awareness, longing gripping me so intensely in my gut that I'm surprised my knees don't buckle. Fuck, I haven't just been fostering a crush on this sweet, perfect puppy. I've fallen in love with him. Every shy smile and disobedient word has taken root in my heart without my permission.

"Do you want anything to drink?" My voice sounds rusty to my own ears. His smile widens, beckoning me closer.

"Does your cum count?" He licks his lips.

I take a step toward him, meeting his fiery smile with one of my own, and catch him around his thighs. I hoist him against me, forcing him to wrap his arms and legs around my waist.

"You're insatiable." I kiss his lips, savoring the flavor of him, memorizing the feeling of his mouth moving against mine as I carry him down the hall toward my bedroom.

"Guilty," he agrees breathlessly between kisses, his tongue teasing mine, his cock growing hard, pressing against my stomach.

I kiss him deeper. I was planning to drop him onto the bed, but now that I have him in my arms, the thought of putting him back down is the worst idea ever. I suppose I'll have to in order to get him naked, and while the naked part sounds perfect, I'm not crazy about the putting-him-down part.

"Listen, puppy," I say in a gravelly voice. "I'm going to set you down, and you're going to strip faster than you've ever stripped in your life because I'm pretty sure I'm going to go fucking insane if you're out of my arms for more than thirty seconds. Then I'm going to pick you back up and fuck you against the wall until you can't even remember what it feels like *not* to have me inside you."

Byron's breath catches, and he nods, his nose bumping against mine. "Yes, Sir," he agrees with a rasp.

I kiss him one more time and then ease my grasp on him, letting him unwrap his legs from around me so he can stand. As soon as his feet touch the floor, he tears off his clothes. I do the same, dropping everything in a pile without care and then grabbing the bottle of lube and a condom from my dresser.

I rip open the condom and roll it on while Byron whines impatiently, seemingly vibrating with need, his cock hard between his legs, the tip wet with precum. His lips are reddened from our kisses, his cheeks and chin the slightest bit pink from my beard. My cock throbs at the sight. I want to mark him all over with bites and hickeys, put a collar around that pretty neck of his, and tell the world he's mine.

That thought hits me in the chest and nearly winds me. The only sub I've ever collared was my last ex. I didn't expect I'd be so eager to do it again after that horrible breakup, but Byron feels like he was made to belong to me.

He whines again, snapping me out of my thoughts. I squirt the lube onto my fingers and toss the bottle aside, then cross the space between us to lift him up again, taking care to smear as little of the lube as possible on his skin. As soon as I have his weight in my arms, I press his back against the nearest wall and kiss him until we're both breathless, panting heavily. I slip my fingers between his ass cheeks and slick his hole.

He gasps and moans around my tongue as I work a finger inside, and then two, his hot hole taking me in greedily. He tugs at my nipple rings with his fingers, sending sparks of heat down my spine and straight to my balls.

"Please, please, please," he begs between kisses. "I need it, please."

"Greedy boy," I murmur, sliding my fingers out and maneuvering him into position against my cockhead.

"*Yesssss*," he hisses as I slowly thrust inside him. A broken sob falls from his lips, and his legs tighten around my hips. I fill him, stretch him, claim him with my cock deep in his ass.

"Such a good boy," I praise. I pull out and thrust back in, this time faster, harder, jarring him against the wall and earning another desperate-sounding cry. "You're Master's good, perfect boy, aren't you?"

"Yes, yes, yes," he pants, digging his fingers into my shoulders, his eyelids fluttering closed.

"Eyes open," I command. "I want you to know who's holding you, who's fucking you."

"I know it's you. No one else ever made me feel like this." He punctuates his words with a moan.

My muscles burn with the exertion of holding and fucking him at the same time, but it's a good burn, especially when Byron's cock bounces against me with every thrust, smearing precum against my skin.

"I'm so close," he gasps as I pound his prostate each time I rut into him. Sweat beads on my skin, my balls are tight, and heat pools in my stomach as I lick and kiss this throat. "I can't wait. *Please*."

I gently nip at his skin and fuck him harder, deeper, pushing him right up to the edge where I know he won't be able to hold on for another second. "Come for me, puppy," I growl, and he lets out a strangled cry, tensing almost instantly, his hole clenching hard around me and then pulsing as he paints my stomach with his hot, sticky release.

I fuck him through it, not relenting until he goes limp in my arms, his cock giving one last helpless twitch, a trickle of cum dribbling out and rolling down his softening shaft. I slam my hips forward, once, twice, a third time, and the heat deep inside explodes in a wave of pleasure, my orgasm crashing over me hard.

As much as I hate to set him down, by the time my orgasm ebbs, my knees are like Jell-O and my arms aren't doing much better after holding Byron up for so long. He's breathing hard as he gets his legs under him. I take off the condom and tie it off, dropping it onto the floor, and guide him over to the bed. I stop for a second to grab my shirt off the floor, using it to mop up the cum on my stomach, then toss it aside.

I climb in next to him and pull him close so I can wrap my arms around him. Byron rests his head on my chest, tangling our legs together, and lets out a happy sigh. I press a kiss to the top of his head and drag my fingers up and down his spine, soothing him to sleep. His body relaxes, and his breath grows slow and heavy. If there's a better feeling than my puppy in my arms like this, I can't think what it would be.

The fact that I'm not planning to stay in Vegas forever and six months seems to be flying by a lot faster than I expected nags at me and tries to steal all the peace from this moment. But I mentally bat my worries away. That's a problem for another day.

17

MARSHALL

I check the time and curse under my breath. I'm supposed to pick Byron up in ten minutes, and I just got back from running a few errands. This damn heat has me sweating like a motherfucker. No way am I showing up to take him out tonight, smelling like I just ran a marathon.

I pull my phone out of my pocket and press the Call button, stripping out of my clothes and making my way toward the bathroom while it rings.

"You're running late?" he answers.

"It's not my fault. It's too damn hot out."

"I'm not seeing the connection, but I'll take your word for it." He laughs. "Aren't Doms supposed to be really responsible and punctual?"

"And subs aren't supposed to call a Dom out on his shortcomings. We both have something to work on," I tease back. "Seriously, though, you don't mind if I jump into the shower real quick before I swing by to pick you up?"

He lets out an exaggerated sigh. "That's fine. I was going to let you put the plug in for me so I can attach my new tail when we get to the club, but I guess I'll have to use this time to do it myself."

I groan, my cock twitching at the image of my sexy boy fingering himself open and then working a plug inside that tight, hot hole of his. "You do that, but hands off that pretty cock. I want the pleasure of taking you apart later."

"Silly Master, you know I don't have *any* problem making myself come without a hand on my cock," he taunts, and I growl.

"Behave, pup."

He giggles. "Fine, I'll be good. I'll see you soon."

"See you soon." I hang up and set my phone down so I can take that much-needed shower.

I diligently ignore my erection while I make quick work of making myself nice and fresh for our date tonight.

In my bedroom, after the shower, with a towel wrapped around my waist, I rummage through my dresser and pick out some clothes for tonight. My fingers brush over the box I stashed in my top drawer a few days ago, and my heart flutters. I know it's too soon, but I saw a collar that screamed "Ziggy," so I went ahead and bought it for him. I may have gotten an engraved tag to go on it too. We haven't been seeing each other long enough for something like that, but it can't hurt to have it. Hopefully, I can give it to him someday soon.

It's equal parts thrilling and terrifying to even think the word *someday*. So many things can happen between now and then. Not in the least the fact that I'm more than halfway through my time in Vegas, and if I'm being honest, I'm itching to get back to New York. Not that I haven't enjoyed working for the studio, but I miss the seasons and the buildings and being able to step outside without instantly bursting into flames. I miss my overpriced loft and my favorite bagel place on the corner of my street. I miss my jogging buddies and the club and my friends. But where would that leave Byron and me?

I shove the box farther back into the drawer. Now is not the time to think about all that. Tonight we're going out and enjoy his first time playing with other puppies at the club, and we'll worry about the future later.

When I pull up in front of Byron's place a short time later, he's waiting outside the building with a duffel bag thrown over his shoulder. He's wearing a T-shirt that says "bad to the bone" with a little dog bone on the front, and I chuckle. He's bouncing as he climbs into the car, carefully setting his bag in the back seat.

"Hey, pup," I greet him, leaning over for a kiss. I feel the curve of his smile against my lips. "Excited for tonight?"

"Yes." He nods emphatically and wiggles in his seat. "Do you think the same puppies I met before will be there or maybe new puppies?"

"Probably the same. There aren't too many pups, so I'd be willing to bet the same ones come to every event around here, with a few newbies of course."

"I hope they like me," he says with all the anxiety of a kid on their first day of school.

I chuckle and squeeze his leg. "They'll love you."

When we get to the club, Byron scrambles out of the car. I hurry out after him and snag him by the back of his shirt before he can rush off without me. I drag him back toward me until his back is pressed against my front, and I bend down so my lips brush against his ear.

"We're at the club. Let's try to pretend like I'm actually the one in charge of you, huh, pup?" I tease in a low voice.

"Yes, Master." He huffs impatiently.

"Good boy." I release him, and he manages to contain his

excitement enough to stay beside me as we walk to the entrance. I put a hand on the back of his neck, and he relaxes into my touch.

Once we're inside, we find a private spot where he can get changed into his puppy stuff. He shimmies out of his jeans, and I bite back a groan at the sight of his jockstrap with the perfect bulge in the front and framing his ass in the back like a work of art.

He wants to leave his T-shirt on, so I put the harness on over it, then help him into his hood, mitts, and kneepads, sparing a second to kiss his snout once the hood is on. He rewards me with a wet swipe of his tongue over my cheek. Last but not least, I attach the furry tail to the base of the plug he inserted at home.

He looks over his shoulder at his tail and gives it an experimental wag. With a delighted bark, he starts to chase it, moving in a tight circle in an attempt to catch it between his teeth.

"Silly puppy." I pet his head and attach a leash to his harness. "Come on, let's go make some friends."

He yips and trots alongside me to the puppy playroom.

Ziggy seems a little unsure of himself as we step into the room, pressing himself against my leg and shrinking down a little as if he's hoping to make himself less noticeable. I stoop down, unclip his leash, and run my hand down his back.

"We're here to have fun. If you want to leave, come back over to me, and we can have a drink at the bar in the lounge instead. Now, go play." I stand up and give him a little swat on his butt to get him moving. He yelps indignantly but scampers off like I told him to.

It doesn't take long before he's made a few friends and is tussling around with them. I feel warm and happy inside watching him play. He looks so carefree, and why shouldn't he be? He knows I'm here to keep him safe so he can let go of everything and just enjoy himself.

A few of the other handlers and I wander near each other, making idle conversation while our pups have a good time.

"You two are new here, huh?" one of the Doms asks.

"Yeah. Both to the area and to puppy play," I admit. "Well, he's new to puppy play. I've dabbled over the years."

"Oh, really? I wouldn't have guessed. He seems so relaxed. Usually, it takes a while before they really get the hang of letting go and leaving all their awkwardness behind."

"Yeah, shyness has never been an issue for Ziggy as far as I can tell." "That's great. My Sparky always loves making new friends. Let me give you my number. Maybe we can set up a playdate outside of the club sometime. A bunch of us usually get together a few times a month for dinner, drinks, puppy time for our boys, whatever."

"That sounds fantastic." We exchange numbers, and after some time, Ziggy makes his way back over to me, looking happy but exhausted.

"Time to rest?" I guess, and he lies down at my feet. I chuckle and pet him while he catches his breath. "All done playing, or do you want to go back?" I ask after a few minutes.

He stands up and nudges me toward the door with his head. "Okay, I guess we're going. It was nice meeting you, and I'll be sure to call so we can get our pups together again soon."

I get Ziggy out of his puppy gear, packing it back into his bag with care. I'm about to detach the tail when he says, "Stop."

"Something wrong?"

"No, I was just wondering..." He blushes a little. "Can I leave the tail on while we get a drink in the lounge and then take it off before we leave?"

"Of course, sweetheart." I leave it in place and help him to his feet. He looks absolutely mouthwatering, his hair all mussed from the hood, wearing nothing but his T-shirt and jockstrap, the tail peeking out from between those perfectly curved ass cheeks.

I'm not imagining the envious looks I get walking my boy into the lounge, and I don't bother to hide my pride in having him at my side. I keep a hand on the back of his neck, both because he likes it and because I love showing every other Dom in here that this pretty boy is all mine.

"Can I ask you a question?" he asks after I order us drinks and find us a place to sit.

"Yes, but only if you're sitting on my lap," I tease, patting my leg. He smiles as he scoots closer and climbs onto my lap.

"I was wondering, most of the other puppies have collars. Should I have one? Or is the harness enough? Is it usually either-or?"

"It depends. Most of the time, a sub with a collar on means something special."

"It does?"

"Yes, it's a sign of commitment when a Dom collars his sub."

"Like an engagement ring?"

"Kind of." I chuckle. "Puppies can wear collars they pick out themselves. If you want to get one, I'd be happy to help you pick it out, but for me, a collar has a significant meaning."

"I'd like that." He leans against me as he sips his drink. "I'll wait, then."

"Oh, you will, will you?" I tease. "So sure we'll get there?" My tone is light, but my heart is beating harder as I ask the question.

"I hope so."

"Me too, puppy." I press a kiss to the side of his head. "Me too."

18

ZIGGY

Ever since he mentioned it, I've been thinking about that collar. I did some research online—finally, I might add—and discovered that Marshall was right. Collaring is something special indeed, both within the BDSM community in general as in puppy play. I never knew.

I have to admit that after everything I read—I got a little sucked into a rabbit hole once I found the blog of a sub detailing his experiences with pretty much everything, and boy, that rabbit hole was deep—I feel even more stupid for how I approached the Kinky Boys job. I've gotten lucky that Marshall stepped in because honestly, that could've gone horribly wrong.

Well, the more I've gotten to know Daddy and the others, even Harley, the more I know they would've picked up on it as well, but it probably would've taken me longer. And I would maybe have never discovered how much I love being a puppy, and it's the best thing in the world.

As I walk up, Marshall is at the door, and as always, he greets me with a deep kiss. This man never does anything halfway, and my heart speeds up at the greedy way he takes my mouth. By the time he lets go of me, I'm panting a little, and his eyes have darkened in a way I recognize by now.

"I don't know what I want more, to fuck you or to play with my puppy first and then fuck you," Marshall says, then kisses me again.

"You could fuck me first. Then we could play, and then you could fuck me again?" I say with a hopeful smile.

He smiles and ruffles my hair. "I could, puppy, but once you're in my bed, the temptation would be too big to stay there. And I want to see you as a puppy again."

Gah, that is the most perfect answer. "You really like me as a puppy, don't you?" I feel a little shy.

Sometimes it's still hard to imagine that this magnificent man wants me not just as Byron but also as Ziggy and as puppy. Or is Ziggy the same as my puppy? I don't know how to distinguish between those three sides of myself.

He folds his hands around my neck and looks me deep into my eyes. My heart skips a beat. "I love it when you're a puppy."

He gives me one last kiss, then lets go of me and smacks my ass. "Time to change, pup."

I strip in the living room, where he has pushed the furniture to the side again and has draped a sheet over the floor, god bless him. Colorful toys are waiting for me, and I yip in excitement as I sink to my hands and knees, completely naked. Marshall sits down on the couch, then beckons me with one finger. "Come here, puppy."

I consider it for a moment, my mind already changing into that different mode where I'm only half Byron, and my other half is this happy, playful puppy. Then I scramble away, letting out a bark.

Marshall chuckles. "Feeling a little disobedient, pup? Remember, only good puppies get treats."

He holds out a bit of chocolate, but this time, it's not a Hershey's Kiss. No, the man has gone for the real thing: Godiva, the one filled with caramel. My mouth waters at the sight.

"Chocolate is bad for real puppies, but I know a puppy who'd love this," Marshall coos. "But you only get it if you're a good puppy."

I crawl back as fast as I can, then sink back so I sit on my feet, sticking my tongue out like a puppy would. He scratches my head. "That's better. Do you want Master to put your puppy gear on?"

I bark, and as a reward, I get my piece of chocolate to keep me occupied while Marshall dresses me.

My harness goes on first, and I love the smell of the real leather. The black straps contrast with my skin, framing me and making me look gorgeous. Marshall runs a hand down my back, then lower down my ass. "Mmm, beautiful."

He has knee protectors for me as well so I can stay on my knees longer and a pair of puppy mitts for my hands. Once those are on, I'm dependent on him because they're not easy to take off by myself. For a brief moment, I remember kneeling for Marshall in that club the first time, the way he immobilized me with that rope within seconds.

He was right. Being a sub is all about trust, and I can say from the bottom of my heart I've never trusted anyone more than I do Marshall. I don't feel frightened or powerless now. I feel safe, protected. Happy in the hands of my Master.

Marshall puts my mask on, then gently removes the plug from my ass and replaces it with a bigger one that holds my black, furry tail. I barely have the patience to sit still, my body vibrating with the need to move while he's checking me over. He slaps my ass. "Go play, pup."

Before the last word is even out of his mouth, I'm gone, heading straight for the toys he put out. Oh, he has a rope to play tug-of-war. I take it into my mouth and bring it back to him. He laughs as he grasps the other end, then gently tugs, not so much it hurts my teeth but enough to make me work for it.

When I grow bored with it, he starts throwing the ball for me. All my worries disappear into the background as I fully sink into my puppy headspace. When I get tired of running, Marshall snaps his fingers, and I obediently drop onto my back.

"Time for belly rubs," Marshall says, his voice so wonderfully low and sexy. I'm not wearing underwear this time, so my dick has been swinging free the whole time. I was at half mast, but once Marshall starts rubbing my stomach in slow circles, I instantly grow hard. I can't explain it, but it feels so dirty when he touches me like this when I'm geared up.

I sigh with happiness as Marshall keeps stroking my stomach, my chest, my nipples. He's touching me everywhere except where I want it the most, and I'm pretty sure he does it on purpose.

"Such a good boy," Marshall praises me. I force myself to stay still, even though all my muscles are tense in anticipation of feeling his hand on my cock. "So obedient to your Master."

Honestly, when he talks to me like that, I'd do anything for him. He could command me to crawl through broken glass, and I'd do it, which goes to show how heavy his responsibility is. My whole system is overloaded with happy hormones, and I drift on cloud nine.

Marshall, dressed in a pair of tight jeans and a form-fitting T-shirt that shows off those sexy nipple piercings, grunts, a sound full of want and need. I watch through heavy eyes as he unbuttons himself, then takes out his cock and strokes it. He's hard, so hard, and wet with precum already. I lick my lips. God, I want him. Will he let me suck him?

For a few minutes, he continues to stroke me all over while he's slowly fisting himself. Wherever his fingers roam, my skin is burning hot, but he's still not touching my dick. He's playing with himself, flicking his piercing, and spitting in his hands to make his cock slicker. I don't think I've ever wanted dick as much in my life as I want now.

When he finally says, "Hands and knees, puppy," I scramble up as quickly as I can, and the way I present myself to him, pushing my ass back as far as it will go, is nothing short of slutty. But I. Don't. Care. I need him, and I need him now.

He whips off his shirt, followed by his jeans, and oh my god, the man was commando this whole time. Sexy fucker.

Thankfully, he's done teasing me. He suits up and slicks himself, then pulls out my tail-plug. "I need to be inside you." The words come out like a growl.

I brace myself as he drops to his knees behind me. The way he slides inside me is graceful yet forceful at the same time. He's a man who knows what he wants, and he's going right for it. I whimper as he pulls back and surges back in, hitting my prostate head on with his piercing. I'm already on the verge of coming, and we've only just gotten started.

"This is not gonna take long," Marshall says, and I would've kissed him for that if my mouth was anywhere near his, but it's not. It's on the ground, holding the sheet I'm kneeling on as best I can with my puppy mitts still on. He's fucking me in full puppy gear, like a Master owning his puppy, breeding me, and I never thought that term sexy until now.

He fucks me hard, the slaps of our flesh meeting echoing through the room. I can't touch myself, not with mitts on, but I don't need to. Hands-free orgasms are not easy, but the way Marshall taps my happy spot directly with his piercing, it's more than likely I'll get one.

He grunts, and I whimper in response. I'm so close, my balls tight and ready, my dick begging to be touched. One touch and I'll explode. If Marshall so much as puts a finger on my cock right now, I'll detonate.

In the end, I don't need it. He slams in hard, then again, and his whole body tenses. He's coming, but so am I. My cock jerks, then releases, spurts of cum flying onto the white sheets. Marshall makes minute moves inside me, shaking with the force of his orgasm.

When he's done, I sag to the floor, unable to hold myself up any longer. Marshall rolls off me, takes off the condom and ties it, then pulls me into his arms, puppy gear and all. We're both panting, our bodies slick with sweat, and I could sure use a shower.

He must've read my mind because a minute or two of cuddling later, Marshall says, "Come on, puppy, time to get your gear off and take a bath."

"A bath?" I perk up. "Together?"

Marshall turns onto his side and chuckles. "We're not gonna fit in my tub, but I'll bathe you, puppy. You'll love the bubbles I got you."

He's right. I adore the bubble bath bomb he bought for me. It smells like the ocean and makes me think of Venice Beach for a moment. I sink deep into the water—lukewarm, at Marshall's insistence. He has a point because his AC is not the best, and I'll be sweating for hours after.

"Mmm, such a pretty puppy." Marshall folds a thick towel up and puts it on the floor to kneel on so he can take care of me. I love the tender way he scrubs me clean with a loofah.

I blow bubbles at him, and he laughs. I can be so playful with him, and he doesn't think it's childish or immature. With him, I can be myself, as Byron and as a puppy. He accepts all of me, and he makes me feel safe and taken care of. He makes me feel…

I love him. The thought pops into my head, so crystal clear, and it sinks deep into the very core of my soul. I love him. How could I not? It may be fast and complicated, but it's the truth.

I turn my head. "I love you." For once, I don't regret being impulsive. "I don't know when it happened, and you don't have to say it back or feel obliged in any way…but I love you. With all my heart."

I don't have a moment of doubt. I'm not afraid. Marshall beams at me, eyes sparkling, giving me his answer before he opens his mouth. "I love you too, puppy. More than I ever thought possible."

He yanks me up out of the bathtub, and I wrap my arms around him as he kisses me. Then he slides into the water with me, and a massive gulf of water splashes over the side. We laugh but never stop kissing each other, and we make out in the bathtub for a long time.

Marshall was wrong. His bathtub is big enough for both of us. Just not with a lot of water in there as well, but who cares?

19

ZIGGY

Time has flown by. Marshall and I have done four more shoots, and tomorrow, we'll film the last one. In the last one, we did a paddling, and though I wouldn't volunteer for that again anytime soon, Marshall made it good for me. He makes everything good for me, and yes, I do realize how incredibly sappy that sounds.

I'm happy. Happier than I was in California even. I found a second job as a sales clerk at Macy's, and my manager is so satisfied with my performance so far she said she'd recommend me for their manager promotion training. It's not my dream job, but between that and Kinky Boys, I'm climbing out of the financial hole I was in. And I have to say that feels really, really good.

I'm not even worried when Daddy asks me to drop into his office.

"Ziggy, thanks for stopping by," Daddy says, and I sit down across from him in his office. The first time I sat here, I was so nervous, hoping he'd hire me. How things have changed.

"You said nothing was wrong, right?" I ask, even though he'd literally put that in his text.

Daddy smiles. "Nothing is wrong, I promise. I just wanted to talk to you in private about what's next for you."

I frown. "What do you mean? I have one more shoot."

"Yes. And what about after that? Have you decided what you want to do after this series is done? I'd be happy to schedule you for some size slut scenes with Max."

Right. Of course. Why hasn't this even crossed my mind? Probably because I've been too blissed out in my little bubble of happiness with Marshall to even give it a thought.

My first instinct is to say yes because why not? I'd love to see what Max is packing and, what's more, feel it for myself. I'm not as needy as I was. Between the shoots and what Marshall gives me at home, it's not like I can complain about my ass not getting what it needs. But come on, the guy packs a ten-inch cock. What power bottom wouldn't say yes to that?

Except it's not that easy anymore, is it? "I think this is something I have to talk about with Marshall," I say hesitantly.

"I think so too." Daddy's voice doesn't hold a trace of mockery.

I ponder it as I drive home—and that very word shows how much has changed. When did I start to think of Marshall's boring apartment as home? I haven't slept in my own bed in weeks, though I'm still paying rent for the crappy studio.

An idea begins to form. Maybe it's time to take things between us to the next level. Marshall has indicated he's ready for something long term, and I'm more than primed for that stage as well. Wouldn't it make sense to make our relationship more official? It's kind of tacky, inviting myself to move in with him, but I'm practically living there already, so what objection could he possibly have?

When I get back, Marshall sits on the couch, on the phone with someone. The call is over by the time I've taken off my shoes and put my car keys in the designated place on top of the dresser in the hallway.

"Hi, puppy," Marshall says as I plop down on the couch next to him and raise my mouth for a kiss.

He obliges with a soft, sweet kiss, and I sigh a little into his mouth and snuggle against him. It's pretty damn perfect what we have, isn't it?

"What did Hunter want?" He scratches my neck, and I'm seconds away from purring in contentment.

Here's my opening. "He wanted to talk about what I wanted to do next."

"And what did you tell him?"

Marshall's intonation is neutral, not giving away anything, and I hesitate for a moment. But how can he say no to this? I know he wants to be with me. And so I jump in with both feet.

"I told him I needed to talk to you first." I sit up straight and turn toward him, pulling up my legs. "I was thinking that I'm spending most of my time here anyway, so what would you say if I moved in officially? I could end my lease, and that would save me a lot of money. I'd pay part of your rent, of course, but it would be less than two separate apartments. And I know we both want something more, that we're ready for something long term. And I'm in for that...with you...if you want..."

Marshall's expression is not what I expected to see and definitely not what I hoped to see. Uh-oh. My stomach plummets. Once again, I've ruined everything by being impulsive. He isn't ready for this yet, and now I've fucked it all up.

"Or we can wait, if you want," I say quickly. "Like, if you're not ready for this, I can wait. I'll happily wait until you're—"

He places a finger on my lips. My eyes fill with tears because I know I'm about to be rejected.

"Puppy, I'm leaving in two weeks. I'm going back to New York."

He's leaving? It sinks in. He was only supposed to be here for six months, and that time is almost up. I knew this. Of course I did. I just thought he'd change his mind.

"You don't want to stay?" I hate how close I sound to begging.

Marshall looks pained. "I wish I could. This town...it's not for me. I miss the seasons, the cold, the bluntness of New Yorkers. This town is too...too fake. Too happy. And too fucking hot. I couldn't live here."

"Not even with me? For me?" I whisper.

He takes my hand, which is shaking as much as my voice is. "That phone call I just ended? That was the confirmation that I got a job I'd applied for. Head of security for a big law firm in the city. I wanted to wait until I knew I had a job to ask you to move back with me..."

My heart skips a beat. "You want me to come with you?"

"Yes. I don't want to be apart, puppy, but I can't live here. Please come with me."

"But I have a job here. Two, actually."

"You can find a job in New York. There's plenty of work for someone as talented as you. If you want to stay in porn, I know some great studios operating out of the area. And if you don't, I make enough to support whatever you want to do."

He's saying all the right words, and yet my heart feels deadly cold. This is not how it was supposed to go. "I just moved here from LA. I can't pack up everything and move yet again. Why can't you stay here?"

Marshall's face is tight with pain. "I can't. I can't function here. I have a life back in New York. I miss my mom, my sisters, my friends."

"I've just started to make friends here. How can I leave all them behind and uproot myself yet again? What if we don't work out? I'll be left with nothing, in a city where I don't know anyone."

"It's kind of pessimistic to assume we're not gonna work out, don't you think?" Marshall says, and for the first time, there's an undertone in his voice. Irritation, maybe. Frustration. I don't know, but I don't like it.

"No, it's realistic. My last boyfriend fucked me over good, and if I'm not mistaken, so did yours, so forgive me for being careful now. I'm not gonna get heartbroken all over again because I made the stupid, impulsive decision to go along with what some guy suggested."

Marshall's eyes harden. "I'm not some guy, and I don't appreciate you comparing me to that dickwad who violated your boundaries and your privacy. You know I'd never do that."

"No, but you do expect me to drop everything and follow you like an obedient puppy, don't you? I made the mistake once of trusting everything would work out fine. I'm not doing that again."

"I don't think that's a fair representation of the facts. You could also see it as proof of how much I love you that I'm asking you to come with me."

I'm so cold now I'm shivering. "If you loved me that much, you'd be willing to stay here for me. You'd be willing to compromise rather than expect me to bend to your wishes. I may be your puppy, Marshall, but this is not an area where you can order me around." I get up from the couch and straighten my shoulders. "Now, if you'll excuse me, I think I'm going home to sleep in my own bed tonight, since it seems I have to get used to that again anyway."

Marshall doesn't say a word as I grab my stuff and walk out, my heart breaking into a million pieces.

Marshall

It's astonishing how quickly that conversation went south. I heard myself being a complete asshole, but I couldn't seem to switch gears as things escalated. I'm sure it had something to do with the fact that Byron was right. I'd expected him to jump with joy when I asked him to move with me or, at the very least, accept the decision and come along like a good puppy. When put that way, I feel like an even bigger dick.

Staying in Vegas was never part of the plan. To be fair, falling in love with Byron was never part of the plan either. But I have a life in New York. He was right about that part too. We've both been burned in the past, and it doesn't make a hell of a lot of sense to make a huge decision like where to live or what job to take based on something as fragile as a few months old relationship.

I look down at the phone still clutched tightly in my hand. I could call Ben back right now and tell him I can't take the security job. I could call the leasing office and see if I can extend the lease on this apartment another six months and see where we stand then. But I really don't want to do any of that. Homesickness settles heavily in my stomach, warring with the very horrifying realization that if I choose to go home, I'm going to lose Byron.

"Fuck," I mutter, dropping my phone with a soft *thud* on the floor and covering my face with both hands.

Am I too old to want my mom? Because I could *really* use one of those perfect mom hugs right now. My phone vibrates on the floor. I pick it up and smile at her name across the screen. My mom is clearly psychic.

"Hey, Mom."

"Hi, sweetie. I had this feeling that I should call you, and you know how seriously I take gut feelings. Is everything okay?"

I give a somewhat watery chuckle, leaning back against the couch with one hand on the phone, running the other over my head.

"Not really, but I'm not sure I want to talk about it."

"If you're afraid to tell me that you're in porn now, your sister's husband already told me."

"What? Which one?"

"Tony."

"Well, you might want to ask Vicki what her husband was doing on a gay porn site. But no, I wasn't worried. I just didn't think that was the kind of thing you'd want to know. I'm just..." I let out a long sigh. "I'm ready to come home, I think."

"Good. Six months is too long for me to go without seeing my favorite son."

"I'm your only son," I point out with a laugh.

"Exactly. You'll come for our big Sunday dinner once you're home, right?"

"Wouldn't miss it for the world." I was planning to bring Byron to that dinner to introduce him to my family for the first time. I guess that won't be happening. My heart aches as all the things I've been picturing since I applied for the security job fall apart. I've been making a long mental list of all the places I wanted to take Byron in New York, and now I'm not going to get to do any of it.

"We can't wait to see you."

"Me too, Mom. Listen, I'd better go, but I'm glad you called, I really needed to hear your voice."

We say our good-byes and hang up. I feel a little lighter after hearing from her, but it doesn't change the fact that I can't have both my puppy and my home.

If it wasn't hotter than Satan's asshole outside, I'd go for a run to clear my head. My other go-to when I need to think is the club, but it doesn't feel right going without my Ziggy. So, where does that leave me? Sitting in my apartment all alone with the feeling of an elephant on my chest. I groan and slump down farther on the couch, grabbing the remote and turning on something stupid just so the noise will drown out my thoughts for a while.

∼

When I wake up the next morning, some of my self-pity has dissipated. The only way we're going to get anywhere is to have a calm conversation. I shoot Byron a text, asking if he'd meet me for coffee. After a few minutes of making me sweat, he sends an okay back.

We meet at the coffee shop near the studio. The same place I agreed to film more scenes with him. If I could turn back the clock to that day, would I've made a different choice? I could've saved myself from getting closer to him, saved myself from being caught in this choice I wish I didn't have to make.

Everything inside me rebels at the thought of erasing

everything we've shared. I've been with plenty of people in my life, but none of them held a candle to him. I wouldn't trade the memories we've made for the world. But I want so much more than just memories with him.

I sit at a table with a coffee and one of the sugary abominations he loves in front of me. When he walks in, he looks around for a second. Then his gaze lands on me. My heart hammers hard against my ribcage, and I give a weak smile and wave him over.

He's stiff as he takes a seat, his face carefully neutral with none of his usual sweet smiles.

"Thank you." He folds both hands around his drink.

"Of course." He lowers his eyes and shifts uncomfortably in his seat. It's up to me to take control of this conversation, and I'm more than happy to. "I don't like how our conversation ended yesterday. I thought we could try again."

He scoffs, fiddling with his straw but not taking a drink. "You weren't happy with it because I didn't go along with what you wanted?"

"I wasn't happy because I acted like a prick, and I don't think either of us fully had the chance to lay out our points of view and find a compromise."

He slumps a little, some of the fight leaving his expression, his jaw losing its tension.

"Fine, tell me your point of view." He waves his hand impatiently.

"I never intended to stay in Vegas permanently. My family and my life are back in New York. I understand you feel the same way about Vegas at this point, but I am hoping you'd at least consider making the move with me. I have a good job lined up and an apartment I've been subletting while I was in Vegas."

Byron narrows his eyes. "See, that's the problem. This is

all about *your* life, *your* job, *your* apartment. I love being your puppy, but that's not *all* I am."

"I know that."

"I'm just starting to get my feet under me here, and I don't want to leave yet. Maybe in the future, I'll feel differently, but right now, I want to stay."

Maybe in the future. It's a small life preserver, a tiny ray of hope that there might be a compromise somewhere in this mess.

"What if we tried to make it work long distance?" I suggest.

Byron sighs and finally scoops some of the melting whipped cream onto his straw to lick off. "It's so far. When would we even see each other?"

"I'll pay for flights. We can do two weekends a month, one where I come here and one where you come out to see me."

He sways his head back and forth and eats some more whipped cream while he seems to consider the proposal.

"Being apart would suck," he says eventually.

"Breaking up would suck more," I counter.

"Yeah, it would. Okay, I guess we can *try* long distance." He doesn't look thrilled about the idea, but I'll take it. At least it's a chance to make it work rather than throwing in the towel.

"I love you, puppy." I reach across the table and take his hand. "We'll make this work."

He squeezes my hand and gives me a sad smile. "I love you too."

20

ZIGGY

I now understand what people mean when they say a cloud is hanging over them. This has been my reality for the last ten days. Two more days and Marshall is leaving, and every time I think about that, my heart stabs with pain, and my throat tightens.

He loves me, I'm sure of that, and my feelings for him haven't changed either. They're still this big force inside me, making me long for him all the time. How will I ever cope with him being so far away? He seems confident we can do it, but I don't share that faith in our relationship.

Or maybe it's faith in myself. I don't doubt him. He wouldn't cheat on me or anything. He's too honest for that, too honorable. And I'd never go behind his back either. That's not what I'm worried about. It's just that...

I need him. It may not be healthy to feel that way, let alone admit it, but I need him. He's my rock, my safe place. He's my Master, and there's no one else I can be myself with the way I am with him. If he's not here with me, how will I survive? How will I find that freedom to be me again? I like who I am with him. He's given me back my confidence. I'm just so scared I'll lose that when he leaves.

Maybe that's why I reacted so emotionally when he said he wasn't willing to stay here. I know I had as little right to expect him to stay as he had for me to move with him, but I'm just so scared. He's the best thing that ever happened to me, and what if we can't make it long distance? The thought makes my heart cold.

Tonight he's taking me to the club again for another puppy playdate. It'll probably be the last time. No way in hell am I going there without him. Not only wouldn't it be the same, but I could never show up there without my Master to take care of me and protect me.

I'm at my own place for the first time since we fought twelve days ago. It's only because he's already packed most of his stuff and has had a cleaning lady come in to do a deep cleaning before he leaves. It's strange being here again, especially on my own, but I guess I'll have to get used to it.

At least my new roommate seems like a sweet guy. Much better than the last one, who was an inconsiderate ass. Gregory is kind and nice, so I'm not expecting any issues with him.

"I thought your boyfriend was gonna pick you up at eight?"

Speak of the devil, Gregory sticks his head around the corner into the hallway where I'm waiting. "He's always late," I say with a smile. "If it's by only five minutes, that's on time for him."

Gregory steps into the hallway, and my eyes widen as I take him in. When he's home, he usually wears PJs. He has super cute ones with Minions on them, which seems to be his favorite thing anyway, considering how many shirts he has with the little yellow imps. But tonight, he's wearing a pair of pink leggings that fit him like a glove, combined with a white crop top with the word "Baby" in glittering pink letters.

I whistle between my teeth. "Looking hot, baby."

From the moment we met, I'd him pegged as gay, which was another reason why I was happy to have him as a roommate. And since we're clearly not each other's type, we're almost destined to be friends, and I like that idea. Maybe having more friends will help fill the void Marshall will leave.

Gregory twirls around, smiling a little shyly. "Thank you. I'm going out tonight as well."

"Hoping to score, judging by your outfit."

He nods, and I love that he's unashamed about it. "Yeah. My D...boyfriend and I broke up recently, and I miss it."

Am I getting too focused on kink that it sounded like he was about to say his Daddy rather than his boyfriend? Not really something I can ask. "Ugh, I'm sorry. From the look on your face, I'm guessing it wasn't your choice?"

"We weren't a good fit, but it still sucks."

I hum in sympathy. "Been there, done that. Another time, I'd love to keep you company, but tonight is not good."

He makes a face. "Erm, not sure if you'd be okay with where I'm going."

I raise an eyebrow. "Where's that?"

He shuffles his feet. "I go to a club...a kink club."

My mouth drops open. "Get out of town. You're not talking about Ball and Chain, are you?"

His eyes widen. "How do you know?"

"That's where we're heading tonight. I'm a puppy, and my Master is taking me to play with other puppies. So what's your kink if I may ask?"

"That's so cool. Being a puppy fits you. I'm a boy looking

for a Daddy. My previous Daddy only wanted to be a Daddy in the bedroom in the end, and that's not what I'm looking for. I want a full-time Daddy. I need one."

I love how simply he puts it out there, without any shame. "I'm sure you'll find someone. You're super sweet and nice. Surely there must be a hot Daddy looking for a sweet boy."

He smiles at me, his eyes sparkling. "If you happen to know any candidates, send them my way."

My phone dings with a text message from Marshall, saying he'll be here in two minutes. "Wanna catch a ride with us?"

Gregory shakes his head. "No, but thank you. I already called for an Uber. But I'll see you there, I guess."

"See you there."

I go downstairs so Marshall can pick me up right at the curb and doesn't need to waste time to park.

"I'm sorry I'm late. I was—" Marshall says when I get into the car.

"It doesn't matter. You're here." I lean in for a quick kiss.

His smile is warm. "I brought your gear, puppy. Make sure you take it with you when we go to your place tonight."

I nod, sadness filling me all over again. Marshall takes my hand and puts it on his thigh. "We'll make this work." With the way he says it, I almost believe it.

The club is busy, as it usually is on the weekend, and when I see the puppy pit, I'm bouncing with excitement. Marshall helps me put my gear on, and as soon as he gives me the all-clear, I'm off.

I'm in my happy place, and I play for an hour, fetching the ball when Marshall throws it, tumbling with other puppies, chasing each other, and then trotting back to Marshall where I plop down at his feet, exhausted.

"Did you have fun?" he asks as he rubs my belly.

I let out a brief yip of agreement, moving into his touch. For a few minutes, he keeps rubbing me while I calm down, my eyes closed as I lie on the floor, perfectly content.

"Puppy, I have something for you." I open my eyes. What did he bring me? More yummy chocolate?

"Kneel for me," Marshall says. Something in his tone puts me on high alert. I'm sure it isn't chocolate, but what is it?

I scramble up, then present myself to him the way he taught me. He hums in approval. "Beautiful, my puppy. You're so beautiful."

My heart explodes with the warm and fuzzies.

"I'm gonna take your mask off for a moment, okay? I need to see your face for this."

I'm getting more and more curious. He's making this into a moment, but what…? It hits me. Oh my god. He's gonna…

He takes off my mask and puts it next to him on the bench he's sitting on. Then he reaches into the bag he brought, and he takes out a collar. He's gonna collar me. My Master is collaring me.

My eyes fill with tears, and around me, it quiets down as people pick up on what's about to happen. Marshall holds out the collar to me. "I want to make you officially mine, puppy. I want to claim you as my sub, my puppy. I promise to always take care of you, to respect your boundaries, and to do my very best to make you happy. I'll be the best Master for you I can be. Will you accept my collar?"

With tears streaming down my face, I nod, then realize that won't do and say, "Yes, Master. I'm yours. I promise I'll be the best puppy I can be…and I love you."

It's not as eloquent a speech as his, but it'll have to do.

Marshall's eyes grow moist as he shows me the engraved

tag on the beautiful black leather collar. "Ziggy" it says on one side, and when he flips it over, I see the other side. "Marshall's puppy." It's perfect, absolutely perfect.

I straighten my neck so he can fasten it, and all around us people cheer in joy as Marshall officially makes me his. When the collar is tightened, he inspects it, slipping two fingers underneath to make sure it's not too tight.

"Gorgeous, puppy. You're all mine now."

"I'm all yours," I affirm, and for the first time, I believe that we'll make it, even hundreds of miles apart.

He drags me onto his lap and kisses me until I'm melting against him. The high I'm experiencing isn't even sexual, though I am rock hard. Being officially his fills me on an emotional level much more than sex ever could. I love him, and he loves me. I'm his. I have to believe that love will conquer all.

21

MARSHALL

As soon as I step off the plane in New York, an overwhelming feeling of *home* crashes over me. I take a deep breath, and a weight falls off my shoulders. The only problem is an even heavier weight still presses on my heart.

I shoot Byron a quick text, letting him know I've landed and that I'll call him in a bit once I'm settled in at my apartment. People bustle around me as I grab my bag off the conveyor belt and head outside to get a cab.

As I step outside, I nearly laugh with relief, the relative coolness of the air compared to what I've been living in for six months. Hell, I almost need a sweater, even though I'm sure it's at least sixty-five or seventy. Without the desert sun beating down on my head, it's downright chilly. I'm already fantasizing about tomorrow's run in Central Park as the cab pulls away from the curb. It's a bit of a ways from my apartment but totally worth it.

I lean back and watch the buildings flying by outside, wishing like hell I had my puppy here with me to point out landmarks to and share stories from my life as we pass meaningful places. My chest aches with missing him, my throat tight.

We pull up in front of my building, and I pay, leaving a hefty tip, and get out of the cab.

I've been dreaming about my New York apartment for six months. Giddy with excitement, I slide my key into the lock, but as soon as I swing the door open and step inside, my mood falls flat.

It's exactly as I remember it. All my furniture is here, and I can get the rest of my stuff out of storage this weekend. It'll be like I never left. My stomach sinks. Fuck, I'm starting to think none of this is going to feel right without Byron here. He's never been here, but somehow it's absolutely wrong without him. Giving him the collar before I left is the only small comfort I have right now. I could tell by the way he accepted it that he understood the full significance of the gesture. If I have to be apart from him, I need to know he is really and truly mine, no matter how many miles separate us.

My mood is sour as I unpack my bag and text my mom and sisters to let them know I'm home and can't wait to see them this Sunday for dinner. I place a delivery order at my favorite Thai place. Then I stand in front of my living room window, looking out at the city and mentally poking at the raw edges in my chest that won't seem to be appeased with all the things I've been anxious to get back to.

After my food is delivered, I set up my laptop on my coffee table, kick back with my food, and hit FaceTime to chat with Byron.

It takes a few seconds for him to answer. Is he busy with something else? I try to remember his work schedule for this week or if he mentioned any plans, but I come up blank.

Finally, he accepts the call, his face filling the screen with a big smile.

"Hey, hold on. Let me get comfortable. I was just walking in the door."

I dig into my food while I wait for him to get settled.

"Were you working?" I ask once he's on his couch.

"No, I was hanging out with Glam. How was your flight?"

"Good." The ache worsens at being able to see him but not reach out and touch. "Did you have fun with Glam?"

"Yeah." He shifts in his seat a little and readjusts the camera. "What are you eating?'

"Thai food."

We both fall silent for a second, and Byron sighs.

"Why does this feel so weird?"

My shoulders sag, and I set my food aside. "It'll take some getting used to, that's all."

"What if we don't get used to it?" he asks, pulling his knees up to his chest, his smile dropping entirely. "I want to crawl into your lap right now. It sucks seeing you and not being able to touch you."

"I know, puppy. I don't like it either," I admit. "But this is the best compromise we have right now. I don't want to give you up." A desperate feeling claws at my chest. Is that what he wants? Is that what he's trying to say right now? That he changed his mind about making this work?

"I don't want to give you up either. I just hate this, but I want to try."

I let out a relieved breath. "It'll get easier." I'm not sure if I'm trying to convince him or me.

"Yeah."

"And in two weeks, you're flying out here, and we'll have a long weekend together. I already have some ideas of places I want to take you and things to show you."

Byron's sad expression morphs into a flirty grin. "What if the only place I want you to take me is your bed?"

"We'll definitely be going there," I assure him in a deep voice, my cock reacting to the mere thought of my puppy here in my apartment, in my bed, all mine to touch and kiss and fuck. "Rest up before your visit because I can promise you that you won't be getting much sleep while you're here."

He rests his chin on his knees, still pulled up to his chest, and looks at me with a kind of sad longing. "I can't wait."

"Me either." After that, things *do* get a little easier. He tells me about some adventure he and Glam went on today, and I tell him all about the things I'm planning to do this week when I'm not working.

We're FaceTiming for two hours. Then I reluctantly let him go so he can have dinner and wind down for the night.

"I love you, Master," he says before we sign off.

"I love you like crazy, puppy." I kiss my fingers and press them to the camera, and he does the same.

The second the screen goes blank, the pain in my chest comes back tenfold. *Only two weeks until he comes.* We'll make this work. We have to.

∽

ON SUNDAY NIGHT, I walk into my mom's place without knocking. She lives in a townhouse in Brooklyn she bought with my stepdad's life insurance money after he passed, but not until my sisters and I strong-armed her into it. She didn't feel right spending the money at all, but we convinced her it was exactly what he would've wanted her to do.

I wander into the kitchen, where I find her and two of my sisters, Becky and Theresa, working on dinner alongside my mom.

Becky spots me and lights up, but I put a finger to my lips to tell her to keep quiet while I sneak up behind my mom and wrap her in a hug. She shrieks, dropping the spoon she's using to stir whatever she has on the stove.

My sisters and I laugh, and my mom swats my arm. "Are you trying to scare me half to death?"

"Nah, just missed my mom." I give her a squeeze and then let her go. She turns around to face me.

"Well, let me get a good look at you. Have you lost weight?"

"Vegas is hotter than Satan's asshole. I probably lost ten pounds just from sweating."

"And you haven't been sleeping." She squints at me.

"It's been a little tough adjusting to the move," I say vaguely.

I can tell she doesn't buy that as the full excuse, but luckily she drops it. I wash my hands and jump in to help with cooking. Vicki and her husband, Tony, show up a few minutes later, and Tony goes to join my other two sisters' husbands in the living room while Vicki hangs out in the kitchen with us.

Chatter fills the house along with the delicious smell of my mom's chicken pot pie and fresh biscuits. My biological dad might've been shitty, but I couldn't ask for a better family than my mom and sisters. Vicki pours glasses of wine all around, and we move into the living room while everything cooks, to catch up on the past six months. I've called and texted with them all fairly regularly, but nothing comes close to competing with Sunday night dinners as a family.

My phone vibrates in my pocket, and I pull it out. A text from Byron. It's a selfie of him lying in bed with his puppy ears on and the caption "I miss my Master." My smile drops from my lips, and my heart aches. I drag my index finger over the screen, wishing like hell I could reach out and touch my puppy.

"So there *is* a reason for the lack of sleep," my mom says knowingly. I jump, closing the picture and shoving my phone back into my pocket.

"What?" I feign ignorance. It's not like I've been planning on keeping him a secret or anything. I just wasn't sure I wanted to dampen the mood by telling them about our long-distance relationship and seeing pitying looks from everyone.

"Did you meet someone in Vegas?" Theresa asks, wearing that same I-can-see-right-through-you smile my mom always gets.

"Yes, I did. He's amazing, and I'm completely in love with him, and he didn't want to move here."

"Oh no," my mom says, and everyone gives me that damn sympathetic look I was hoping to avoid.

"No, it's fine. We're going to make it work long distance for now."

"I'm sure that's going to work out just fine," Becky says encouragingly, but I don't miss the look she exchanges with Vicki.

"How'd you meet him?" Theresa asks.

"Um..." My face heats up, and I take a sip from my wine. "Through work."

"As a porn star?" Vicki arches one of her neatly tweezed eyebrows at me.

"Yeah, hey, are we just not talking about your husband checking out man-on-man porn or what?" I glance in Tony's direction, and he doesn't seem the least bit ashamed, nor should he as far as I'm concerned.

"I was curious." He shrugs. "I certainly didn't bargain for

seeing my brother-in-law's dick, though. I can tell you that much."

Everyone bursts out laughing, and I just shake my head with a grin.

"Well, in any event, I'm sure he's a lovely person," my mom says.

"He really is. He's coming to visit in a couple of weeks. I'll try to bring him to Sunday dinner if I can."

"Good, because anyone who was able to talk you into doing porn is someone I'm curious to meet," Becky says.

Dinner is loud and wonderful, and when we're finished eating, we play a game together. By the time the night winds down and we all head out, I'm full of a warm, peaceful feeling, which only lasts until I get back to my empty apartment.

I take off my shoes and head straight for the bedroom. I strip out of my clothes and crawl into bed. Lying back, I FaceTime Byron.

He answers quickly, his smile lighting me up inside.

"Hey, puppy. How are you? I miss you."

"I'm good. Did you like the picture I sent?" he asks. It looks like he's in bed too. I roll onto my side and prop my phone up so I can pretend we're lying right next to each other.

"I loved it. I told my family all about you tonight. They can't wait to meet you."

"Yeah?" he seems uncertain, biting his bottom lip.

"You don't have to worry. They're the best. You'll love them."

"I believe you. How was dinner?"

"It was great. I can't believe how much I've missed in six months. Becky and her husband are trying for a baby now, and Vicki got a big promotion. And I can't believe how much I missed hugging my mom." I smile fondly as I recount bits and pieces of the evening to him. There's a hint of sadness in his eyes as he listens and nods.

"I'm glad you had a good night."

"Thanks." I sigh. "It's late, even there. I suppose I should let you go."

"Yeah." He doesn't seem any happier about the idea than I am.

"Or...would it be lame if we left FaceTime going while we both go to sleep?" He grins again and shakes his head.

"I'd love that."

"Me too." I switch off my light, and he does the same on his end. The picture looks strange with only the light of the phone cast over his skin. I close my eyes, and the soft sound of his breathing is all it takes to lull me to sleep in no time.

22

ZIGGY

As soon as I see my friends all show up unannounced, I know I'm about to be subjected to an intervention. I've been absolutely miserable since Marshall has left, and they've all seen it. When I open the door, they pile into the hallway.

Glam is first, and he hugs me tightly. "We're here for you, boo."

Baby is next, and he holds on long, pouring his concern in me. I love it.

They brought Max as well. I guess they took his friend Benton's car because he's here too, looking a little sheepish. "I offered to go home and pick them up later, but they insisted I come along."

"The more, the merrier," I say, and I have never meant that more. Lonely doesn't even begin to describe how I'd felt in the last week without Marshall. I'm counting down the days until I fly in to see him. Six more nights.

I let them into the living room, where they squeeze onto the couch or on the floor. Then Glam pulls a massive bottle of tequila out of a bag, followed by a big container of limes, plastic cups, and a salt shaker.

"All I need is a knife and a cutting board, and we're open for business," Glam declares.

"I'll get it," Gregory says, standing in the doorway, in his Minions onesie. I hadn't noticed him yet, but it makes sense he'd come out of his room to check out on the noise.

"Guys, this is my roommate, Gregory. Gregory, these are my friends and coworkers Glam, Baby, Thunder, and Benton."

I told him about Kinky Boys a few days ago, and he had a good laugh about it. It turns out he's a massive Ballsy Boys fan but hadn't heard about the Kinky Boys yet, so he's been teasing me with my career ever since, but in the best way. I'm not sure if everyone is okay with him knowing their real names, so I figured it'd be best to use their porn names.

Gregory waves at everyone as they say hi in chorus. Then he hurries off to the kitchen and returns with the items Glam asked for.

"Come join us." Luckily, I don't have to insist, and he immediately lowers himself to the floor. He really is the cutest and the sweetest guy.

"I feel like I need a porn name too," Benton complains. "Like, my name doesn't match all your names at all."

"Hmm, how about Maniac…'cause you certainly drive like one," Baby says, rolling his eyes.

Everyone chuckles, but Benton looks mock-offended. "I'll have you know I've—"

"—never been in an accident," Max takes over. "We know. Not as much of a reassurance as you think, unfortunately."

"Bitch, you don't get to complain. I've been driving your

sweet ass all over town for years now," Benton fires back, but his eyes sparkle.

"It's not his ass we're worried about. He has more valuable assets we need to protect," Glam quips while pouring all of us our first shot of tequila, and that has everyone laughing again.

"We could call you Bitch," Max suggests. "Because lord, do you know how to bitch."

Benton waves his hand. "Don't be so negative, honey. I'm a fucking ray of sunshine, and you know it. Sunshine, rainbows, and freaking unicorns, that's me."

"I still say Baby was onto something," Glam says. "My heart rate has only now come down from the way you drive. One of these days, your guardian angels are going on strike or plain quit their jobs, and you'll get us all killed."

Benton perks up. "That's it. Angel. That'll be my porn name."

Max scoffs. "I hate to bring it to you, but you ain't no angel, sweetcakes. Not unless angels have become horny little fuckers since the last time I read the Bible..."

Benton seems unfazed. "Aren't they supposed to be in heaven and all that? Well, my idea of heaven is a place full of horny men who want to get it on."

And with that, we're all in stitches, and his nickname becomes official. Angel. It suits him somehow. "Do you need a porn name too, sweetie?" Glam asks Gregory, who laughingly shakes his head.

"I'm perfectly happy being the baby boy of whoever will be my next Daddy."

Glam whistles. "Girl, I like you already."

As our tequila intake increases, so does the laughter, but I grow quieter and quieter. This is why I didn't want to leave Vegas. These men are my friends in a way I never thought

I'd have friends again after what TJ did. They're amazing, and I don't want to lose them.

Glam scoots over next to me, then puts his head on my shoulder. "How you feeling, boo?"

"Happy that you guys are here. Sad that Marshall is not."

"He didn't want to stay?" Baby asks, and the room goes quiet.

I bite my lip. "New York is his home. He was only here for six months, and he was homesick. I get that. His whole life is there. His family, his friends, his job."

"So why didn't you go with him? Or didn't he want you to?" Max wants to know.

"He did, but I didn't want to uproot my whole life again." Much to my frustration, tears well up in my eyes as I gesture around the room. "How can I leave all of you behind just when I feel like I've found friends who get me?"

"Ziggy, sweetheart, we'll still be here," Glam says, his voice warm and kind. "It's much easier to maintain a friendship at a distance than a relationship. You need your man much more than you need us. You could fly here every few months to hang out with us, and in between, we can FaceTime and shit."

"But what about my jobs here?" I protest.

"Were you gonna keep doing porn?" Baby asks, sounding surprised.

I think of the discussion Marshall and I had about it. Neither of us was sure how we felt about it, which surprised me. Marshall didn't flat out say he didn't want me to, though he did suggest I might want to try something more vanilla. He had a point there, but I'm not even sure if I want to stay in porn at all.

"I don't know. Marshall isn't dead set against it, but it's

hard for me to see myself with anyone else, especially in a kink setting."

"I'm sure Daddy would shoot you in a plain porn scene for the Ballsy Boys," Baby says.

I nod. "Yeah, he already offered that, but I haven't decided yet. I'll have to make up my mind soon, though, since I don't make enough as a sales clerk to pay for everything." That reminds me of the ad I found online that I did some research into. "I did see something else that might work for me. They're looking for online English teachers for kids abroad, like teaching English to kids in Japan or something. You need to be a native speaker and have experience teaching, and I have both. I sent in an application because the money is great, and I think it would be fun."

"That's right up your alley," Glam says. "And that's something you can do from anywhere, right?"

He's right, of course. If I quit porn and do that job instead, what would keep me in Las Vegas other than my friends? I could get a job in retail anywhere. I let out a deep sigh. "I'm from LA. How the hell would I ever survive in New York?" The words sound weak, even to my own ears.

"Sweetheart, you miss him so much that all week you've been walking around like a zombie with a dark cloud hanging over him. Could whatever struggles you may have to adapt to New York feel worse than this?" Glam says kindly.

"Of course it would be a big adjustment, but you'd have Marshall there. It's not like you'd be alone, and you did that when you came here, and look how that turned out," Baby piles on.

The way they put it makes it a no-brainer, but I'm so scared of making the wrong choice. Again. I've made a few too many impulsive decisions that either did go wrong or could've ended in disaster, and I'm scared to jump in without thinking again.

"What if we break up? I'd be stuck in a strange city, one of the biggest on earth, all on my own."

Glam pats my back. "Boo, it's not like you'd be stuck there. First of all, I don't think you guys will be breaking up, but even if you did, you could always come back. It's not permanent, sweetie. Las Vegas will be here waiting for you."

I lean against him, savoring the feeling of being heard and understood. I have the best friends in the world. "I'll have to see how it goes when I visit him."

Max nods. "I've been to New York a few times, and I'd move there in a heartbeat. It's an amazing, vibrant city, and I'm sure you'd fit right in. Just go there with an open mind."

By the time they leave, it's two in the morning, and we're all drunk except Max, who, for some reason, doesn't drink. He's actually called an Uber for him and Benton, who's clearly too wasted to drive, but neither of them seems to mind. When I drag myself into bed, the dark cloud has lifted just a little. I miss Marshall like crazy, and I'd kill to be in his bed right now, but maybe, just maybe Glam and the others were right. I'll have to wait and see how New York treats me.

23

ZIGGY

My face is practically pressed against the window as we approach Newark Airport. That's Manhattan, right there below me, and it's an incredible view. I've never been to New York, but I kinda expected it to be like LA, but even from the air, it looks completely different. It's so small, such a tiny island stuffed to the brim with millions of people. But I'm only here for one person.

Missing Marshall is like this giant gaping hole inside me. It aches in a physical way, like I'm constantly aware that a part of me is missing. I knew I'd fallen hard for him, but I hadn't realized how much of my happiness was linked to him. It's been a painful confrontation, though it has also made me realize how shallow my previous relationships have been. I've never ached for someone the way I do for Marshall.

It takes forever to get off the plane, and I'm like an impatient toddler, practically stomping my feet in frustration. I'm grateful I'm flying with carry-on only so I don't have to wait for my luggage. As soon as I walk through the doors, I see him, and I'm running before I even consciously make the decision.

When I jump, he catches me, and I sling my arms around him, holding on tight. His smell surrounds me, then invades me, comforting me that he's really here. We're together again.

"God, I missed you, puppy." Marshall sighs into my ear. It's such a rush that he says it first. He's told me on the phone, but right now, I hear the emotion in his voice. I feel the tension in his body as he says it, and I know he's telling me the truth.

"I missed you too." The ache that's been stabbing my soul is gone, replaced by joy. "I missed you so fucking much."

"I know. Come on, puppy, let's go. I need you all to myself."

He takes my bag from me, gentleman that he is, then laces our fingers. He only lets go when our train arrives, and we embark. We find two seats together, and as soon as we sit down, I put my head against his shoulder.

"I can't believe you're here," Marshall whispers, kissing the top of my head.

"Sorry for not asking you which airport was the easiest before I booked my ticket," I say, and he chuckles. "I hadn't expected it to be this big of a deal."

"For tourists, Newark is the easiest because it has an easy train connection to the city, but considering I live in Queens, this is a little out of the way for me. But, puppy, I would've picked you up from anywhere to see you."

My man knows exactly what to say to make me feel better. "So, are we going to your place?"

He hesitates. "That's up to you. We could do some sightseeing in Manhattan first if you want, since we have to switch trains in Penn Station anyway. From there, it's a short walk to see the Empire State Building and Macy's, and it's not far to Times Square either."

"Can we do that later? Like, tomorrow, maybe? For now, I just wanna be with you...be held by you." My voice is small, and Marshall's arm around me tightens.

"I want nothing more than that, puppy."

We barely speak on the long journey to his place, content to sit close together and wait until we have privacy. His studio is on the top floor of an old building, and the elevator creaks in protest as it starts the journey downward again.

"I got lucky with this apartment," Marshall says as he unlocks the door. "One of my brothers-in-law is a contractor, and he was hired to fix up this building a couple of years ago. He tipped me off, and I contacted the owner and traded a shitty fourth-floor apartment in a stuffy building without AC and an elevator for this. It's fairly spacious for a studio, and it's super light."

We step inside. He's right. The light streams in from several large windows. It's definitely bigger than I expected it to be, and a hell of a lot better than the depressing apartments many of my friends in LA live in. The kitchen looks new, and so does the laminate floor.

"My brother-in-law put in some extra things for me when they were redoing this, like more expensive kitchen appliances and a better floor. I paid for it myself, which was a win-win for my landlord and me. It'll increase the value when I ever leave, and it's far more homey and practical for me."

"It's amazing." I walk around, following Marshall. "I like it far better than your place in Vegas."

Marshall laughs. "That's not exactly a high standard. That carpet was..." He shudders. "Ew."

I laugh as well. "It was. I like laminate or hardwood floors. So much easier to clean."

His bedroom is semiseparate from the living room by a half wall. "Also something my brother-in-law put in. It's just drywall, so if the landlord would want to take it out again, he easily could."

"I can see why you like this place."

Marshall circles his hand around my wrist and tugs me toward the windows. "You know what I like best? No one can see inside. Not unless they're using a telelens or something, in which case, they're more than welcome to watch me fuck you..."

He wraps his arms around me from the back and pulls me tight against him. His hard cock presses against my ass. "Because that's what I intend to do now, puppy. I need you something fierce," he growls into my ear. "I've had a fucking hard-on all week, imagining what I'd do to you when you got here."

I whimper and push my ass against him. "I'm here, Master. Show me what you want to do to me."

He gently bites my ear. "I hope you've been resting up this week, puppy, because you're not gonna get much sleep here..."

I arch my back, exposing my neck to him, and he immediately latches onto it, sucking gently, leaving wet trails all over. He pops the button on my jeans and slips inside my pants, sneaking under my underwear until he wraps his warm hand around my dick. The moan that escapes my lips is positively sinful, and he grunts in approval.

"Mmm, I'm so happy to have you back in my arms, puppy. This is where you belong."

His words are bittersweet as they confirm exactly how I feel myself, but how can I be with him when he's here and I'm in Vegas? It'll have to wait till later because I want to stay in this moment for as long as I can.

I wriggle my butt, and he tightens his hold around my dick. "I know a place where you belong...that would make both of us happy," I whisper.

He sucks hard on that tender spot behind my ear. "Is that so? And where might that be?"

I turn my head so my mouth is near his face. "Inside me, Master...and I came prepared."

Marshall immediately lets go of my dick and dips down my pants in the back, pushing me slightly off so he has enough room. He goes straight for his target, and the possessive growl he makes as he discovers the plug I'm wearing makes my skin prickle with anticipation.

Then Marshall steps back. I only have a second to feel disappointed about the loss of contact as he drags down my pants and underwear at once. I laugh, relieved, as I step out of them. I whip my shirt over my head without him prompting me while he unbuckles and strips out of his own clothes at record speed, then grabs something from his pocket.

When he presses his body against mine again, he's naked, and I close my eyes as I open for him, my heart as much as my body. He walks me toward the window, where I step onto a little ledge at the bottom. It brings me an inch or two higher, at the perfect height for him.

"Hands against the glass," he commands, and I obey without hesitation.

This time, there's no foreplay, no teasing, no waiting. He finds the plug and pulls it out. The telltale crinkling of a condom packet indicates he's getting ready, and I shiver as I wait for him. He's gonna fuck me here, right against this window, and it's the hottest thing I could've ever imagined.

He enters me with one smooth slide, sinking in deep into my well-prepped hole, plastering his body against mine. We're skin to skin, him buried inside me, his breath hot against my ear. "I can't believe you're here," he whispers. "And if it turns out this is a dream, I don't ever want to wake up."

Marshall's hand skims my hips, then higher up, while the rest of him stays motionless. Then he kisses my neck, featherlight kisses that make me tremble in his arms. "Please," I beg. "Please, Master."

When he finally starts moving, I'm near tears with how perfect this is, how whole my heart feels here in his arms, how natural our union is. I'm where I'm meant to be, and it makes no sense while being perfectly right at the same time.

He fucks me hard and deep, his hips moving in the same rhythm as his hand on my cock. I'm slightly rattling the windows as I hold on to them for purchase. We come at the same time, him unloading in the condom with a loud groan and me spraying the windows with my cum.

Panting, I watch it drip down. I could get used to this. Maybe New York isn't so bad after all.

Marshall

I SWEAR I HARDLY SLEPT, hating the idea of missing a single second of the short seventy-two hours Byron is with me in New York. Waiting for him for the past two weeks has been miserable.

Don't get me wrong. I love my new job. I love that I get to go to weekly family dinners again. I love getting back to my routine of running in Central Park, even if it's a tad far from my apartment. I love that my favorite bagel place has started making breakfast sandwiches with egg whites and turkey bacon. I *don't* love that I'm aching to hold my boy in my arms. And I *don't* love that he's asleep in my arms, happily snoring and nuzzling closer to me every so often, and I already fucking miss him in anticipation of him leaving again.

"Are you watching me sleep?" he mumbles, burrowing his face against my neck and trying to scoot closer, even though he's already flush against me, our legs tangled and our bare skin touching everywhere.

"Yes, puppy," I answer without shame, dragging my fingers through his sleep-messy hair.

"What time is it?" he asks around a yawn.

"Early." I press a kiss to the top of his head. "Go back to sleep."

So he does. I hold him and pet him in his sleep for a few more hours, then slip out of bed and throw on some clothes so I can head down to the end of the block to get coffee and breakfast for us.

By the time I get back, Byron is standing naked in my kitchen, looking a little lost in front of my coffee maker.

"Oh good, you brought coffee. I couldn't figure out how to work this thing."

"It's a bit stubborn, and I thought you'd prefer this sugary crap you love so much."

He grins and reaches for the iced mocha with extra whipped cream. He takes a sip and moans happily, tempting me to lean over and kiss him. I taste the sweetness on his lips and feel the curve of his smile against mine.

Ziggy

"You'd better go get dressed before I drag you back to bed," I say.

"You wouldn't hear me complaining," he assures me breathlessly.

"There's a lot I want to show you. I promise we'll have plenty of time for sex after everything I've planned today."

He sticks out his bottom lip in a pout but sets his drink down and scurries over to his suitcase and pulls out clothes to wear. I take a sip from my own black coffee, watching happily as he wiggles his ass seemingly subconsciously while he dresses. I bite back a chuckle and shake my head. Once he's dressed, he bounces, yes *bounces*, back over to the counter and digs in the bag I brought back with me. He unwraps his sandwich and takes a huge bite.

"Oh my god, this is amazing," he says through a mouthful of food.

"They are. And just one of the *many* wonderful things New York has to offer." I told myself I wouldn't bring up the idea of him moving again this weekend. We only have a short time together, and the last thing I want is to spend that time fighting. But I can't help slipping in a *tiny* sales pitch when it's handed to me on a silver platter like that.

He looks away, seeming determined not to acknowledge the comment, so I follow suit and dig into my own sandwich, dropping the subject for now.

Once breakfast is out of the way, our first stop is Central Park.

"This is nice," Byron says as we walk hand in hand through the park.

"You should see it in the fall. It's gorgeous when the leaves all change."

"I've always wanted to see leaves change like that. They

do some out in California, but only in certain areas, and they don't last long."

"We have all *four* seasons here in New York. Just saying."

Byron gives me a look that says he knows exactly what I'm doing. "Yeah, and a million feet of snow from what I hear," he counters.

"The snow isn't so bad. We could leave the city and find somewhere to go sledding. Or we could come right out here to Central Park to build a snowman or have a snowball fight."

He wrinkles his nose, but I swear a small spark of interest flashes in his eyes.

I make it my mission to give him the full New York experience complete with a stop at a classic New York pizza place for lunch and then a trip to Times Square.

"That's the other great thing about New York..." I'm saying as we step into my apartment after our long, eventful day.

"Ugh." Byron chuckles. "I get it. New York is fantastic."

I draw up short, grimacing at myself. Shit, I definitely overplayed my hand. He kicks off his shoes, sending one of them flying. It thuds against the wall and then clatters to the floor.

"You're right. I'm sorry. I told myself I wasn't going to push you." I guide him over to the couch. We both sit down, and to my surprise, instead of keeping his distance because he's upset, he crawls onto my lap and rests his head on my shoulder. "It's been hard being apart, but I know you need to see this thing through in Vegas."

"Yeah," he agrees, but it sounds halfhearted.

"Talk to me, sweetheart. What are you thinking?"

"I'm thinking..." He sighs, biting his lip and squirming in my lap. "I'm thinking that I'm miserable without you."

"Me too." I kiss the top of his head. I knew this would be difficult, but I never expected to miss him *this* much. It's like I'm missing a limb without my puppy at my side. I love New York; it's my home and always has been. But maybe, if Byron can't leave Vegas just yet...maybe I could go back and try to hang in a little longer.

I open my mouth to suggest just that, when he blurts, "Fine, I'll move here."

"You will?" I ask, stunned. He nods. Jumping up and down with glee seems like an appropriate reaction. But I hold back. "Are you sure? You don't have to do this, you know. I could come back to Vegas. Not forever, but I could probably survive another year."

He smiles and surges forward to kiss me.

"I was scared to make such a big move," he admits. "But I really do want to. I've been thinking about it since you left, and this is what I want."

"You really do?" My chest feels like it's full of helium. "You're *positive*?"

He giggles and presses his lips to mine again, sweeping his tongue into my mouth and then nipping at my bottom lip. "I've never been more sure of anything."

I pull him into my arms and carry him to the bedroom. This calls for a celebration, and I know *exactly* how my pup likes to celebrate.

Now that I know I'll have all the time in the world to show him around New York, I'm much more amenable to his stay-in-bed-for-the-weekend plan. And that's exactly what we do.

When I drive him to the airport on Monday morning, it still sucks, but knowing that he'll be back in a few more weeks so we can start our life together for real makes it a hell of a lot more bearable. I brought him to dinner with my family on Sunday night, and he fit in just as well as I thought he would. My mom adored him, and my sisters told me I'd better not screw things up with him. Needless to say, they were thrilled when we told them Byron would be moving here, but not as thrilled as I was to be able to make that announcement.

"Call me as soon as you land, and if there's anything I can do to help you get things wrapped up in Vegas, let me know."

"Yes, Sir," he says with a grin, looping his arms around my neck. I pucker my lips for a kiss, and he surprises me by licking them instead, giggling like crazy at the stunned look on my face.

"Behave, puppy. I'll see you in a few weeks."

"I love you," he says, his playful mood sobering.

"And I love you, pup. More than anything."

EPILOGUE

MARSHALL

I check my watch for the hundredth time in the past five minutes and then glance anxiously in the direction Byron should be appearing any second. The past three weeks have been absolute torture while he's been back in Vegas, getting everything wrapped up to move.

I spot him in the crowd, and my heart jumps into my throat, a smile spreading over my face instantly. It takes a few seconds before his eyes land on me, and I love that I can see the instant his expression changes from anxious and searching to one of pure joy.

He picks up his pace, walking quickly through the crowd until he's in an outright run, not stopping until he gets close enough to launch himself into my arms. I stumble back a little, but he barely gives me time to regain my balance. He's raining kisses all over my face, making a sweet little whimpering sound as he wiggles in my arms. The jingle of the tags on his collar fills me with happiness.

"Oh, puppy." I sigh and claim his lips with my own, my heart bursting wide open at having him in my arms where he belongs.

"I missed you," he murmurs between kisses.

"Not more than I missed you," I tease as he nips at my bottom lip.

"Take me home, Master," he says against my mouth. *Home*. Fuck that word sounds perfect on his lips.

With one more hard kiss, I set him down, then take his small suitcase from his hand and put my other hand on the back of his neck to lead him out.

He sits so close in the cab he's practically on my lap. Not that I'm complaining about that *at all*. Like the last time, I point out a few landmarks, because I didn't hit them all before. He rests his head on my shoulder and nuzzles my neck every so often. I'm not sure if he's even listening to my little New York City tour or not, and I don't mind either way.

When we get up to my apartment, I want to help him unpack, lead him to the window to enjoy the fantastic view I pay an arm and a leg for, and sit him down on the couch for a back massage to ask about how his flight was. Byron has *very* different plans.

As soon as the door is closed behind us, he jumps on me again, forcing me to drop his suitcase in order to catch him in time. His mouth is hot and hungry on mine as he tugs at my clothes helplessly, even though he's clearly not about to get them off when I'm holding him. He whimpers and wiggles, pressing his hard cock against my stomach, reminding me of when we had sex after our first date, up against the wall in my bedroom.

I carry him down the hall to my bedroom and toss him onto my bed. He squeaks with surprise as he hits the mattress, bouncing a little.

"Strip, puppy," I say roughly, wasting no time tearing my own shirt over my head and flinging it aside. My jeans and underwear follow my shirt, and I wrap my hand around my cock, looking down at my boy with his messy hair and kiss-swollen lips, giving myself a few slow strokes.

He stares at my cock, licking his lips hungrily. His own clothes are long gone, his cock flushed and hard, lying against his belly, a clear strand of precum hanging from the tip, reaching toward his skin.

"Master," he says in a shaky voice.

"Yes, puppy?"

"My ears are in my suitcase. Can I have them?"

"You want to be a puppy while I fuck you?" His breath hitches as he nods. I lean over the bed and gently bite his throat, just over his collar. "Stay here, and don't you dare touch yourself."

I hurry back to the living room, where I dropped the bag. I roll it over and unzip it. It takes a minute or so of rummaging around before I find the ears. I left all his puppy stuff with him back in Vegas, but I'm glad he packed his ears in his carry-on. He must have the rest getting shipped with his other belongings.

I step back into the bedroom with his ears in hand and find my naughty puppy with his ass in the air, shamelessly humping a pillow, his ass flexing with each thrust, little whines and whimpers falling from his lips.

"What a bad puppy," I scold, giving him a hard smack on the ass. He moans loudly and tilts his ass up in a plea for more.

"You said not to touch, and I'm not." He glances over his shoulder with a wicked glint in his eyes.

"No loopholes allowed. Follow the spirit of the law, not the letter of it." I give him a stern look and another couple of spanks, then slip his ears into place. "Come, puppy." I crook my finger at him, and he climbs off the pillow, his cock swinging between his legs as he crawls close to the edge of the bed where I'm standing. I grip the base of my cock and stroke myself again. His eyes are trained on my cock like it's his favorite treat. "Lick it, puppy," I command.

He doesn't need to be told twice, descending on my erection with wet, eager, puppy-ish swipes of his tongue from base to tip, over and over. He laps at my PA piercing and nuzzles my balls, then licks my shaft again, humming happily and wagging his butt. I wish he'd brought his tail too, but that's okay, we can work with what we have.

"Stop," I growl when my balls start to tighten and my cock tingles with my impending orgasm. Ziggy makes an indignant noise and looks up at me with innocent eyes, his mouth wet and tempting. He tilts his head to one side, and affection bursts in my chest.

"God, I love you, puppy." I plant a tiny kiss on the tip of his nose, and he gives a small bark. "If you want to fuck the pillow so badly, then climb back on, naughty pup." I jerk my head toward the pillow still lying in the middle of the bed, awkwardly smushed by his previous assault of it.

Ziggy does as I say, scrambling back onto the pillow, his hips twitching helplessly as if he can't stop himself. He presses his nose into my other pillow and groans, humping the pillow harder.

I climb onto the bed behind him, grabbing his slightly reddened ass cheeks in my hands and kneading them. As they part, I spot the base of his plug peeking out. I groan, my cock jerking at the sight. After a few more swats of my hands against his ass and the backs of his thighs, I carefully tug the plug free and drop it onto the floor in the vicinity of our clothes. His soft, ready hole twitches as I run my thumb along the rim.

I shove my thumb inside. He whimpers, thrusting against the pillow again as I work my thumb in and out shallowly, feeling the heat of his body and the impatient clench and release of his hole.

With my other hand, I reach for a condom from the nightstand. I tear it open and roll it on one-handed. I leave my thumb in place, pressing it against the lower part of his entrance as I notch the head of my cock into place. He pants harder and then moans as I push inside, stretching him wide as I enter him in a smooth movement.

With my cock buried to the hilt, I tease his rim with my thumb, still buried inside him, tugging and stretching him. Ziggy moans and gasps, vibrating as he tries his hardest to hold still for me.

I lean over him, pressing my lips against his ear. "Make yourself come, naughty puppy."

He groans and does exactly as I tell him, desperately fucking himself between the pillow and my cock, making strangled noises of pleasure, a thin sheen of sweat forming on his skin as he writhes under me. Heat grips me, settling in my core. My balls constrict, and my cock aches as he uses me to take his pleasure.

"Good boy," I praise, my voice gravelly and tight. "Such a good, filthy boy."

He whimpers and whines, moving faster and faster until he cries out, throwing his head back and nearly howling as his channel clenches tight around me. His chest heaves as he drags in harsh breaths, humping the pillow through his orgasm, his inner muscles pulsing around my cock, dragging my own orgasm violently from my balls.

I collapse against him, my lungs burning as I try to catch my breath, aftershocks still sparking along my spine.

After a few minutes, I manage to disentangle from him, roll onto my back, and get rid of the condom.

He scoots close, and I wrap my arms around him,

pressing my nose against the top of his head to fill my lungs with him. I'm not sure how long we lie like that, just listening to each other's breathing and holding each other. Eventually, his stomach growls, and he laughs.

"Sorry," he says. "And sorry about your pillow." He glances back at the pillow lying on the other side of the bed now, rumpled and covered in his cum.

"I'll wash it," I assure him. "And I'm going to order dinner because I can't have my pup going hungry."

I order from my favorite Thai place again while Byron and I lounge naked on the couch, and I tell him all about the things I want to take him to see that we didn't have time for during the weekend when he visited. This is what my first night home was *supposed* to feel like. But I get it now. New York is my home, but Byron is my home just as much now. I find myself reaching out and touching his bare skin as often as I can, unable to get my fill of him.

I still can't believe he's staying. I lean over and kiss him, just because I can.

"I'm happy you're here, puppy."

"Me too," he agrees with a smile, snuggling close and letting out a happy sigh.

The last thing I expected when I fled New York seven months ago to take a temporary job at Kinky Boys studios was to meet and fall in love with the man of my dreams. I drag my finger along the smooth leather of his collar, and my heart swells in my chest. From here on out, it's just my puppy and me. Forever.

The End

BOOKS BY NORA PHOENIX

🎧 indicates book is also available as audio book

Perfect Hands Series

Raw, emotional, both sweet and sexy, with a solid dash of kink, that's the Perfect Hands series. All books can be read as standalones.

- **Firm Hand** (daddy care with a younger daddy and an older boy) 🎧
- **Gentle Hand** (sweet daddy care with age play) 🎧
- **Naughty Hand** (a holiday novella to read after Firm Hand and Gentle Hand)
- **Slow Hand** (a Dom who never wanted to be a Daddy takes in two abused boys)

No Shame Series

If you love steamy MM romance with a little twist, you'll love the No Shame series. Sexy, emotional, with a bit of suspense and all the feels. Make sure to read in order, as this is a series with a continuing storyline.

- No Filter 🎧
- No Limits 🎧
- No Fear 🎧
- No Shame 🎧
- No Angel 🎧

And for all the fun, grab the **No Shame box set** 🎧 which includes all five books plus exclusive bonus chapters and deleted scenes.

Irresistible Omegas Series

An mpreg series with all the heat, epic world building, poly romances (the first two books are MMMM and the rest of the series is MMM), a bit of suspense, and characters that will stay with you for a long time. This is a continuing series, so read in order.

- **Alpha's Sacrifice**
- **Alpha's Submission**
- **Beta's Surrender**
- **Alpha's Pride**
- **Beta's Strength**
- **Omega's Protector**
- **Alpha's Obedience**
- **Omega's Power**

Ballsy Boys Series

Sexy porn stars looking for real love! Expect plenty of steam, but all the feels as well. They can be read as stand-alones, but are more fun when read in order.

- **Ballsy** (free prequel)
- **Rebel** 🎧

- **Tank** 🎧
- **Heart** 🎧
- **Campy** 🎧
- **Pixie** 🎧

Kinky Boys Series

Super sexy, slightly kinky, with all the feels.

- **Daddy** 🎧
- **Ziggy**

Ignite Series

An epic dystopian sci-fi trilogy (one book out, two more to follow) where three men have to not only escape a government that wants to jail them for being gay but aliens as well. Slow burn MMM romance.

- **Ignite** 🎧
- **Smolder** 🎧
- **Burn** 🎧

Stand Alones

I also have a few stand alones, so check these out!

- **Kissing the Teacher** (sexy daddy kink between a college prof and his student. Age gap, no ABDL) 🎧
- **The Time of My Life** (two men meet at a TV singing contest)
- **Shipping the Captain** (falling for the boss on a cruise ship)
- **Snow Way Out** (snowed in, age gap, size difference, and a bossy twink) 🎧

BOOKS BY K.M. NEUHOLD

Stand Alones
   Change of Heart

Love Logic
   Rocket Science
   Four Letter Word

Four Bears Construction
   Caulky
   Nailed

Heathens Ink
   Rescue Me
   Going Commando
   From Ashes
   Shattered Pieces
   Inked in Vegas
   Flash Me

Inked

Unraveled
Uncomplicated
Unexpected

Replay
Face the Music
Play it by Ear
Beat of Their Own Drum
Strike a Chord

Working Out The Kinks
Stay
Heel

Ballsy Boys
Rebel
Tank
Heart
Campy
Pixie

Kinky Boys
Daddy

Short and Sweet Stand Alones
That One Summer
Always You

You Can Also Find My Audiobooks HERE

MORE ABOUT NORA PHOENIX

Would you like the long or the short version of my bio? The short? You got it.

I write steamy gay romance books and I love it. I also love reading books. Books are everything.

How was that? A little more detail? Gotcha.

I started writing my first stories when I was a teen...on a freaking typewriter. I still have these, and they're adorably romantic. And bad, haha. Fear of failing kept me from following my dream to become a romance author, so you can imagine how proud and ecstatic I am that I finally overcame my fears and self doubt and did it. I adore my genre because I love writing and reading about flawed, strong men who are just a tad broken..but find their happy ever after anyway.

My favorite books to read are pretty much all MM/gay romances as long as it has a happy end. Kink is a plus... Aside from that, I also read a lot of nonfiction and not just books on writing. Popular psychology is a favorite topic of mine and so are self help and sociology.

Hobbies? Ain't nobody got time for that. Just kidding. I

love traveling, spending time near the ocean, and hiking. But I love books more.

Come hang out with me in my Facebook Group Nora's Nook where I share previews, sneak peeks, freebies, fun stuff, and much more:
https://www.facebook.com/groups/norasnook/

Wanna get first dibs on freebies, updates, sales, and more? Sign up for my newsletter (no spamming your inbox full... promise!) here:
http://www.noraphoenix.com/newsletter/

You can also stalk me on Twitter:
https://twitter.com/NoraPhoenixMM
On Instagram:
https://www.instagram.com/nora.phoenix/
On Bookbub:
https://www.bookbub.com/profile/nora-phoenix

MORE ABOUT K.M. NEUHOLD

Author K.M.Neuhold is a complete romance junkie, a total sap in every way. She started her journey as an author in new adult, MF romance, but after a chance reading of an MM book she was completely hooked on everything about lovely- and sometimes damaged- men finding their Happily Ever After together.

She has a strong passion for writing characters with a lot of heart and soul, and a bit of humor as well. And she fully admits that her OCD tendencies of making sure every side character has a full backstory will likely always lead to every book having a spin-off or series.

When she's not writing she's a lion tamer, an astronaut, and a superhero...just kidding, she's likely watching Netflix and snuggling with her husky while her amazing husband brings her coffee.

Stalk Me
Website: www.authorkmneuhold.com
Email: kmneuhold@gmail.com
Instagram: @KMNeuhold

Twitter: @KMNeuhold

Bookbub: https://goo.gl/MV6UXp

Join my mailing list for special bonus scenes and teasers: https://landing.mailerlite.com/webforms/landing/m4p6v2

Facebook Reader Group Neuhold's Nerds: You want to be here, we have crazy amounts of fun: http://facebook.com/groups/kmneuhold

Printed in Great Britain
by Amazon